BLOOD WAGER

CONNIE SUTTLE

Print Second Edition (2018)
Print ISBN: 1-63478-057-4
Print ISBN-13: 978-1-63478-057-5
Ebook ISBN: 1-93975-900-5
Ebook ISBN-13: 978-1-93975-900-9

Published by:
SubtleDemon Publishing, LLC
PO Box 95696
Oklahoma City, OK 73143

Cover art by Renee Barratt @ The Cover Counts

To Walter, Joe, Larry, Lee, Dianne, Sarah and Mark.
Thank you.

ACKNOWLEDGMENTS

As always, this book is the result of collaboration. If it weren't for the support of my editor, my cover artist and my beta readers, it would be less than it is. All mistakes, as usual, are mine and no other's.

About the Author:
Connie Suttle lives in Oklahoma with her husband and a conglomerate of cats. They have finally banded together to make their demands, which has proven disconcerting to all humans involved.

You may find Connie in the following ways:
Facebook: Connie Suttle Author
Twitter: @subtledemon
Website and Blog: subtledemon.com

R-D Series:

Cloud Dust

Cloud Invasion

Cloud Rebel

Latter Day Demons Series:

Hot Demon in the City

A Demon's Work is Never Done

A Demon's Due

Seattle Elementals Series:

Your Money's Worth

Worth Your While*

BlackWing Pirates Series

MindSighted

MindMage

MindRogue

MindMaster*

* * *

Black Rose Sorceress Series

The Rose Mark

Rose and Thorn

Black Rose Queen

Queen of Thorns and Roses

* * *

Future Wars Series

Buffer Zone

Black Zone*

* * *

Other Titles from SubtleDemon Publishing:

Malefactor

Transgressor

Underhanded*

by Joe Scholes

*Forthcoming

CHAPTER 1

wo vampires walk into a bar. Sounds like a joke, doesn't it?
It is. A gloriously heartbreaking joke—on me. The punchline for that joke will be delivered in the form of a sentence, but not
one that might end with laughter. No, this sentence will determine
whether I live or not. If I were to bet honestly, my money would be on
the latter. My mistake? Walking into a bar. Four glasses of wine and
poof, I was vampire. Now, wedged tightly in a corner of a nine-by-
nine cell lined with steel and titanium, I wait for a punchline to
conclude my life. But I'm starting near the end and not the beginning.
Let's go with that. *The beginning.* The thing that led to this pivotal
scene in my life. The event that snatched away my heartbeat and sent
me running into darkness.

* * *

I NEVER DRINK. Never. But I did that evening. The bartender had taken
one look at my red nose and blotchy, tear-stained face before setting a
napkin in front of me. "What can I get for you?" His voice was low
and kind.

"I don't drink," I sniffled. "What do you recommend?" The bar

1

closest to the hospital was the one I'd chosen. Some of the medical facility's personnel were regulars; I'd passed a doctor I recognized on the way in. This place was nicer than most of the bars closer to home —I saw that right away. It boasted polished wood floors and upholstered barstools neatly lined up along the bar. Tall, round wooden tables dotted the remainder of the floor and prints of western scenes hung against walls painted a forest green. Several people were already seated comfortably and drinking, although it was barely six.

"Let's start you off with a glass of wine," the bartender offered a sympathetic smile and selected a bottle of white from a fridge below the bar. "This is a Riesling and those are usually a little sweet. You might like it," he informed me as he uncorked and poured. I watched a few bubbles rise in the crystal glass as I impatiently wiped away another tear. Lifting the wineglass, I gulped down half its contents right away. "Hey, now, let's slow down a little," the bartender cautioned. Nodding my head at his words, I set the glass on the bar, my hand shaking a little. I kept my eyes down, attempting to get myself under control.

It was early January, which is generally Oklahoma's worst time of the year, weather-wise. A light snow was threatening to blow in, bringing sub-freezing temperatures with it. Night was coming early too, along with the heavy cloud cover and I shivered every time someone walked into the bar. I'd chosen the seat directly in front of the door but I wasn't about to move. It was easier just to sit there, I think, huddling into my misery and hoping wine would dull its sharp edges. Pushing my empty glass toward the bartender, I silently asked for a refill.

"What's your name?" The bartender set my third glass of wine in front of me.

"Lissa," I gave a half-hiccup, half-sob.

"Is that short for Melissa?" he asked gently. "I'm Warren by the way."

"No, Warren." I wiped a stray tear off my face with the heel of a hand. Warren handed over a fresh cocktail napkin since I'd run out of tissues. "My father had a terrible sense of humor," I added, accepting the paper square gratefully. "He named me Lissa Beth." The napkin scratched raw skin when I wiped my face with it.

"Maybe he did have a terrible sense of humor," Warren agreed, looking up as the door opened behind me. "I'll be back," he said. After a few seconds, I heard him asking the new arrivals what they wanted. I turned to look; I couldn't help myself. Two men were now seated at one of the round tables off to the side. Warren was taking their order when one of his customers turned toward me, stopping my breath for a moment. Images of black-as-sin hair, exotic features and a Latin background washed over me. Dark eyes narrowed in contempt as the man studied me, his eyes meeting mine for the briefest of moments. A smile quirked at lips that might be both sensuous and cruel. Turning back to my drink, I shivered again and it wasn't because the door had opened.

"That gentleman over there wants to buy you a drink," Warren was back and holding up the bottle of wine.

"No, Warren," I gestured for him to set the bottle down. "Tell the gentleman thank you but no," I said as firmly as I could. "I don't think a woman should accept a drink from a stranger on the same day her husband died, do you?" I lifted my wineglass and drained it. "I'll pay for the next round myself." Numbness clouded my brain after a fourth glass of wine so I sat there, waiting for my head to clear a little before attempting to make my way outside. While I waited, I caught snatches of conversation between the one who'd offered to buy my drink and his companion.

"I say seven days," one of them said.

"Nine," the other countered. I had no idea what they were discussing. At the time, I didn't really care. As it turns out, I wish I had known what they were talking about and I wish I had cared. I have no idea if it might have changed anything, but at least I would have known.

CHAPTER 2

Cold air served to wake me up a little as I sat inside my car. The small parking lot was filling up around me as night deepened, cloudy and moonless. Holding keys in my hand, I eventually recalled that placing one of them in the ignition would make the car start. My Honda was ten years old and dated, but still ran like a top. With Don's illnesses over the years, I hadn't been able to afford a new one. Yes, I know I should have been thinking about funeral arrangements and calling friends and relatives, but I wanted one final bit of space for myself—a suspension between what was real and what I wished were real before dealing with any of it. We had no children but Don had a brother. Both sets of parents were dead and we'd lost contact with most of the cousins and other family. Sighing, I slipped the key into the ignition on the third try. Honestly, I intended to close my eyes for a bit before trying to drive home. My car would warm up after a while and it wouldn't hurt to let it sit and idle while I sobered up. I was too drunk to drive right then and I knew it.

I sat there, blinking stupidly as the locked metal door of my car was torn away as easily as a tissue is lifted from a box. Mutely I listened while it clattered across the hard surface of the parking lot. A tall form crouched down beside me and dark eyes found mine. I was staring at the man who'd offered to buy my drink and his smile was just as cruel as I'd imagined it might be. Lifting a hand to rub my eyes, I desperately fought to convince myself that reality had not just shifted and I truly wasn't seeing what I imagined I was seeing. That brief glimpse of the impossible, trailed by the slightest moment of self-delusion, was the last thing I remembered before I died.

* * *

CONCRETE IS COLD IN WINTER. Icy cold when the temperature falls to twenty-three degrees, even if you are inside. And I was inside. It was dark, too; I knew that somehow, although my vision was perfectly clear. I found myself in some sort of cellar or basement warehouse, I couldn't tell which. There were plenty of boxes and crates surrounding me, stacked up here and there within walls formed of cinderblocks painted black. The funny thing? I knew it was cold. Bone-freezing cold. That didn't seem to matter. I didn't even have a goose bump as I sat up and looked around. I'd been left in the floor, wherever I was. Rising easily, I made a full turn to get my bearings. My prison couldn't have been more than a twelve by twelve square, and an old desk with newspapers stacked atop its dusty surface sat nearby, amid a pile of boxes. Wondering if the newspapers were recent, I navigated the clutter to take a look. The paper on top was printed five days after Don was removed from life support—January ninth. I had no idea if that was today, yesterday or ten years ago. Don't get me wrong, my mind was perfectly clear. I merely had no memories past getting into my car after drinking four glasses of wine. As my first-ever drinking binge, it sucked.

Now, I had no idea where I was, no idea how I'd gotten there and no idea how to get out. There weren't any windows and I couldn't see a door anywhere. Setting the newspaper down, I noticed a cocktail napkin lying nearby that someone had written on. Lifting it up, I began to read. Horrified is a tame word to me now. Any thesaurus has an alternative listing of words one might use and all of them are woefully deficient. I'd read that napkin—over and over—and still the words petrified me. I recalled hearing something about curing phobias once, where at times the sufferer is flooded or immersed in whatever it is they fear. Nothing might cure what I felt after reading words carelessly scrawled across a stained paper napkin.

"I agree to pay Sergio Velenci one million pounds if the female takes less than nine days to fully turn." They'd wagered my life. I didn't learn until later just how serious that wager truly was. A signature was beneath the agreement, written in beautiful, old-world script—*Edward Desmarais.*

Those lengthy, needle-sharp teeth I'd imagined while sitting in my car? I hadn't imagined them. They'd belonged to a vampire. I laughed humorlessly. The movies and television shows? They had it all wrong. Those weren't fangs they were showing us. Those were ridiculous compared to the real thing. While pondering how long it had been since my attackers left me in my makeshift prison, another thought wriggled its way into my brain. If they were betting on how long it would take me to become vampire, what were they planning to do with me afterward?

Scrambling off my perch on the edge of the desk, I placed the napkin as close to its original position as I could before straightening the newspapers. I'd leafed through them briefly and they'd gotten scattered a little. No, I can't say why I bothered. Perhaps it was to give myself a little time to think, and I was thinking now. Desperately. Furiously. Whatever their ultimate purpose, I had no desire to meet up with either vampire. Ever. That decision made, I went in search of a way out.

If I hadn't smelled the scent of garbage, I would never have found the door. It was designed to blend in with the rest of the wall and nearly undetectable. I followed the scent instead, sensing a slight bit of air sifting through a crack between a wall and the nearly invisible portal. I couldn't locate a handle, a knob or anything else that might be used to open it. If it hadn't been for my desperation, I might have remained rooted in that spot, waiting for Edward and Sergio to return. If I had, I'd have met my final death right then.

Instead, I whimpered and clawed at the crevice with my fingers, not expecting anything to come of it. Surprisingly, bits of concrete were crumbling away in my hands. I stared at my fingers in amazement; they'd grown so strong I could tear into cinderblocks as easily as if I were digging into soft earth. As soon as I had a large enough hole hollowed out, I placed one hand around the edge of the thick door and yanked. It flew behind me at least ten feet and the noise it made as it landed offended my ears and made me cringe. Dust clouded around the severed door and I think a couple of crates were crushed beneath its weight when it fell. Beyond the empty doorway were narrow stone steps leading up and to the outside. I climbed them swiftly, bursting through another door and into a cold, crisp night.

The garbage I'd smelled was overflowing a metal bin behind a nearby Asian restaurant. Someone was shouting in Vietnamese inside the restaurant kitchen. Another voice shouted back. *Time to get the hell out of there.* I jogged down the adjoining alley for several yards, thinking while I ran that I hadn't been able to run anywhere in a very long time. My age, my weight and my lack of exercise had seen to that. After coming to the end of the alleyway, I cautiously stepped around the last building, hoping to find an address or a street sign that would tell me where I was. I found both.

Downtown Oklahoma City was where I stood, at the corner of Mickey Mantle Drive and Flaming Lips Alley. If I hadn't been so dazed and frightened, I might have held onto the nearby lamppost and laughed myself silly. Flaming Lips Alley was named after the Oklahoma band that had made a name (and an alley) for themselves.

Even so, I was still too close to the cellar I'd just escaped so I jogged a little farther until I reached Reno Avenue. I knew where I was, then. I wasn't looking forward to walking the remaining ten miles to my house in Midwest City, but I didn't have a choice. I had no money, no purse and no cell phone; nothing belonging to me had been left inside the cellar. A search for those things had yielded no results while I explored my little cave. My vampires had taken them. Amusing, I know, calling them *my* vampires. I had no idea if they were anyone's vampires, other than their own. A thought hit me as I jogged the ten-mile trek to my house, dodging traffic at times and running across lawns at others—if Edward and Sergio had my purse, then they had my license and a lot of other things. *They knew where I lived.*

The back door into my garage was now hanging on its hinges, but I didn't take time to worry over the damage I'd caused. The exercise I'd gotten on the way home had made me thirsty—*extremely* thirsty. I blasted into the house like a hurricane and nearly tore the door off the fridge getting it open. Ripping into the carton of orange juice, I swallowed a mouthful and immediately became ill. I was coughing up orange juice—the sticky, orange liquid was pouring from my throat and nostrils as my body rejected it. And while that usually burns, it really burned now. After rinsing my mouth out with water when I coughed up the last of the OJ, (I was careful not to swallow any of the water) I sat down miserably on the living room sofa, grabbed the remote and turned on the television.

The news anchor was expounding on something he thought important enough to do an editorial over and then asking viewers to send e-mails with their opinions before getting back to the news. Staring in disbelief, I gaped at a photo of myself; it was flashed there on the television screen while the female anchor was discussing my disappearance six days earlier. The most recent newspaper I'd seen in the cellar was from the day before, which meant that Ed and Serge had been visiting me every night. There'd been a newspaper purchased and left on the desk for each day I'd been gone. The vampires hadn't arrived before I'd wakened—there was no current newspaper. They could have gotten there shortly after my escape, though. That thought had me motivated right away.

Upending the top drawer of my dresser in the bedroom, I peeled off the envelope taped to the bottom and then grabbed an empty purse out of the closet. I wanted to take a shower but figured I was living on borrowed time as it was. A comb and brush followed the envelope into my purse as I spared a glance at my reflection in the bathroom mirror, receiving the second largest shock of the evening. The face I now wore? I didn't recognize it. Vampirism had restored my youth, but that wasn't the biggest surprise. I'd never had the facial features the mirror reflected as I stared at my image in amazement. My clothing? It hung off me. I just hadn't taken the time to look at any of it. Nothing in my closet would fit me now. The last thought that went through my mind before I grabbed a coat out of the closet and hauled ass out of there, was that I'd just put paid to the theory that vampires don't cast a reflection.

Don's car hadn't been driven in a month, probably. I couldn't remember when I'd last started or driven the thing. It was red and ancient—a 1959 Cadillac with fins and everything. My husband had loved that car. I kept trying to get him to sell it and buy something a little more reliable and fuel friendly, but he'd ignored me. One of my favorite phrases when I teased him about it, was, "*Donald Workman does what Donald Workman wants to do.*" He'd laugh and do exactly that.

"Come on, you eccentric behemoth," I begged, trying to get the Cadillac's motor to turn over. It finally did start and I apologized silently for not allowing it to warm up a little before shoving it into gear and backing out of the garage. I was still so thirsty I thought I might go crazy as I hit the button on the garage door opener, closing down the door and mutely bidding my house and my life goodbye.

Where do you go to find a blood donor? There wasn't any way I wanted to prey on some of the homeless population and with the weather as cold as it was, they probably needed everything they had. My thirst warred with my fear of killing someone if I did drink from them. I'd experimentally rolled down the window while driving through a twenty-four-hour pharmacy parking lot at one point. I heard—actually *heard*—the blood rushing through the veins of the woman who'd passed close to the car. The tires of the Cadillac left marks on the pavement as I screeched out of there.

Time was my enemy as well. The bank clock proclaimed that it was four-thirty and dawn would be coming soon. Were all the vampire stories true? Was I going to fry if I didn't find a deep, dark place to hide during the day? Where was the fucking manual for new vampires? I drove past a bar—it was a dive located on a remote corner in the southeastern part of Oklahoma City, boasting only one light pole to illuminate the parking lot. The bar was closed but there were still two cars in the lot. I found out why a few seconds later. I'd shown up just in time for the local dealer to pass off a baggie of drugs. It was marijuana; I could smell it when I rolled down the window.

Is that frightening? I could smell it? I also smelled the deodorant on the teen buying and the stale, pungent body odor of the one selling. I was out of the Cadillac so fast I must have been a blur because I caught both of them unaware and had fangs sunk into the neck of the dealer before the teenager could even squeak.

A second squeak caused me to look up as I dropped the dealer, who fell to the ground with a bemused smile on his face. At least he was still alive. The teenager was backing away from me though, his baggie of weed clutched tightly in his hand and a horrified expression on his face. I'd gotten enough to drink, however. "Go home!" I shouted at the boy as he took another step backward. He turned and ran, leaving his car behind. The dealer was still sitting there on the cold, blacktopped surface of the parking lot, a look of worship on his face as he gazed up at me.

"Wow," he breathed, "that's the best orgasm I've ever had."

"Get up from there," I muttered. Reaching down, I grabbed his arm and pulled him upright, setting him on his feet in less than a blink. "Let's just keep this between the two of us, all right?" I said, dusting him off a little and turning him toward his car. "And stop selling to that kid. He still has pimples, for Christ's sake."

Another myth dispelled, I know, I'd just said Christ and hadn't gone up in flames. "Oh, yeah, thanks for the uh, you know," I couldn't bring myself to say it.

"Baby, you can give me a hickey any day," the man was grinning and dazedly attempting to open his car door.

"Well, we'll see," I told him. "Now, go home and take a bath, willya?"

"Sure," he laughed, flopping onto the car seat. I closed the door for him and trotted toward the Cadillac. The car was still running obediently in the middle of the road where I'd left it, the driver's door hanging wide open. I climbed in, checked my appearance in the mirror and discovered a tiny bit of blood drying on my chin. Wiping it off, I adjusted the mirror and drove away, wondering where I might find a place to spend my daylight hours.

While I drove, I did have a thought—one of my neighbors had an outside storm shelter. I didn't want to go back to my neighborhood but I knew plenty of people in Oklahoma had storm shelters. It was a good bet there wouldn't be any tornadoes during the day; the weather was still too cold. I found a shelter about a mile away after parking the Cadillac in a strip-mall parking lot. The lock on the shelter door twisted off easily in my hand and I climbed inside half an hour before dawn, determined to stay awake as long as I could. It wasn't long, as it turns out. I was out like a light the minute the sun peeked over the horizon.

* * *

"You're only *now* looking at her license?" Harry stared at the older vampire who held a purse in one hand, an Oklahoma driver's license in the other.

"We overestimated her age," Edward Desmarais grumbled as he frowned at the birth date. The driver's license indicated the woman was forty-seven years of age, when he and Sergio had believed her nearly sixty. Shoving the license inside the purse, Edward handed the bag to Harry and instructed him to destroy it. Edward wasn't quite as handsome as Sergio, although he still turned heads with blond hair that curled slightly and gray-blue eyes that might smile if the woman was pretty enough.

"You know the Council is going to ask how you managed to turn a female before they take your head, don't you?" Harry asked a second question while stuffing the purse inside his briefcase.

"The Council need not know," Edward sniffed. He was more than three hundred years old and felt superior much of the time, while Harry was a mere eighty-four and beneath Edward's notice. "Sergio and I intend to track her down and eliminate the problem." Edward examined his fingernails. They were perfect, as usual.

"Edward, you know how scarce females are among our kind," Harry was nearly begging. "At least turn her over to the Council—anonymously if you can."

"There is too much danger that we will be discovered. She was, as you might say, not an ideal candidate in the Council's eyes."

"That doesn't alter the fact that she exists," Harry pressed. "For good or bad, she's vampire. Can't you give her a chance?"

"We dare not. There are more lives at stake than hers." Edward was finished with the conversation, Harry could tell. He sighed a little. "Fine. If I hear anything, I'll let you know."

"See that you do," Edward gave Harry a final look and turned quickly, leaving the younger vampire standing in the alley outside the cellar. Harry was originally from Missouri, born in an era when Jazz and Swing were popular. He'd never even heard of the Flaming Lips.

* * *

THE HUNGER WASN'T DEBILITATING when I woke at sunset so I lay there, staring at the ceiling of the circular, prefab tornado shelter I'd slept in while thinking about Don. Since everyone knew I was missing, I wondered if Don's brother David had gone ahead and planned a funeral. Sighing, I slipped off the small bench I'd slept on and walked up steep, narrow steps, cautiously lifting the door. My ears and nose told me more than my eyes; except for a dog barking far off, it was safe to come out.

Once outside the shelter, I headed toward to the Cadillac. It sat there, thankfully, in the same spot I'd left it. A trip to Walmart was in the offing—I couldn't keep wearing the same clothes and I needed a shower. The synthetic, elastic-waisted slacks I wore were threatening to drop if I moved too quickly and my blouse had twisted around me while I'd slept in it.

The envelope I'd taken from home held exactly six thousand dollars in cash. It was Don's funeral expense money, but what else was

I supposed to do? Wandering the aisles in Walmart later, I picked up jeans, blouses, socks, bras and underwear. A couple pairs of athletic shoes—white and black—went into my basket, too. A coin-operated Laundromat was my next stop, where I washed my new clothes. Perhaps someone else can wear new jeans without washing them. I can't. The smell of the dye alone offended my senses now. I'd picked up a cell phone too, while I'd been at Walmart, the kind you can pay for your minutes in advance. I called David's number on it, since that was the only way to find out where things stood.

David was Don's only brother, and he'd be the one making arrangements in my absence. We'd never been close, but I had to find out what was going on. David's wife, Sara, answered the phone. Disguising my voice as best I could, I identified myself as a cousin from out of state.

"I just heard the news," I said. "Can you tell me what's going on?"

"Well, we buried Don two days ago," Sara replied. "They found Lissa's car in the Oklahoma River, but they haven't found her body yet."

I had to clap a hand over my mouth to hold back the gasp that threatened to escape. The Oklahoma River was several miles away from the bar where I'd been attacked. Ed and Serge had gone to great lengths to hide their crime. "So, they're pretty sure she's dead?" I asked after getting myself under control.

"Yes. A shame, don't you think? Probably suicide." Sara clucked for a few seconds as she imagined a more mundane death for me. "Lissa and Don were really close, you know," she continued. "We've already talked to her place of employment—Lissa took a leave of absence while Don was in the hospital. She worked for one of the judges downtown, you know."

"What's next, then?" I asked, working to keep the quiver from my voice. My job, my friends, my home—everything was gone, now. I knew David and Sara would have to get the courts to declare me legally dead before claiming any insurance money, but I figured that was already in the works.

"David's already got a lawyer," Sara was reading my mind. "We're working on getting everything straightened out. You're not going to believe this, though. Somebody broke into the house, stole Don's old Cadillac and a few other things and then ransacked the place. We have to put new doors on and we're getting a security system installed so it won't happen again." My house was worth around two hundred thousand and it was paid for. Yeah, they'd get a security system to cover their assets. I also had two hundred thousand in a life insurance policy. Sara had always been a little on the mercenary side, so it was no surprise that they had a lawyer. I'd have to ditch the Cadillac, too, since it was reported stolen.

After loading my freshly laundered clothing into the Cadillac, I drove to a nearby motel, hoping I could get a room without having ID or a credit card. The young man behind the front desk might have been torn between calling the police and hiding behind the counter when I walked in. Getting a good look at myself in the mirror behind the desk, I could see why. My eyes were red. Not red from lack of sleep or crying for hours. These eyes were bright red. Blood red. I'd smelled blood the minute I'd walked into the place. Someone had been bleeding. I caught sight of the desk clerk's hand; two fingers were bandaged. It was his blood I'd scented.

"I need a room," I almost growled at him.

"Y-yes ma'am," he stuttered.

"Stop being frightened, I'm not going to hurt you," I snapped. The immediate difference was astounding. The guy straightened right up and became professional.

"I'll need your ID and credit card," he said.

"I don't need to give my ID and credit card. This will be cash only, for one night," I growled.

"Yes ma'am," he tapped at his computer. "Your name?"

"You don't need my name. Give me a key."

"Yes, ma'am." More tapping. "Room 206. Elevator is around the corner. He handed a key card over. I gave him cash for the room.

"You don't remember what I look like," I added as a precaution and went to get a few things out of the car.

The shower felt really good. Vampires clearly appreciate warm water as well as anyone. I changed into new jeans and a long-sleeved T afterward. I hadn't been able to tuck in my blouses since I was in high school but I did now, taking a good look at my image in the mirror. My hair was strawberry blond again, like it had been in my youth and my eyes were a clear blue. My skin was now flawless, whereas it hadn't been before and well, I had a figure. A nice one. I was having difficulty reconciling what I'd been only a few days before and what was reflected in the mirror now. My jeans? A size six, thank you. When Ed and Serge had attacked me, I'd been a size sixteen and for somebody five-one, that's big. I'd always joked with my co-workers at the courthouse that I resembled an egg. No more egg. And I looked to be in my early twenties, on top of that. Trashing my old clothes on the way out of the motel, I slid into the Cadillac and went looking for a place to leave it.

There's a cemetery on Sunnylane Road in Del City that you can drive around in. It's pretty in the spring and summer with all the trees and sculpture. Now it was dead grass and darkness. I left the Cadillac parked on the south end and took the keys with me when I walked away. Don's key ring was probably the only thing belonging to him that I could keep. I couldn't see that the police would come looking for me either—my fingerprints would have been in the car anyway. After all, I was Don's wife and I'd driven the car a few times just to keep the battery charged up. All I had to do now was find somebody who wanted to donate blood and then find a place to stay while the sun was up.

"I WAS HOPING she'd return and make things simpler for us," Sergio glanced around the cellar. He and Edward had rented it as an emergency hiding space and it would have been the perfect place for the female to spend her daylight hours. Instead, her scent had gone cold inside it. She hadn't come back.

"She can't be all that intelligent," Edward said. "Did you see her? She looked like hell, didn't take care of herself and didn't have a drop of make-up on. No wonder we both thought she was nearing sixty."

"See her?" I turned her, if you'll recall," Sergio snorted. "I almost gagged doing it, too."

"I cannot understand this," Edward raked fingers through his hair. "She hadn't changed all that much when we saw her last. How did this happen, my friend?"

"No idea. I've been checking the local news for any information regarding unexplained deaths or missing humans, but have found nothing out of the ordinary. If she's feeding and killing, she hasn't yet done anything to raise suspicion."

"You know that's all it will take to bring the Enforcers in," Edward paced inside the cellar. "We must find her first and eliminate our little faux pas."

He and Sergio walked out into the alleyway only a short time later. The woman had one advantage over them; she'd lived in the city all her life and they'd only been there a short time, stopping briefly on their way to the west coast. Their stop had been extended due to their own foolishness. Now they had to eradicate the evidence of that foolishness before moving on.

"HEY, SUGAR, WHAT'S YOUR NAME?" The man's breath was so loaded with alcohol I almost choked. I'd decided earlier that a drunk might not remember much if I bit him, and with the little bit of persuasion I seemed to have, that would make it even easier.

"How about you and me, over in that corner?" I had to get close to the man's ear; the music was playing so loudly inside the dimly lit western bar it was painful to me. Smells too were assaulting my now-sensitive nose—perfume, beer, sweat and sex. The man I'd chosen was plastered already and willing to agree to anything, especially if a female proposed it to him. I took his hand and led him over to the darkest corner, got him settled into a booth and waited until nobody seemed to be looking to do my thing. I was holding his head while I drank so any casual observer would think we were necking. I licked the last few drops of blood off his throat afterward and let him sit back in his seat. He blinked at me a few times while a slow grin spread across his face. "Sugar, that was some kiss," he slurred. I patted him on the shoulder and got up to leave the bar, learning quickly once I was outside that drinking from a human that was already drunk makes the vampire drunk as well. I wobbled my way across the street that ran alongside the bar. There were businesses and furniture outlets nearby and I wanted to see if any one of them might have a spot where I could sit for a while until the drunk wore off.

* * *

DRINKING from a drunk was now on my list of things never to do again, I vowed when I woke the following evening. I'd gone to bed in the basement of a warehouse under renovation, and since it was Sunday, nobody was scheduled to work. I was lucky to be in one piece —I'd gotten into a car the evening before with four crazed frat boys from a local university after a tiny bit of coaxing. They'd slowed down as I'd walked toward one of my targeted furniture stores, asking if I needed help or a ride. The young men were out looking for fun, and after they'd convinced me to ride with them, we'd done a bit of a pub-crawl. I know. I'd intended to go looking for a place to sober up, but alcohol inhibits your judgment just as they always said it would. I did have something I didn't have before, though. Pulling the fake ID out of my jeans pocket, I examined it carefully.

My frat boys knew somebody that might help me, they'd said after mentioning their goal of going to as many bars as possible during the evening. Since I had no ID, I'd lied to them and spun a tale of woe about having my purse stolen. I'd gotten my meal in the first bar by using the mojo I seemed to have, but that didn't guarantee it would work everywhere. Plus, I was learning to lie like a professional, I suppose, and those boys ate it right up. They had a friend who was in the business, they'd said. For two hundred dollars, that friend fixed me right up. The braces-sporting geeky youth cranked out a new ID for me in a matter of minutes. It even had the hologram that everybody checks.

I was Lissa B. Haddon, now. We'd lived next door to some Haddons when I was little and the name just popped into my head. According to my ID, I was twenty-three and weighed one-ten with blue eyes and blond hair. I hoped the ID was good enough to get me out of town—Ed and Serge had to be looking for me still and I didn't want to hang around and wait on them to show up. A cab drove me to Target where I purchased a rolling suitcase and then asked the driver to take me to the bus station. If you have a sensitive nose, the bus station might be the last place you want to go. I shoved all my clothing into my new suitcase and used my new ID to buy a bus ticket. I was heading to Denton, Texas, just as fast as I could get there.

There was a bus heading out at three in the morning and arriving in Denton around six. According to the schedules, Denton was as far as I could go with the amount of time I had. It also left me a little time to find a place to sleep once I got there. My blood donor for the evening was hanging around a bar about a block over, and he had a big grin on his face when I left him.

AFTER MY ARRIVAL IN DENTON, I found a nearby hotel to spend the daylight hours. I figured I was risking my life sleeping in a motel room to begin with, so I made sure the door was locked and the drapes drawn. Even then, I curled up on the windowless bathroom floor, wrapped up in all the bedding I could drag off the bed before I went to sleep. Well, sleeping might be a misconception. One minute I'd be awake, the next I was unconscious. I know I breathed while I was awake, that allowed me to speak. As far as a heartbeat went, I didn't have one. That myth was no longer a myth. Whether I breathed or not while I slept—I had no way of knowing.

The newspaper crackled as I turned the pages after nightfall at the nearby Denny's, searching for a job. The money I had would only get me so far, after all, and clothing, hotel rooms and bus tickets had already put a hefty dent in my cash. A job was in order so I could take some time, build up a larger reserve and review my limited options. It would have to be a night job, too—that was a no-brainer. After all, plenty of people worked at night; hotel desk clerks, all-night service station attendants, fry cooks at Denny's—the list was narrow and far from perfect. I sighed, pretended to sip my black coffee and kept looking.

One job fit my requirements; cleaning offices at night. The work hours were ten at night until six in the morning. I circled that and hoped somebody would be there before dawn or late at night so I could interview. I also circled a waitress job, a job delivering bundles of newspapers to hotels (I'd need a car for that one) and a night security guard. That was a possibility since it was for a nearby college. Belatedly, I wondered if I needed to know how to shoot a gun. There was also an ad for a personal bodyguard, asking for night hours. I circled that.

My evening meal came from a man in the motel parking lot who was climbing into his car to go barhopping. He was smiling and asking me to go with him after I finished. "No, I just want you to go have a good time and forget about me," I instructed, patting his shoulder cordially. His eyes went blank as he started his car and drove away, almost running over my toes when he left me standing there. After hopping aside to keep my toes from becoming tread toast, I resolved to phrase my instructions more carefully from then on.

The phone rang four times at the number for the personal bodyguard before somebody picked up. It was the last and only number answered by a human on my list. "Yeah?" The voice didn't sound happy.

"I was calling about the bodyguard position listed in the paper," I said.

"A girl?" He sounded a little snarly.

"Yes."

"Be at this address in an hour." He gave an address, which I hastily wrote down and hung up immediately after verifying. Not one for words, I suppose. A cab dropped me off at the designated address and the driver handed off a card with his cell number so I could call when the interview was over. I didn't know whether I liked all the male fawning and attention or not; it was certainly a new experience for me. We'd pulled into a circle drive after passing tall, wrought iron gates that stood open. Wondering if the gates were normally shut, I stared around me as I walked to the front door of the huge, three-story mansion and pressed the doorbell. Somebody had lots of money; there was no doubt about that.

The door opened and I found a tall, very nice looking man with black hair and nearly black eyes standing there, dressed completely in dark clothing. He didn't have time to say anything, merely drawing in a sharp breath before another man, dressed in denim head to toe, rocketed through the door and barreled right into me. My reflexes were much faster now, I discovered as I flung the attacker to the side. He snarled and came right back after me. I backhanded him, knocking him into the wall beside the door. That slowed him down a bit. The tall, dark-haired man watched the drama unfolding before him on the wide verandah, his arms crossed casually over his chest as if a battle weren't going on all around him. His lips curved in an amused smile as my assailant slid down the wall. My attacker was a little stiff when he rose and lurched toward me, so I grabbed him by the collar of his denim jacket and tossed him easily off the porch. He landed with a satisfying crunch a good ten feet away, right in the middle of the paved circular drive.

"What the hell was that?" I asked, staring at the crumpled heap in the driveway.

"Your new boss," the tall man replied, grinning. "Davis, get up and get back in here!" He shouted at the man.

"Maybe I should go help him," I said, thinking I wasn't making any points by beating the crap out of the guy.

Davis rolled over on his side, managed to come up on all fours and then slowly stood. He looked at me and then wobbled over. "Where the hell did you learn how to hit like that?" he asked, wiping his bleeding lip with a knuckle.

"It's a newly acquired skill," I replied.

"I am William Winkler," the tall man said, offering his hand. I took it.

"Lissa Haddon," I gave my new name.

"Come in, Lissa, and we'll talk salary," William Winkler said, so I followed him inside the house. Davis came in behind me, a little slower than he'd gone out.

CHAPTER 3

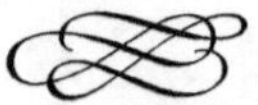

"*D*avis and you will be the night guards, Glen and Phil are the day guards," Winkler informed me after we settled on thirty-seven thousand as a starting salary. It included a room in the guesthouse so that was all right with me; I just hoped there weren't too many windows to block. Winkler owned a nationwide electronic security company plus an armored car service and farmed out security guards to banks and the like. Having a bunch of personal bodyguards seemed a little paranoid to me but I kept that to myself.

"We patrol the property," Davis informed me, rubbing his left shoulder as we walked around the edges of Winkler's expansive grounds later. The house was huge, sitting on four acres of well-kept lawn. An eight-foot concrete and stucco wall surrounded the property and the iron gate that had been open when I arrived was now closed and would require a code to get in. "Nobody comes in unless we're expecting them," Davis added. "Winkler has a personal assistant who answers calls and the like during the daytime. You're lucky I was there to get the phone when you called."

"Sorry about the shoulder," I said. "I had no idea who was attacking me. It was reflex."

"I'll remember not to jump you next time," he rotated his arm a little, trying to get his shoulder to loosen up. "The other guys come on around six-thirty," he said. I mentally gulped, hoping I could get to my room before the sun came up and that I wouldn't fry if I had to go on duty before the sun was completely down. I'd find out, I suppose. Again, I wished for the latest version of the Vampire Manual.

My hand covered a yawn the next morning as I was introduced to Glen and Phil, the day guys. Seems I had the whole top floor of the guesthouse to myself. Glen and Phil, having seniority, got bedrooms inside the house and had the extra duty of jumping and running at night if anything got past Davis and me. I also discovered that I could deal with a bit of muted light but the brighter it was, the more uncomfortable I became. I was glad to hole up in my top floor guest-house suite where there were light blocking shades, installed specifically for day sleepers. My alarm was set for six so I could grab a quick shower before going to work. The only remaining dilemma was finding a meal.

* * *

"WE'VE GOT PROBLEMS," Edward informed Sergio as he watched the evening news. The anchor was describing a young man from a local community who had posted an unusual account on MySpace.

"We're trying to contact the young man for an interview," the anchor was smiling, refusing to take the whole thing seriously. "The teen claims he watched a female vampire bite someone else before chasing after him. He says the vampire didn't kill the man, she just took blood from him." The anchor and his female counterpart were both laughing. "That's all for tonight, and fangs for watching," the anchor said.

"Fuck!" Sergio shouted. "Where the hell is Harry? Isn't he supposed to be out looking for her?"

"We have no idea when that teen saw her, if he did see her," Edward was calming himself. "You know those young ones that do what they call Goth? Who knows what kinds of tales they are capable of spinning? I suggest you get Harry to track down this young man. A little compulsion will tell us right away if he's being honest or not."

"Fine," Sergio snapped angrily, pulling out his cell phone.

Harry had gotten information from the Del City Police Department after they located the Cadillac. It had been abandoned in a cemetery near the center of town and he'd employed a little compulsion of his own to examine the vehicle while it was impounded. It definitely had the smell of a vampire about it. He was just about to call Edward with the news when his cell rang.

"Harry, here," he said after checking the ID.

"Harry, we have another assignment for you; a human that may have spotted our quarry," Edward informed him.

Harry blinked at Edward's news. "I was just about to call you, the police found the Cadillac abandoned in Del City and it has the scent all over it."

"Where was the car?" Edward asked.

"In a cemetery," Harry replied.

"Meet us at the house," Edward instructed. "And bring your laptop. We have information on someone who may have seen her."

Harry was in his car within seconds and on his way to the house that Edward and Sergio had been forced to rent. There were three safe houses in the area but those generally required checking in with the Council. Edward and Sergio wanted to avoid that at all costs.

* * *

"SIR?" Charles stood in the doorway to Wlodek's study, a sheaf of papers in his hands.

"What do you have, Charles?" Wlodek, Head of the Vampire Council, looked up at his personal assistant. For nearly three hundred years Charles had been his private secretary, but times and labels had changed. Charles didn't seem to care one way or the other what he was called. Anywhere else, Charles would be considered the biggest snoop anyone had ever seen. He was also discretion itself and often provided Wlodek with information and insights that he might not have gotten otherwise.

"These papers are for you to sign," Charles handed the pages he was holding over to Wlodek after walking up to Wlodek's huge, antique desk. "And there's something else you should know."

"And that is?" Wlodek quirked an eyebrow at his assistant.

"You know about MySpace?"

"Your space?"

"No, Honored One, MySpace. It's a networking website where anyone can post just about anything. I keep a lookout on all those websites and blogs, sir, in case anything pops up that we should be interested in."

"I'm assuming you found something?" Wlodek's eyes were nearly black, they were so dark, and only his hair was darker in color. He was more than twenty-six hundred years old and his origins were Greek. His name, however, had been something other than Wlodek in the beginning. After Poland became a country, he'd settled there for a time and changed his name. He'd been known as Wlodek ever since.

"Yes, Honored One," Charles continued. "A human teen claims to have seen a female vampire drinking from a man." Charles was holding back a smile, but amusement danced in his hazel eyes anyway. Wlodek wasn't particularly fond of merriment in such close quarters. He cleared his throat to bring Charles back to the issue at hand. "Did he say if the man still lives?" Wlodek asked, his face betraying no emotion.

"That's what he said. Of course, we have no way of knowing whether this might be true or not." Charles nearly bounced on his toes. A *female* vampire. What news!

"If he saw a female, then it likely isn't true," Wlodek sighed. "We have so few females." Charles nearly deflated at Wlodek's statement.

"I wonder why they're so hard to turn?" Charles mused aloud. He knew very well that a female hadn't been successfully turned in more than seven hundred years. Wlodek would know that better than anyone, so Charles kept the information to himself, schooling his features. He'd allowed himself a bit of excitement. Now it was time to deal with reality.

"A question I have often asked myself," Wlodek answered. "Find out as much as you can about this rumor, young Charles, and keep me posted. If I feel this merits investigation, I will send an Enforcer."

"Of course, Honored One." A bit of Charles' former excitement returned and he smiled to himself as he left Wlodek's office. Wlodek leafed through the papers Charles left with him before picking up a pen and signing his name.

* * *

I HAD to be swift and cautious. The mansion that bordered Winkler's was having a party and some of the guests had gone outside to smoke pot at the back fence. Scaling the eight-foot wall in two blinks, I silently dropped down on the other side, three feet away from the two twenty-somethings who were lighting a joint. I ordered one to look away while I helped myself at the throat of the other. He enjoyed it more than I did, sighing lustily when I licked his throat and pulled away. I was over the wall again in another blink as the other young man turned to his companion and offered him a hit.

"We're going out," Davis announced, calling me in on his walkie-talkie a few minutes later. He'd given me a little time earlier to go and retrieve my suitcase from the motel room and check out.

"Where are we going?" I asked. "I warn you, I only brought jeans with me."

"That'll be good enough for tonight, Winkler just wants a beer," Davis said. "I'm driving, you sit in the back." A Mercedes waited on the circular drive when Winkler walked out of the house dressed in a designer shirt and jeans, wearing loafers that probably cost more than I used to earn in a month. He moved with a casual grace, sliding his wide-shouldered frame into the front passenger seat. Winkler wasn't hard to look at, so I reminded myself that it wasn't polite to stare. Dutifully I loaded into the back of the car. I'd never ridden in a Mercedes before and wanted to explore the vehicle a little. I figured that would be rude so I folded my hands politely in my lap and listened while Winkler told Davis where he wanted to go.

A nightclub in Dallas was our destination for the evening and it was definitely upscale with what I considered high-class call girls at the bar. Winkler got a table while I asked Davis if he wanted me off to the side or somewhere else to keep a watch on things. "No, sit at the table with Winkler," he said. "Just make sure nobody approaches him unless he wants it." Davis sat down between Winkler and me. He was facing the door, I had the bar area.

"Hooker at two o'clock," I leaned in and muttered to Davis who passed the message off to Winkler.

"Let her come," Winkler drank from the bottle of beer he'd ordered. I watched the woman anyway as the dyed-blonde sauntered toward Winkler, wiggling suggestively as she settled beside him. Red lips pouting a little, she maneuvered her body as close to Winkler's as she could. He bought a drink for her and it wasn't long before she was doing her best to rub herself all over him. Projectile vomiting came to mind as I struggled to scan the room and ignore the implied sex. My chair overturned as I leapt up to snatch the cell phone out of a customer's hand; he was about to snap a photograph of Winkler and the woman. Yeah, I thought she was a hooker, but I had to give her the benefit of the doubt until I knew for sure.

"You don't want to do that," I was afraid I'd crush the cell phone just by squeezing it a little while the man backed away from me. "S-sorry," he said.

"I'll just bet you are," I slapped the phone into his hand. "Tell me who you are and why you wanted that picture," I growled.

"R-reporter, *Dallas News*," he mumbled.

"Well, reporter, *Dallas News*, don't you think it's time you left?" I gave him the nastiest glare I could conjure. My life had certainly changed in the space of a few days. Before, I would have apologized to a fly for swatting at it.

"Sure," the reporter agreed breathlessly, backing away from me a little more.

"And you can forget you saw any of us," I added, following him until he was out the door and heading down the hall toward the elevator. The nightclub perched on the top floor of one of the many tall buildings in Dallas, with a nice view of the entire city. There wasn't time to stare out the plate glass windows next to the bank of elevators; I had a job to do. Sighing, I walked back to the bar. The hooker was now attempting to taunt me, licking Winkler's earlobe when I sat down again. I just rolled my eyes a little and looked the other way.

"Who was the jerk?" Davis asked, leaning over so I could hear him. Actually, I could have heard him just fine anyway, but he didn't know that.

"Reporter for *Dallas News*," I informed Davis.

"Did he get the picture?"

"No."

"Good."

Winkler ordered another beer and the hooker asked for another fruit drink. Davis and I were served club soda. I pretended to drink mine. "He's taking her home," Davis grimaced when Winkler indicated he was ready to go.

"Fuck," I muttered. Who can account for the taste in men? I certainly couldn't. And the fact that my language had now descended all the way into the gutter didn't help matters, either. Some other woman might have handled becoming vampire with grace and dignity. I wasn't that woman. I hadn't gotten to mourn my husband, go to his funeral, or fight for what should still be mine. That was taken away. I had no idea if I could put up a good fight against Ed and Serge, but as far as I was concerned, they had a lot to answer for.

I sat up front with Davis this time while Winkler and his hooker du jour necked in the back of the car. I caught Davis glancing into the rear-view mirror from time to time and briefly wondered what he was seeing. After thinking about it for a moment, I realized I didn't want to know.

Phil and Glen had taken the night off so Davis and I checked the house over while Winkler poured out a drink for his lady friend. When we gave the all clear, he escorted her to his bedroom on the second floor. I wanted to put a finger down my throat and gag. "Do you want to stay inside and guard the house or go outside and walk the perimeter?" Davis asked me.

"If it's all the same to you, I'll go outside," I said.

"Take a jacket, it's getting cold out," he called after me. I just waved a hand and walked out the door. Davis wasn't bad looking as men went, but for me, it was still much too soon after losing Don, even if he had been unconscious for two full months before he died. Davis had wavy brown hair and light brown eyes that tended to sparkle a little if he was amused. He was around six feet tall and in good shape. He worked out with weights; I'd seen them on their racks inside his downstairs guesthouse apartment.

Instead of walking the perimeter the first couple of rounds that night, I jogged a little, making a full round in a short period of time. It gave me time to think and I wondered what was worrying Winkler. I also wondered why a reporter wanted a photograph that badly. And four bodyguards? Did the president have that many swarming around him all the time? Six-thirty rolled around and Glen and Phil took over while Davis informed them that the boss had a sleepover. Phil grumbled a little—somebody would have to take her home and he figured it would be him.

"HAVE YOU TRACKED DOWN THE TEEN?" Edward asked Harry when Harry arrived with the cooler of blood.

"Not yet," Harry replied. "And I had to lie and tell the supplier that my fridge broke down so he'd send more blood." Harry's complaint was ignored. Edward could have ordered it himself from the Council-owned blood bank, but that would tell them where he was. Edward had no desire for the Council to learn his whereabouts.

"I HAVE THE INFORMATION, HONORED ONE," Charles was back with more papers. Wlodek had to think for a moment to determine what Charles meant.

"Well?" he asked. Charles smiled. Wlodek knew that smile. Charles could charm or bribe information from just about anyone, and since compulsion didn't work over the phone, those skills were often quite useful. Wlodek never asked how Charles did it; he really didn't want to know.

"The teen described it quite accurately," Charles was still smiling. "And I managed to learn from him that the man bitten provides the boy with his weekly supply of marijuana. The man is still supplying him, although he seems reluctant to do so."

"So, have either of them seen the vampire again?" Wlodek didn't know whether to express his growing interest to Charles.

"The teen says no. I haven't spoken with the dealer."

"Why don't you attempt to do so and we will go from there?" Wlodek glanced at the papers Charles handed him to sign. "What does Gilbert want this time?" he held up the request for an audience with the Council.

"He swears he has created a device that will warm a unit of blood in less than ten minutes," Charles snorted. "You know how many times we've tried something like this and it just ruins the blood."

"I realize that. Why don't you ask him to submit the schematics instead and we will decide whether to allow him inside the Council chamber."

"I'll do it." Charles held out a hand and Wlodek handed the paper over, holding it by a corner with an expression of distaste. Gilbert wasn't one of his favorite vampires.

"Has Radomir arrived, yet?" Wlodek asked. "I wish to speak with him."

"I'll find out," Charles said, lifting the walkie-talkie from the holster at his belt. "Rolfe, has Rad come in?" he released the button on the walkie-talkie.

"Not yet," came the crackling reply.

"Send him up when he arrives," Charles said.

"Will do," Rolfe sent back.

"Anything else, Honored One?" Charles asked.

"Nothing at the moment," Wlodek told him. Charles turned quickly and left the office.

Radomir, the youngest of Wlodek's three remaining vampire children, arrived in Wlodek's study less than fifteen minutes later. "Father?" Radomir dipped his head respectfully to Wlodek.

"Child, I want you to contact Gavin Montegue," Wlodek sighed. "And keep it quiet. This must be between the three of us, do you understand?"

Radomir's eyes widened only a fraction but Wlodek caught it. Radomir knew things were serious if Wlodek was asking for their most effective Assassin. Gavin had served the Council as an Enforcer for three hundred years before taking on the assignment as Wlodek's elite Assassin. If Gavin went after a rogue, their death was assured and would come swiftly.

"What shall I tell him, father?" Radomir asked.

Wlodek watched his youngest turn carefully. Radomir was more than eleven hundred years old. Flavio was nearly eighteen hundred. And the other—only that child and Wlodek knew that Wlodek had made him. He was quite old indeed.

"I have had word from someone operating on my behalf in the U.S.," Wlodek shuffled papers on his desk. "He tells me that two of ours accidentally turned a female and she is running loose and feeding from the populace without guidance."

"Do you know where she is?" Radomir wanted to know. His breath had caught when his sire said *female*.

"Not exactly," Wlodek frowned and signed his name to the top paper. "We've narrowed it down to a general area. I also want those two imbeciles taken into custody and brought to me. I wish to question them before we pass sentence."

"And the female?" Radomir was still holding his breath.

"She will be eliminated," Wlodek said softly. "If those fools had taken responsibility in the beginning, this might have been avoided. As it is," Wlodek signed his name to another paper, "I am considering her rogue, my child. That is why I'm calling Gavin."

"I'll bring him tomorrow evening, father." Radomir nodded to Wlodek again and left the study. Radomir knew why Wlodek was asking him to contact Gavin. All of Wlodek's calls came through Charles. Wlodek didn't want to upset Charles with this for some reason. Radomir would never say it, but he found Gavin's involvement and Wlodek's decision just as distasteful as Charles might.

* * *

DAVIS WAS FORCED to take Winkler's date home. He'd grumbled about the assignment and then Phil had done a little grumbling of his own so Davis loaded the woman in the car and pulled through the iron gate. She was humming and applying lipstick when he dropped her off. Davis made a mental note and pulled away a little, turning a corner before stopping to watch the woman.

"We need to run a check on the person living at this address," Davis walked into the kitchen later with a slip of paper in his hand, interrupting Winkler at breakfast.

"What's that?" Winkler wiped his hands on a napkin.

"The real address of your lady friend from last night," Davis growled. "She asked me to drop her off at an apartment complex in Fort Worth, but I pulled around and waited while she made a call on her cell and a cab came to pick her up. I followed until the cab dropped her off at this address." Phil and Glen were helping themselves to pancakes the cook had just served up, but Phil was the one who reached over and took the address from Davis.

"Lissa was about to have a hissy fit over the woman last night," Winkler smiled and cut into his own pancakes.

"Maybe you should listen to Lissa more often," Davis said. "She had that reporter collared before he could even blink."

"And that's why there's no footage of me all over the news this morning," Winkler agreed. "Perhaps we should make ourselves a little more public. Do you think she'd like to go to a basketball game? I have tickets for tonight."

"Are you sure this is what you want? You know they'll broadcast your image all over the place."

"A game is harmless," Winkler observed. "Lissa can appear to be my date. She's quite attractive."

"I haven't failed to notice," Davis said dryly. "But she said last night she only has jeans to wear."

"Here," Winkler passed over his credit card. "Go find something for her. Size six."

"How do you know these things?" Davis muttered, slipping the credit card into his pocket.

"Why do you think they're all after me?" Winkler replied, grinning. "I'm a genius."

* * *

DAVIS WAS POUNDING on my door when I got out of the shower at six-fifteen. Yeah, I know I hadn't bought a robe and the motel room I'd rented hadn't been classy enough to provide one that I could steal. And yes, I'm probably going to hell for even thinking about stealing a robe. If hell exists. Truthfully, I think I've been there for a while. "What?" I flung the door open, clothed only in a big, fluffy towel that I'd wrapped around myself. At least Winkler provided his guests (and employees) with big fluffy towels.

Davis just stared for a minute, shut his mouth a few seconds past that and handed a bag over to me. "We're going to a Mavericks game tonight and Winkler wants you to pose as his date. Wear something in the bag." He turned to leave. I was too shocked to thank him at first. In my experience, men didn't normally buy anything you'd pick for yourself and it usually didn't fit on top of that. Remembering my manners when it was nearly too late, I yelled, "Thanks," at his retreating back. Davis just flung up a hand and kept walking toward the stairs.

Okay, the long-sleeved top was really pretty. A royal blue with some sort of beading, designed in a crossover style that would accent the breasts. There were two other tops; one pink, the other a plum color, but I liked the blue best. Then there were two pairs of slacks and a skirt. The skirt I tossed aside right away—it was short. The shoes at the bottom of the bag were only a half-size off. Davis must be good at sizing people up; the clothes were all in a size six.

The blue top and the black pants were what I chose to wear. I wasn't sure if I'd ever worn anything that I liked so much or had more than likely cost so much. The shoes were Christian Louboutin, in black with a kitten heel. The bag came from Saks, so some money or serious plastic had changed hands. I French braided my hair, too. An old friend I worked with at the courthouse had shown me how, once. Gloria was a tall black woman who had enough confidence and charisma for six ordinary people. I always admired her for speaking her mind and having what it took to look everybody in the eye when she said it. Gloria never minced words and she could braid hair better than anybody I'd ever met.

Too bad I didn't have any earrings, they might have completed the outfit but I was hoarding the four thousand dollars in cash I still had left. I had no idea if or when I would find myself on the streets again. Winkler seemed satisfied with what he saw when I showed up inside the house a little while later. "You clean up nice," Phil wandered out of the kitchen carrying a sandwich on a plate in one hand and a soda in the other. I wanted to snap at him for some reason.

Don's Cadillac came to mind when Davis drove a new model around front and I was more than happy to sit in the back seat on the drive to Dallas this time. I also listened in on his and Winkler's conversation, learning only then that little miss spread-legs from the bar was a spy of some sort. Since Davis had been in the house all night, she hadn't been able to poke around like she wanted.

"She came out twice, once to get a drink in the kitchen and the second time to find the bathroom down the hall. That's what made me suspicious," Davis observed after Winkler said that Phil had gotten information on her. The bathroom inside Winkler's suite should have been just fine. She was an industrial spy, I learned, and was thinking about how far over my head all that was. Her real name was Merlia Tomkins. Yeah. *Merlia*. Mer-lee-uh. Go figure.

Winkler had seats on the first row, of course, so close to the team we could reach out and tap them on the shoulder if we wanted. Just before the game started, Winkler's face and mine were splashed across the screen at the top of the arena for the entire nation to see. Lovely. Just fucking lovely. If Ed and Serge had any idea what I looked like now and just happened to be watching, well, *ESPN* was about to get me killed. Plus, I was hungry, my stomach clenching in near-pain. There'd been no time to feed before we left for the game and I desperately needed my blood fix. No way could I ever be vegetarian; I was hooked on a protein diet now. Excusing myself at the beginning of the second quarter, I rose from my seat, telling Winkler that I had to visit the ladies' room. That was the first time I drank from a woman. The guys might have welcomed me in the men's room, but it would have been much more noticeable. If I'd been giving the males orgasms, the girls got them too, I learned.

My blood donor was plump and pretty, dressed in a white and blue Mavs jersey with Dirk Nowitzki's name spelled across the back. She'd stepped inside the handicapped stall (more room, you know). I moved so fast nobody could see me and got her as she was sitting down. I had to cover her mouth; she wanted to moan with her orgasm. I licked her neck afterward—I'd noticed the punctures healed up almost instantly when I did that. My donor blinked and nodded when I whispered the instructions to forget about me. I stepped out the door first, washed my hands and returned to my seat beside Winkler.

"You're going to be on national television," Winkler observed and leaned over to kiss me. Our faces were spread across the giant screen at the top of the arena during a lull in the game. The cameras were searching for couples to kiss while the lenses were trained on them. Forced to smile afterward, Winkler went one better and rubbed my nose with his. The crowd loved it. I was scared witless.

"I can't say I'm all that pleased about it," I grumbled in Winkler's ear. He laughed. The Mavericks played Golden State that night and trampled all over them. Davis and I had to fend a few people off Winkler as we made our way to the car after the game, but the drive home was uneventful.

CHAPTER 4

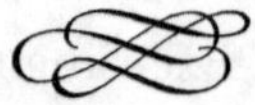

"So, this is the young man?" Gavin paced the length of the teen's small bedroom. The boy was sitting at his computer, swallowing with difficulty as the tall, wide-shouldered man examined him and growled.

"Yes." Harry might have been sweating, just as the boy was, if he'd been able. The Council had sent an *Assassin*. Harry expected an Enforcer to come after he'd contacted them, sending the female's purse and personal effects to London along with the message. Schooling his face, Harry turned his attention to the business at hand.

"What did she look like? This *vampire* you claim you saw," Gavin growled.

"Uh, really pretty," the boy shuddered. Compulsion had been placed by Harry, which forced the young man to answer every question Gavin asked.

"Describe her!"

"I can show you. I saw her at a basketball game and got the image off the internet. She uh, was with some famous guy," the boy quavered.

"Show me. Immediately."

"Okay." Harry had to back up so the boy could get to his keyboard.

The teen pulled up the image quickly. "I was about to put this on MySpace," he said, "So everybody could see what she looks like."

"Get a copy of this," Gavin ordered. Harry took a flash drive from the kid to download the images.

"See, that's her, right there," the boy pointed out the strawberry blonde sitting next to the tall, dark haired man on his computer screen.

"Who is she sitting with?" Harry breathed, crouching next to the boy to get a better look.

"William Winkler," Gavin growled.

"The one who's putting the recognition software together that's supposed to catch criminals ninety-eight percent of the time? The software that's supposed to be ten times better than anything else on the market? That William Winkler?" Harry's voice almost shook as he stared up at Gavin. The vampire community lived in fear of that software. If anyone started hunting them, it could be used effectively to track them down.

"That would be the one," Gavin agreed. "This is becoming more complicated by the minute."

Harry pulled the flash drive from the boy's computer. "Now, young man, you are going to remove those images from your computer and you are going to put up messages that you didn't see anything and that you lied, do you hear me?" Harry ordered.

"Yes, sir."

"Good. We'll wait while you do it."

The boy had everything done roughly half an hour later. "Now, you will forget you ever saw us, won't you?" Gavin placed compulsion this time.

"Yeah." The boy's eyes went blank. Gavin and Harry walked out of the teen's bedroom, breezing past parents who wished Mr. Smith and Mr. Jones goodbye. The two vampires climbed into the rental Gavin had gotten at the airport to drive away.

"I have the name and phone number of his dealer," Harry held up a slip of paper.

"Good. Let's take care of that next," Gavin said. They met the dealer in the parking lot of a nearby bar. It only took a bit of compulsion to get the man inside the rental with the two vampires. "You're the one who was bitten by the female vampire?" Gavin demanded.

"Did she bite me? I thought she kissed me. Man, that was the best sex I ever had with my clothes on." Gavin expected the man to smell of stale sweat and marijuana. Surprisingly, his scent was fresh, smelling of body wash and freshly laundered clothing instead.

Harry snickered a little at the dealer's comment but cut it off at Gavin's frown. "You will no longer remember the incident and you will not recall meeting us. Get in your car and go home." Gavin was finished with this one.

They watched as the dealer drove out of the parking lot. Harry sighed. "She really hasn't done that much damage, if you think about it," he said. "I mean, that had to be her first time and the compulsion wasn't strong enough to take completely. Apparently she's gotten better at it."

"Those fools botched this," Gavin growled. "And now I've been sent to terminate her. If they'd shown even the slightest bit of responsibility," Gavin didn't finish.

"At least we know where she is," Harry sighed again. "She was lovely, wasn't she?" Gavin didn't reply. He couldn't consider any target lovely. He had to kill them. Gavin left Harry at his home in Moore before driving to the airport. The Council's private jet was there, waiting for him to check on the prisoners before they left for London.

"Russell, Stephan," Gavin nodded at both Enforcers. Edward and Sergio were chained with silver and titanium while the Enforcers prepared to load them onto the jet. "Too bad we weren't allowed to kill you; I think I might have taken pleasure in doing you both," Gavin showed his fangs to the captives. "But Wlodek wants to question you instead. Perhaps I'll be back before he passes sentence."

Edward Desmarais hissed at Gavin. Grinning, Stephan cuffed Edward for his impudence, his white teeth a contrast to flawless black skin. Russell, slightly taller than Gavin but not as wide across the shoulders, snickered, slapping Stephan on the back. The hard blow failed to shift Stephan's solidly muscled frame.

"There's more where that came from, so you'd better behave your-self," Russell informed the prisoners.

"I don't believe you wish to tangle with either Stephan or Russell," Gavin warned Edward, who'd been knocked off balance by Stephan's blow.

"Why aren't you returning now?" Sergio had the temerity to ask.

"Because I have to stay and clear away your little fuck-up," Gavin growled. "If you'd had the balls to take responsibility, this might be turning out a bit differently. As it is, she's not going to live over it. Doubtless, that was your plan all along but I find it dishonorable and unjustified. You took someone who wasn't a viable candidate according to the laws, and a female in addition to that. If she'd not accepted the turning, you'd be just as guilty of murder and potential exposure of the race as any of the rogues we kill. And then you allowed her out on her own. Every sire is obligated to watch over his turns. You left her locked in a cellar while you amused yourselves. Which one of you turned her, anyway?"

"He did," they each pointed at the other.

"It matters not to me at this point," Gavin growled. "Wlodek will be asking and there's no way you can deny his compulsion. I warn you to be honest so your death might be swift. He can draw it out, you know."

Sergio shrank back at Gavin's words. Gavin knew then who'd done the actual turning. Edward and Sergio were loaded into the plane and extra chains were placed on both, holding them to special seats inside the jet. Prisoners were always transported in this manner. "Good luck with that filth," Gavin told Russell, Chief of Enforcers for the Vampire Council. Russell nodded, flashing a grin at Gavin and waving as he leapt up the steps. The door closed shortly afterward and the plane rolled out toward the runway. Gavin heaved a sigh and walked toward his rental. The Skirvin Hotel in downtown Oklahoma City was his destination, where he planned to spend the night. The cellar where the female had been kept was his chosen objective after checking into the hotel. Gavin wanted to visit it one last time before flying to Dallas the following evening.

* * *

GAVIN SNIFFED his way through the cellar. It held a musty odor, overlaid with that of Sergio, Edward and Harry, even. There was a lighter scent, too, that belonged to the female. It was a more exotic spice than that of the males. Vampires always knew one another by scent. Humans sensed it too, at some level. It was designed to attract them to vampires so they might feed. A female vampire's scent was an aphrodisiac to some males of the species. Gavin had been close to Ilaisaane and Susila many times—they were both female Council members and he'd not felt as much pull from either of them as this slight scent from the cellar. He reminded himself to be careful; she was a kill and he was going to get this over with quickly.

Back inside his hotel room, Gavin downloaded the information from the flash drive he'd gotten from the teen into his laptop, sending that plus the other information to Wlodek's personal computer. Feeling restless afterward, Gavin walked the streets and wandered the canal that wound its way through Bricktown. Two women offered themselves to him as he walked through the nearly deserted sidewalks. Gavin growled at both of them. One of the women called him an unkind name as he left her behind. She was of no consequence; tonight he had other things on his mind.

Gavin's cell was ringing the moment he stepped out of the shower the following evening. Recognizing the number immediately, he tapped the button to answer. "Yes, Honored One?" he said.

"Gavin, I appreciate the information you sent," Wlodek said. "We have a new strategy, now."

"Honored One?"

"Oh, I still expect you to eliminate the girl, but there are other things to accomplish first." There was almost a smile in Wlodek's words and the Head of the Vampire Council didn't smile often. "We learned through channels that she's working for William Winkler as a bodyguard. I want you to get as close to Winkler as you can. Use her, if necessary. Become a bodyguard for him yourself; that might work best. We need to know how well his software is going to work, Gavin.

If it is as good as the rumors make it out to be, you understand how it might impact our race. I expect you to use discretion if it performs as promised. It must not be allowed onto the market."

Gavin stood rooted to the bathroom floor. This was bigger than he ever imagined it might be. Yes, he understood completely how this might affect his race. The Council, the Enforcers and the Assassins all worked diligently to keep the vampire race hidden. This could well be the assignment of his lifetime. "Of course I understand, Honored One," Gavin found his voice.

"Good. Keep me apprised as often as possible," Wlodek instructed. "Through my personal e-mail account."

"Of course, Honored One." Wlodek terminated the call. Gavin shut down his phone a little slower, finished toweling himself off and dressed.

* * *

THE SAFE HOUSE Gavin had been assigned in Dallas was already stocked with blood in both the refrigerator and the freezer. The ground level of the home was for appearances only; the portion of the home Gavin would use was the basement, closed off from the rest with a very thick door. The basement ceiling was reinforced with steel and concrete with the door leading into it controlled by a security-alarmed keypad. He'd gotten the combination from Charles, Wlodek's personal assistant.

A local mall or discount store was Gavin's next objective; he'd brought mostly suits and slacks with him. As a night guard, he needed jeans and casual clothing to wear. He would certainly have to play the part and modify his speech and accent if he were to present himself to Winkler as an addition to his stable of bodyguards. Charles had also given him a phone number and the information that an ad had been placed in the local newspaper for additional bodyguards for the security magnate. Charles thought Gavin was there to keep an eye on William Winkler—he still had no idea that the female vampire was being tracked as well.

* * *

"Yeah, we're looking for two more. Can you come in for an interview tomorrow?"

"Tomorrow evening," Gavin informed the voice over the phone.

"Fine. Be here at eight." The address was given and Gavin committed it to memory; he never wrote anything down. Gavin then turned to washing his new jeans. He hated the stiffness of the new fabric and the jeans that weren't stiff when you bought them looked as if they belonged in the rubbish bin.

* * *

"Lissa, we've got a couple of interviews tonight so you'll be walking the perimeter alone until that's all taken care of," Davis informed me.

"That's all right," I grinned at him. I was getting comfortable quickly, and that probably wasn't a wise thing to do. I'm sure the Vampire Manual, if there were such a thing, would say to trust nobody and always be on your guard. More than likely, it would also say not to take jobs with humans because we were vulnerable in the daytime, but then nobody had been there to hand out a copy of the thing to start with or give me any helpful advice. "And if these two get hired?" I asked Davis.

"We'll be working eight hour shifts instead of twelve and we might even get a day off, now and then." Davis grinned back at me.

"Cool," I said. "Do you intend to interview these two like you did me?"

"Yes, and I hope I can walk tomorrow," Davis laughed.

"Come on, you could walk after I dumped you in the driveway."

"True, but my shoulder wouldn't work for days."

"Poor thing," I said.

"Don't give me false sympathy." He took off toward the house. Turning away, I went to walk the perimeter.

* * *

"WE HAVE a bank of electronic surveillance monitors," Winkler ushered Gavin through the room where monitors lined the walls. "If the fence or the gate is compromised, they're programmed to automatically sound the alarm. The outside guards patrol the perimeter as well in case the system fails for any reason. This property backs up to two others and they often throw parties. I don't want the neighbors fried, shot or otherwise becoming dead if they decide to climb over the back fence as a drunken prank." Winkler smiled at Gavin who didn't smile in return; he merely nodded his understanding.

"Since you only work nights," Winkler went on, "I'm going to pair you with Lissa. You'll be relieved in the mornings by Phil and Glen. Davis, along with James, the other new hire, will be doing the swing. I'm making arrangements to bring in staff that normally work for a bank downtown, just to patrol one day a week. This will give the regular guards a day of free time now and then. There hasn't been much of that, lately."

"Will it be a regular day off or will it be staggered?" Gavin asked.

"Staggered, no sense in letting the enemy know which day the normal staff will be off, now is there?" Winkler was grinning again. "You'll be informed when your day off comes up."

"Very well," Gavin nodded.

"I'll let Davis introduce you to Lissa and you can take the second bedroom in Lissa's top floor guesthouse. Mind you, I expect you to behave yourself. Lissa is a lady and a very good bodyguard. Step out of line with her and you'll be out of a job."

Gavin nodded again while Winkler poked his head out the door and yelled for Davis.

* * *

"HE'LL BE TAKING the second bedroom in your guesthouse," Davis informed me later. I did my best not to stutter as I told him that would be fine. It wouldn't be fine. I slept all day. What if the new guy came into my bedroom when I didn't answer to a knock or something? He'd probably think I was dead. Technically, I suppose I was, but I didn't want to be pronounced by a doctor and wake up in a coffin, or be hauled out in daylight and not wake up at all, I guess.

"Here he comes, now," Davis said. I stared at the man who approached us. He had to be at least six-five and broad across the shoulders with dark hair that curled just a little, along with handsome features and a shuttered look on his face. The other thing I noticed as he drew near, and it almost knocked me to my knees, was the smell. No, he didn't smell bad. He smelled good. *Really* good. And it wasn't from soap or aftershave, either. If he had any on, I couldn't detect it. It was all him and it was spice and amazement, rolled together. It was a good thing we'd only pass each other occasionally while patrolling the perimeter. If I had to stay in close proximity to that, I might be persuaded to lick and nibble now and then and that wouldn't do at all.

Mentally apologizing to my late husband for entertaining such thoughts, I shook Gavin Matthews' hand when he held it out to me. He left after a bit to bring in his clothing and other belongings. Gavin's things were already in the shared bathroom when I got off at six-thirty. He had to be in bed—he wasn't anywhere else—so I took a five minute shower (I can soap and rinse really fast since becoming vampire) and went to bed myself.

Davis left a note under the guesthouse door, telling me that Gavin and I didn't have to be on duty until nine in the evening. I silently thanked whoever was responsible for that. The days were getting longer and I didn't know what I'd do when daylight saving time came along and I was still beginning my shift at six-thirty. As it is, I was up by then and had plenty of time to look for my donor outside the walls. I found one easily enough; there's a service station and convenience store not far away and restaurants and other businesses past that. Sort of a vampire buffet, if you like. After I fed, I went back to the castle of doom (that's what Davis called it on occasion), punching the code on the keypad to let myself back in.

Gavin didn't say anything to me when I walked inside our shared guesthouse. He was busy watching the local news so I left him to it. If he was going to eat, I didn't want to watch. Food was now a forgotten pleasure. I remembered how it tasted and what it was like now. I'd nibbled, here and there, if somebody offered me something inside the house. It all tasted like dust and I'd have to throw it up later, otherwise it just sat in what I had left for a stomach until I got rid of it. One more thing for the Vampire Manual to explain, I'm sure. "Where do you normally start?" Gavin asked me later when nine o'clock rolled around.

"At the gate, but Davis and I switch it up sometimes and start at the back fence," I said. Gavin's scent had permeated the guesthouse; I'd noticed that right away after coming back from feeding earlier. Hoping I'd get used to it, I asked him which side he wanted to take.

"I'll do clockwise," he said, taking off in that direction. I just shrugged and took off counter-clockwise. James, the other new guard, came outside for a smoke a couple of times while Gavin and I worked. He was bunking with Davis, who is a bit of a health nut. I wasn't surprised James got sent outside to take care of his habit.

* * *

GAVIN SILENTLY CURSED WLODEK, Edward, Sergio and all eight Council members every time he passed Lissa on his rounds. Lissa's scent was overpowering and he thought briefly about placing compulsion on Winkler to get a different roommate, but discarded that thought immediately. Where else was he going to get a housemate that slept the same hours and had the same needs? Not that he intended to give himself away to Lissa; it would make it easier to eliminate her down the road. She had absolutely no idea that he was vampire, like herself. A true sire would have taught her that and many other things necessary for her survival. Instead, she was fumbling her way along, blind to all of it.

Gavin saw her during their brief lunch break, sitting on top of the wall near the front gate with her knees drawn up to her chest, staring out over the street that passed before the manor. He'd gotten a little background on her from Harry and wondered what else he might discover about her. The information could be found easily enough on the computer, he concluded, shrugging away the urge to place compulsion and ask Lissa himself.

* * *

"KIDDIES, WE'RE TAKING A LITTLE TRIP," Winkler announced a few days later. "I'm sure you're all tired of walking the grounds here, so we're going away for a bit."

"Where?" Davis asked.

"A little north of the border. We're going to Oklahoma City. I have an associate who owns a large house in Nichols Hills, so I'm going to borrow it for a bit. Ever since I went to the Mavericks game, the media has been bombarding me with requests for interviews and such. If I granted the requests, I'd never get any work done." We stood inside Winkler's kitchen, watching him drink a cup of coffee while he talked.

"Are you moving your equipment up?" Phil wanted to know.

"Yep. Andy and I packed it up this afternoon and you and Glen are going to drive it up. Tonight. In fact, we're all going tonight. It's only a two and a half hour drive. I have vans coming for all of you; I just need to know who is driving."

"You want to drive?" Gavin turned to me, a slight frown on his face. That frown was nothing compared to the one plastered across my face, most likely. Serge and Ed might be there, waiting for me. I'd come to Texas in the beginning to get away from them. Would I be safer if I stayed at the house in Nichols Hills all the time? I hadn't seen or heard anything after they'd shown my face on *ESPN*. Those two didn't seem to be basketball fans.

"I'll drive," I shrugged, since Gavin was waiting for an answer.

"Lissa is from the Oklahoma City area, she can take point in case you have any questions about the local amenities," Winkler smiled at me. I bit my lip instead, truly glad that I'd gone out to feed early.

Gavin and I loaded up our bags and such; I was surprised to see he had a small refrigerator in his room, which he also loaded into the van. Maybe he kept beer and snacks in it. Why would I care? I drove the entire way, stopping only once so Winkler could stretch his legs. "Remind me to get you a real cell phone," he told me. Mine had run out of pre-paid minutes when he'd called to tell us to pull over.

"Whatever you say, boss," I said. He might be saved the trouble and expense if Ed and Serge found me. Gavin was quiet most of the trip, asking only a few questions once we drove past Norman on I-35.

"Norman's a college town," I said. "University of Oklahoma. I have a master's degree from there," I added, realizing immediately that I should have kept my mouth shut. I no longer looked old enough to have a master's degree.

"Which area of study?" he asked, ignoring my discomfort.

"Fine Arts," I said. Yeah. A fine arts degree. Pretty worthless, actually. I'd worked as a clerk for a judge, holding an MFA. Well, it was better than retail management. That's what I started out in and the benefits had certainly been better.

Gavin didn't comment on that. "So, what is there to do in Oklahoma City?" he asked instead.

"They have an NBA team now, if you like basketball. A minor league baseball team which should start playing soon, minor league hockey, lots of fast food restaurants, plenty of sleazy bars and a couple of good bookstores and museums. The museum downtown has a great Chihuly exhibit and I went to see the Roman exhibit they had not long ago; it was definitely worth going to see. There is also a symphony and live stage performances. And if you're ambitious, you could always go to Tulsa. The Philbrook museum is there. If you're into gambling, there are several Indian casinos scattered around, some of them pretty nice, actually." I realized I was babbling a bit while Gavin remained silent, digesting the information I'd given.

"We only get one day off per week and won't know when that is until it is upon us. Not enough time to make many plans," Gavin almost smiled. Almost. I hadn't seen the man smile once since I'd met him.

"I intend to go to the bookstore when I get a little time," I said. "I haven't gotten anything good to read in weeks."

"What do you read?" he asked. Gavin's beautiful, deep brown eyes showed the first signs of interest since I'd met him.

"All sorts of things. Politics, history, humor, fiction, mystery, science fiction, even a little religion and new age from time to time." I also intended to visit Don's grave but I wasn't about to divulge that information. I might have to be careful, too. Ed and Serge could have it staked out, no pun intended, which gave me a new set of worries. What about crosses, stakes, holy water and churches? Damn. Where was that fucking manual? The only two vampires I'd recognize for sure were the ones I was doing my best to stay away from. Maybe there were others out there, but would they help me if I found out whom they were, or had Serge and Ed ruined everything for me? I had no way of knowing. Gavin turned away, lost in his thoughts just as I was.

I followed the van in front of me as we caravanned to Nichols Hills, pulling through yet another gated wall and parking near an enormous house. Many were the times I'd driven through Nichols Hills, just to look at the grand mansions lining the streets. The grounds around this one weren't as expansive as the house in Denton, so I'd have a shorter walk every night. Gavin and I were given the two-bed apartment over the four-car garage and moved our things in. Once upon a time, I'd have huffed and puffed, lugging my belongings up those stairs. Now I could run up them carrying a Mini Cooper if I wanted. Not that it would fit through the door or anything.

"Which bedroom do you want?" Gavin asked, dumping his luggage in the entryway.

"I don't care," I said, and I didn't. It wasn't as if I'd spend much time awake in it anyway.

"They both have a bath and are nearly the same size, so I'll take the one closest to the door," Gavin decided for both of us.

"Good enough," I made an expansive gesture with my arms and then added, "While I realize that many women might have a tape measure out, calculating the square footage of both just to make sure they got the better deal, well, I truly do not care." I picked up my bags and carried them into the second bedroom down the hall. Gavin's laugh followed me the entire way.

After hanging my small wardrobe inside the walk-in closet and setting out my three pairs of shoes, I sighed and decided I really needed to go shoe shopping. The one pair of dress shoes that Davis had bought for me was fine, but I needed other things. The other two pairs were athletic shoes, one pair white, one black, but I was wearing them out quickly, walking all night. I knew where the New Balance store was in Edmond, not far from the Nichols Hills mansion. Maybe I could borrow a van and drive there. Surely, vampires didn't hang around New Balance stores. There was also a mall not far away, where other shoes could be purchased. I had two paychecks already that I hadn't cashed, so finding a bank with late hours was a necessity. There were at least two branches in town that stayed open until eight, I'd just have to find the right day to do it. No way was I opening a checking account; that would surely be a catastrophe of epic proportions.

* * *

"*Honored One*," the e-mail read, "*we are now in Oklahoma City. Secondary has decided to work from here. Am keeping primary under observation. Primary seems completely ignorant, which is most unfortunate. I cannot fault her in her eating habits, however. She is quite careful in that respect. Have learned that secondary is nearing 60% completion. Will keep you advised.*

G."

Wlodek sighed as he read the message. The girl was an unfortunate victim; he'd already questioned Sergio and Edward. He was only waiting until the situation was resolved and she was properly disposed of before he brought the two before the Council for final questioning and sentencing. Gavin would be present for that and would give his views on the entire affair before final decisions were made. Only Nyles Abernathy, Edward's sire, was still alive. Sergio's had walked into the sun nearly a hundred years before. Nyles would be notified at the proper time and Edward and Sergio's assets would be liquidated and added to the Council's coffers. That was standard procedure when a vampire was sentenced as a rogue.

* * *

GAVIN KNEW Lissa had gone out to feed. He felt a bit of guilt over that; he had plenty of blood stocked inside his small refrigerator while she was forced to find a donor. Gavin used the extra time to do research and the more online reports he read on her disappearance, the greater his rage grew. He should never have allowed Edward and Sergio to leave intact. He should have killed them where they stood. Wlodek must deal with the situation, now. Gavin sighed and shut his laptop when he heard Lissa's steps on the stairs.

* * *

DAVIS ASKED Gavin and me to come into the house once we were on duty. Phil and Glen were up still, both of them wearing grim expressions. "Winkler is in his bedroom," James whispered as we walked inside the large kitchen.

"We received death threats today from an unidentified source," Glen said right away. "We came here at the right time; part of the wall around the house in Denton was blasted down and then two letters were delivered, one saying that if Winkler completes the software program and offers it for sale, they'll kill him."

"What does the other one say?" I asked.

"The other one says he's a dead man," Phil answered my question. "They're not waiting. They want him dead now."

"Crime families or terrorists?" I asked. "I know, nobody's told me what it is he's working on and truthfully I can't say I want to know, but even I've figured out it must be important. And since he's in the security business, it has to be bad for them, doesn't it?"

"She's smarter than she looks," Phil elbowed Glen.

"Thanks. Don't think I haven't heard every dumb blonde joke in the book, either," I muttered sarcastically.

James snorted and I felt like elbowing him. Yeah. I got offended every time somebody at the courthouse decided to tell me, yet again, the latest dumb blonde joke. Plenty of dumb blondes started out with dark hair and a bottle of peroxide. Davis must have noticed my anger and discomfort. "They were only teasing, Lissa."

"Now might not be a good time for it," I grumbled.

"Settle down," Gavin placed a hand on my arm. I caught myself before I hissed at him, jerking my arm out of his grasp instead.

Phil cleared his throat. "We have to be proactive about this," he said. "Winkler wants to wire the fence with extra monitors and sensors so a crew is coming up from Dallas to do that. They'll be here for three days and additional security is coming up as well. We also asked for a few handpicked guards that will help us out with this. Bear in mind if you see, hear or suspect anything or anyone, get on the phone right away." He lifted a box from the granite island and tossed it to me. "Winkler said you should start using this immediately." The box held a cell phone and a charger. I wasn't about to say thanks.

I stalked out of the house after the meeting was over, ready to make my rounds. "You must hold your anger in check," Gavin came up silently beside me.

"Trust me, I *am* holding my anger in check," I snapped.

"I understand what you are going through," he added. That brought me to a standstill. I stared at him, dumbfounded. As usual, his face was an expressionless mask.

"Buddy," I said, poking him in the chest with a finger, "You have no fucking idea what I'm going through. Now stay the hell away from me." I nearly ran to get away from him.

Tears aren't easy for a vampire. They are hard for our bodies to make, I suppose, since we don't take in water or anything. At least they were mostly clear and not blood. It was something I learned that night. I wiped them away angrily when Gavin was on the other side of the house and pretended nothing was wrong when I passed him on patrol.

I was sensitive to every rustle, every sound and every little breeze on that February evening in Oklahoma. Perhaps it would have been therapeutic to take out my frustrations on a nameless, faceless enemy, but now, in addition to keeping my eyes and ears open for an attack from Serge and Ed, terrorists or organized crime wanted to come calling. I had to be ready for that. Winkler had hired me almost sight unseen that very first night and I owed him. The other person I felt I owed, however, was me. I don't know why Phil's little dig upset me so much, but it did. Now I had to find a way to get past that. Had to.

Phil and Glen took over at five so I went to my bedroom and shut the door—I wasn't in the mood to talk to anyone. Therefore, it was poetic justice when Gavin came knocking. Sunrise wouldn't come for another hour and thirty-five minutes, so what the hell. Why not entertain company?

"Go away," I yelled.

He opened the door anyway. "What do you want?" my voice was surly. A month ago, I wouldn't have treated my worst enemy that way.

"I thought you might want to talk." His face remained shuttered as it usually did, his dark eyes raking my face.

"About what? And since when do *you* talk? Your stimulating conversation is only outstripped by your sparkling wit," I muttered, refusing to take the bait.

Gavin turned his head and it took me a few minutes to realize he was chuckling. At least the mask had cracked a little. I threw a pillow at his head, which he ducked easily. "Go away," I snapped.

"Is that the worst you're going to do?" he lifted his gaze to me after he ducked the pillow and his dark brown eyes were still laughing even if his mouth wasn't.

"Hmmph," I said. "What did you do to deserve worse? There might be a couple of people I'd like to beat into the ground, but I have no idea where they are and they'd probably get me first," I said. "That might not be a bad thing. They could finish what they started. You know," I pointed my second pillow at him, "It's not dying that worries me. It's the pain beforehand. Now go away. I want to wallow in misery for a while."

"All right." He backed out of my doorway and closed the door.

* * *

"Honored One, I saw her control her temper last evening. I was worried that she was about to attack one of the others, but a brief bout of anger was all she displayed and then calmed herself. It was quite interesting to watch, truly.

G."

Gavin shut his laptop. He had no doubt that the two Lissa had referred to were Sergio and Edward. It was a shame he couldn't tell her that they'd been shipped off to London and locked away until the Council could deal with them. Unfortunately, the Council wouldn't deal with them until after Lissa herself had been eliminated and Gavin had returned to report to the Council. She'd given him important information, however. He would make her death as swift and painless as he could.

CHAPTER 5

*V*ampires don't dream. At least I didn't, and I liked dreams, most of the time. And how old did vampires get? Were they immortal like all the books and movies said or did they die after a while, getting all shriveled and wrinkly until one day, poof? No more vampire? I was beginning to think of the missing manual as the FVM—*Fucking Vampire Manual*. Lists of thoughts and questions felt like a good idea at times. At other times, it seemed like the worst possible thing I could do. What if somebody went through my belongings? Would they find my lists and break out the stakes to stab into my chest or the long, sharp swords to behead me? Maybe my first trip out should consist of a visit to a church, just to see if I could walk into the thing.

"Day off tomorrow," Davis informed us as we showed up for our shift. Gavin was back to his usual, silent self, I noticed. I didn't speak to him, either. "Winkler says you can borrow a van or a car if you want to go out," Davis went on. "The new security guards will be working in your place and the electronics crew will be working round the clock; they're bringing enough people for two full shifts."

A day off. I was heading to the bookstore, first thing. There was a Barnes and Noble nearby; I'd hit that first. And then maybe the church. Or I'd try going to Don's grave. I wondered if I could get flowers somewhere. I didn't want any of those plastic things and the silk ones usually got stolen or trashed later. The real thing was temporary, just like most people's lives. And they generally smelled better. Some of the grocery stores carried flowers, I knew. I'd check into that.

It was while I was making my rounds a while later that I heard rustling outside the fence. Stopping on a dime, I went completely still to listen. More rustling came, and what sounded like footsteps. I pulled out my cell, sending a prearranged text to Gavin—*Help*. He was there in seconds, coming right to me as if he knew, somehow, where I would be. I smelled him before he arrived; that wonderful scent hadn't left him and hadn't dulled with time, either. I'd finally put it out of my mind—it was a mystery I probably wasn't destined to solve.

Gavin heard the shuffling the minute he arrived. Putting a finger to his lips to keep me silent, he ran noiselessly down the wall for around thirty feet before jumping up, lightly catching the edge of the wall and lifting himself to the top. He crouched there once he was up, watching. We heard giggling then, and a lighter clicking. Now I knew what was happening; the unmistakable smell of pot wafted over the wall. What is it with people and their wacky weed? Maybe I was a prude, but I'd never tried it. Honest. And now they were causing me to jump at shadows. Too bad I'd already fed, but then I recalled the drunk at the bar and thought better of that idea.

"Just keep an ear out," Gavin was back at my side, speaking softly. When had he jumped down? I hadn't seen or heard it. I'd have to do better than that. Nodding to him, I went on my way. The smokers were gone when I next passed that spot.

The electronics crew arrived right at five that morning and Gavin and I checked their IDs when they drove in. We also went through their trucks with a fine toothed comb, making sure there weren't any weapons. Phil and Glen were out in the yard helping us before it was all over, checking over the luggage and equipment now scattered across the circular drive. Everybody seemed to be who they said they were, so Gavin and I went to find our beds. Fleetingly, I wondered if he went back to the kitchen to eat or if he had something in the fridge or the pantry. I seldom got into either to check. I did drink hot tea now and then, just to appear normal at meetings held in the kitchen. It felt almost normal, too. Of course, I'd excuse myself and go to the bathroom to get rid of it later.

The van felt big and bulky to me as I drove it toward Barnes and Noble, out by Quail Springs Mall. First, I planned to check out all the new releases. It had been months since I'd stepped inside a bookstore just to browse. Someone tried to strike up a conversation with me from the moment I walked inside the store, so I attempted to ignore the man while I made my way through the new paperback racks. He wasn't giving up that easily.

"She's book shopping, not date shopping," Gavin dropped a hand on the man's shoulder, forcing the man to back away quickly.

"What are you doing here?" I asked, reading the back flap of a mystery and deliberately refusing to look at him.

"I enjoy reading too, when I have time," he said. "I've read that one already," he tapped the book I was holding. "Not as good as some of the author's others, but still a good read."

"Ah," I said. "So, what would you recommend?" I looked up at him now; I couldn't help it. "So I won't waste my money." I watched his face; he so seldom had any sort of expression on it. That didn't keep me from thinking about how nice he looked or anything.

"This one," he lifted another mystery by a not so well known author. "The story is more original than the other."

"All right, but if I don't like it, I'm holding you responsible," I said.

"Feel free. If you can make me feel guilt, I will be much surprised."

"That must be nice, to live in a guilt-free world," I observed.

"I said if *you* can make me feel guilt. I didn't say I didn't feel it."

"Ooh, excuse me. Tarzan not feel guilt Jane heaps upon him," I said. He turned his head but not before I saw a corner of his mouth quirk a little.

I picked up the book he'd recommended and then went wandering around. Gavin went his own way after a bit, which was what I was hoping he'd do. Setting my stack onto the registers about an hour later, I chatted with the cashier while pulling money out of my pocket.

I'd left my purse behind, opting instead for stuffing cash and my fake driver's license in the pocket of my jeans. The cashier bagged up my books and I went out to the van, dropping the bag onto the passenger seat.

My next stop was a grocery store, where I bought a mixed bouquet of flowers before heading out to Rose Hill Cemetery. Don and I had purchased two plots five years before. It was likely I'd never be buried in mine now, if that *vampires turn to ash* thing were true. The headstone had already been inscribed with Don's information; I saw it as soon as I climbed out of the van. The gravesite was near the narrow road running through the cemetery, covered still in a pile of raw Oklahoma dirt and brittle dead flowers. I hugged myself, realizing just how short a time had passed since Don's death. Spring was still teasing and barely making an appearance. There were tight buds on nearby trees and just the hint of green on the ground surrounding the grave, but most of it was still brown grass. Tears fell as I cleaned away old flowers and debris.

"Here you go, honey," I laid the fresh flowers on Don's grave and sat down beside it. Even though it was quite dark with no moon, I could see perfectly well and couldn't help staring at my name, inscribed on the other side of the double headstone. Only my date of death was missing. I wondered if eventually they'd put the same date of death on my side that Don's carried—January fourth.

"I'm sorry I didn't make it to the funeral," I said. "But then you probably know why. I sure hope your brother honored your wishes. And I'm sorry I didn't realize you'd already left me that day. Sorry that the doctor had to tell me instead of my knowing it, like I should have." I wiped my cheeks. "I haven't mourned you properly, either." A sob accompanied those words. "Honey, I'm in such a terrible place now and I don't know what the hell I'm doing," I said when I could speak coherently again. "It's like one of those awful dreams, when you find out there's a test in class that you didn't study for and you don't know any of the answers." I sniffled for a little while longer.

"Anyway, I wanted to come by and say hello," I went on after a bit. "I hope you're somewhere listening. I don't know when or if I'll make it back." I was wiping my cheeks on a sleeve as I made my way to the van, wishing I'd bought some tissues. I needed them now.

* * *

GAVIN WISHED he hadn't followed her. He heard every private word she uttered, and it was sad. Horribly sad. He waited for half an hour after she'd gone to climb into Winkler's Jaguar; Winkler had asked for it to be brought up with the security team. Davis had lent him the keys after Gavin said he needed something smaller than one of the vans. Lissa would have noticed one of the vans more easily than the low to the ground Jaguar. Cursing softly, Gavin put the car in gear and drove toward Nichols Hills.

"Honored One, our secondary is being threatened by other factions and security is tight and quite heavy, now. Additional forces have arrived and our primary is hemmed in. She has developed new skills in slipping away for her meals. Even I am failing to detect her at times and am at a loss to explain this. I will keep you informed to the best of my ability.

G."

She was a ghost. She barely spoke to anyone now, Gavin noted as he watched her slip inside her bedroom after they'd finished their shift. It was a Sunday morning, early, around five-thirty or so. He heard the shower running and knew she was cleaning up. Winkler was also wandering the house like a specter when he wasn't working —Davis informed Gavin that Winkler was working well into the night most of the time. Gavin had no idea if that meant the software was coming along or if problems had developed.

* * *

"I WANT to go out to eat." I hadn't seen Winkler in days, yet he now stood before me, declaring that he was starving and wanting to go out for a meal.

"Where do you want to go?" I asked. Winkler was dressed in a white, long-sleeved shirt with the cuffs folded back a time or two, black jeans and black cowboy boots with silver tips. Well, weren't we western tonight?

"Where can I get a chicken-fried steak?" he answered my question with one of his own while grinning a little, his nearly black eyes twinkling mischievously.

"Several places, but there's at least one that serves up a pretty good chicken-fry and it's a little off the beaten path," I said, appreciating the boyish grin on his face. Days had passed since I'd felt like smiling, but I was foolishly beaming back at Winkler now.

"Good, we'll go there," he said. Gavin appeared beside us, offering to drive.

"I know where we're going," I said, snatching the keys to the Jaguar away from him. He just shrugged and let me have my way. Those words were probably the most I'd spoken to anybody for days. Can vampires get depressed? I sure felt depressed. I'd wondered several times over the past week whether the walking into the sun thing was true and how painful it would be if I did it. Yeah, I was back to the pain thing again.

We all climbed into the Jaguar. Winkler rode shotgun so Gavin was forced into the back seat and it irked him, I could tell. Well, he could drive on the way back. We made our way to I-240 and swung around until we got to the Del City exit, ending up at Don's Alley Restaurant. I know. I used to tease Don all the time about it because we liked to eat there. Unfortunately, it was named after a different Don. "You can get your chicken-fry here," I said, pocketing the keys instead of handing them to Gavin, who lifted an eyebrow a little but didn't say anything. I hate giving people directions while they're driving. I'd rather get myself there if I know where I'm going and the driver doesn't.

"Don't you want something to eat?" Winkler grinned at me over his menu.

"No, I ate already and I'm not really hungry. I'll just take a glass of tea," I said. Gavin got black coffee; he said he'd eaten already, too. Winkler ordered the chicken-fried steak, along with mashed potatoes and gravy, green beans and ranch on his salad. A big dinner roll came with all that and Winkler stared at the enormous pile of food when it came.

"This is enough to feed three ordinary people," he sighed happily, cutting into his steak. "It's really good," he mumbled around his second mouthful.

"I knew you'd like it," I said. I almost added that it had been my husband's favorite but caught myself in time.

Winkler had eyed the pie display on the way in and saved room for a generous wedge of coconut cream. "Man, it was worth coming here just for this," he said. The whole piece was reduced to a few crumbs and the edge of the crust when he declared himself too full to move.

"You want I should carry you?" I teased him a little when he lightly rubbed his flat stomach. Maybe all that typing or programming that he did kept him in shape.

"No, but I do feel like working some of this off. Is there a bar around here?" Winkler was grinning hugely now.

The closest bar that I felt he'd be comfortable in and wouldn't need a leather jacket and a tattoo to get inside was the one I'd gone to the day Ed and Serge had done me in. "Can you follow directions without getting grumpy?" I asked Gavin, handing the car keys over. He looked as if he might have a stroke if he weren't allowed to sit up front.

"I can follow directions. No guarantee on the grumpy part of it," he informed me, snatching the car keys so fast I almost didn't see them leave my hand. The man could crack a joke without even a hint of a smile. I found myself wishing I had control like that.

"I'll settle for what I can get," I said, pointing him toward the southwest part of Oklahoma City.

"You can barely see this from the street," Winkler was looking out the passenger-side window as we bounced our way into the parking lot of Tipzy's Bar. They definitely needed to resurface.

"It's not bad inside," I said. "The first time I ever got drunk was inside this bar."

"No kidding. When was that?" Winkler was laughing.

"About a month and a half ago," I said. "And I've sworn off drinking. To that degree, anyway—ever since."

Gavin turned to watch me when I'd said that but didn't comment. We walked inside and I saw that Warren was still there, tending bar. Of course, he wouldn't recognize me now but he'd been nice to me when I was probably looking as bad as I'd ever looked and feeling worse than that, even. He had shoulder-length dark hair, nice green eyes and a beautiful smile, even if it was overshadowed by a larger than necessary nose. It really didn't detract from his looks at all. The first time I'd seen him his hair was pulled back in a ponytail. He wore it loose now and a couple of women at the bar were batting their eyelashes at him.

Winkler picked a table in a corner and we sat down. A waitress was on duty and she walked over to take our order. I asked for club soda with lime, Gavin ordered a bloody Mary and Winkler wanted scotch and soda. Winkler walked over to the bar after a bit and struck up a conversation with the two women, who were laughing and talking with him and Warren in no time. Gavin and I were busy watching him, making sure he stayed out of trouble when the door opened and someone else stepped in.

I scented him the moment he walked inside. His smell was similar but not quite as exotic as Gavin's. He zoned in on us right away, walking right over to our table. Unsure of what he wanted, I just stared up at him. He was handsome, though Gavin was more so, and he didn't have an edge about him like Gavin did. Gavin *felt* dangerous —fairly vibrated with it, in my opinion. If such a thing were possible, that is.

"Little queen, may I buy you a drink?" The man was speaking to me but I had no idea what he meant. I must have frowned up at him, uncertain how to respond when Gavin said a word, and if that word wasn't wrapped in power then I was dreaming. And like I said before, vampires don't dream.

"Leave," Gavin commanded, forcing the man to turn as quickly as he could and walk right out of the bar.

"Gavin, you scared the bejeezus out of him," I admonished as I watched the door slam shut. Gavin's eyes, including what should have been white, were quite dark. It must have been a trick of the light because they cleared when he turned to me and blinked.

"He should not be approaching you," Gavin declared imperiously, sipping his drink.

"I'm driving home," I said, watching him consume the bloody Mary in a matter of seconds.

"Gavin, Lissa, this is Jeri," Winkler brought his date du jour over to the table. They both had fresh drinks in their hands and Winkler pulled an extra chair over so Jeri could sit with us. I wanted to bang my forehead against the table and wondered if Winkler would ever consider trying for a steady girlfriend before deciding it wasn't any of my business. Or, as Don would have said, "None o' your bidness." I missed him. Gavin insisted on driving home after Winkler and Jeri finished their drinks, and since he'd only had two drinks, I didn't argue. Jeri was duly impressed with the house in Nichols Hills as we drove through the gate.

"You live here?" she whispered to Winkler, her eyes wide.

"Temporarily. I have a larger home in the Dallas area," Winkler couldn't help himself. If it got him a better deal in bed, who was I to argue? Jeri was still sober enough to know what she was doing and I hoped they were both mature enough to use protection. Winkler had an arm around Jeri as he led her toward the front door, making me wonder who would get the pleasure of taking her home in the morning.

"I'm glad to see you more yourself," Gavin came up beside me.

"Talking, you mean," I said, crossing my arms over my chest and watching Winkler grope Jeri's ass as they walked inside the house. "Why do men want sex with women they don't even know?" I searched Gavin's face, watching his jaw work for a few seconds. "Never mind," I said. "Forget I asked."

We returned to our normal job of patrolling the grounds, but we had help now and only took small sections. With my newly acquired senses, I didn't even have to walk anymore if I didn't want to. I could hear everything inside and outside the wall. We had two female security guards who'd come along with the others and that night I heard one of them having sex with a male guard while both were supposed to be working.

I sent a text (the longest one I'd ever sent), telling Gavin what was happening as discreetly as I could. He must have double-checked because ten minutes later Davis was in the yard, chewing out both offenders before firing them. Another guard drove the offenders and their belongings straight back to Dallas. I'd heard what Davis was telling the two when he'd fired them. "I don't give a damn what you do when you're off duty, but when you're working, you're protecting a client. This isn't protecting your client!" Yeah, I got them in trouble. My underlying reason was this: even though Winkler was a hooker-licking sleaze at times, I liked him better.

"You did the right thing," Gavin told me later as I walked into our guesthouse apartment.

"I know, but it still makes me feel like crap. So don't try to cheer me up," I held up a hand to stop him from saying anything else.

"I wasn't going to attempt it," he said.

"Good, because I might have to smack ya."

"You have such interesting phrases," Gavin said. "Smack me? You wish to smack me?"

"Keep talking like that and I'll do it instead of thinking about it," I grumbled. "Leave me alone. I have a headache." I didn't really; vampires apparently don't get headaches. Or any other kind of ache, for that matter. Not normally, anyway. Gavin leapt at the opportunity to refute my statement.

"You do not. Take yourself from my sight," He made a little shooing motion with his hand.

"Now who has the interesting phrases?" I asked. "You sound like King Henry the Eighth, sending one of his queens off for beheading."

"He only beheaded two of them, you know," Gavin grinned wickedly.

"And he didn't divorce anybody, those marriages were annulled," I said. "So there." I flounced away, wanting a shower before I went to bed. The sun was creeping up on me; I could feel it already.

My next day off came three days later and since I was running out of shampoo, I borrowed one of Winkler's ugly vans and went to Target. When Davis found out where I was going, he handed off a list of things to pick up for Winkler and some of the others. Dummy me —I thought the housekeeping staff ran the errands. Now, I had a full page of things to buy. I spent more than an hour trying to find the right kind of deodorant or the specified type of disposable razors for Phil, Glen, Davis, Winkler and some of the add-on security. Davis had given me an envelope full of cash to pay for everything but it was my day off, for cripes sake. He'd also asked me to make a run by the grocery store, handing me another list of things to get there, most of it snacks and junk food plus soft drinks. The van was nearly full by the time I finished and headed toward the house.

An angry anthill best described what I found when I parked in the driveway. Phil, Glen and Davis were just about to tear their hair out, a dozen security guards were on cell phones having a breakdown and Gavin was watching everything from the sidelines. He was standing on the wide porch, leaning against the stucco wall of the house with his eyes half-closed and an unreadable expression in his eyes. Since nobody seemed to notice that I'd gotten back, I went about unloading everything into the kitchen, even placing the perishables inside the fridge. Finding Gavin afterward, (he hadn't moved from his spot on the porch) I asked him what all the fuss was.

"Winkler took off about two hours ago, by himself," Gavin said. "Nobody can find him now."

"What was he driving?" I asked, a bit of fear creeping into my voice.

"The Jag. We only found out a few minutes ago that he had the tracking system disabled."

"Did he do it or did somebody else do it?"

"That's a good question, now isn't it?"

"Your concern is overwhelming," I said sarcastically, pacing in front of him. He was still leaning against the wall, not particularly oblivious to the uproar but certainly indifferent to all of it.

"He's only been gone two hours. Even the police won't start looking for someone unless they've been gone for twenty-four."

"Is that when you plan to look?" I stared at him in disbelief. Gavin just shrugged. This whole thing worried me. After all, Winkler was the man who wouldn't pick up a hooker or an easy lay in a bar without security. I went to find Davis.

"Did we get any response from Winkler?" I asked. Davis looked to be on the verge of an aneurysm.

"We tried his main cell first, but got no answer. Then we tried the back-up—he carries an extra phone with him, usually tucked into the top of one of his socks if he's wearing any, and it's set on vibrate. We got a momentary hit on that, but all we heard was the word *Con—* as near as we can make it out, anyway." Davis' hair was wild and he looked to be at his wits' end.

"Con? That's it?" Now *I* wanted to have an aneurysm. "And no answer on the second try?"

"Or the third or the sixty-third." Davis was truly about to experience some sort of mental event, I could tell.

"Davis, you won't do him any good if we have to take you to the hospital. Calm down, okay?" I patted his arm. "I have to think about this," I said, moving away from him. The tension in the house and the yard was so thick it might have taken a machete to cut it, so I went to the guesthouse and sat down on the sofa in the small living room. Gavin might not be concerned, but I certainly was. What did I know about Winkler that might help? And what did his cryptic message mean? Gavin walked in about that time.

"Did Winkler get any calls or messages before he took off?" I asked.

"Davis said he got two, but he didn't think anything about them at the time and Winkler wasn't upset that he could tell. Nothing to make him run out of here like a frightened hare." Gavin headed toward his bedroom.

"Around here we say scared rabbit," I said distractedly. "Con. Con. Con." I was beating my forehead with a fist.

"Keep that up and you'll have a nice bruise tomorrow," Gavin said, turning toward me.

"Go fuck yourself," I muttered, but somehow he heard.

"I prefer to perform that act with someone else," he retorted, walking into his bedroom and closing the door.

"You would," I grumbled, standing up to pace a little. I did have one thing I knew about Winkler that none of the others did. I had his scent. I could have picked him out of a crowd anytime. Just like I could find Davis, or Phil, or Glen, or Gavin. Especially Gavin. He had a scent that didn't come close to anyone else. The guy in the bar? That was similar but about a hundred miles behind what Gavin had. I put that out of my mind.

"Con," I said again, out loud. "Con. Fuck." I paced a little more. It took me ten more minutes, pacing and muttering to myself before something hit me. "Fuck!" I said one last time and ran out the door.

Yanking the door to the van open and nearly unhinging it in the process, I pulled the keys from my pocket and started the thing before I was completely in the seat. I was fastening the seatbelt with one hand while steering the van through the gate with the other in seconds. Precious time was wasted winding my way out of the Nichols Hills neighborhood but I finally made it, driving straight toward Hefner Parkway. That hooked into I-240 and then I-40; I was making my way westward as fast as I could, holding my speed back enough so I wouldn't risk getting stopped by the Highway Patrol. All I needed now was for somebody to pull me over and then arrest me for carrying a phony driver's license.

Yukon, Oklahoma, is nearly due west from Oklahoma City. I left the interstate and turned north on the exit for Garth Brooks Boulevard. The Flaming Lips had an Alley; Garth Brooks had a Boulevard. Hell, Will Rogers had an airport and Gene Autry had an entire town. Yukon has a population of around twenty-two thousand and it's scattered. First, I drove slowly through the town and the nearby neighborhoods with the windows rolled down on the van—looking for the Jaguar and sniffing the air as I went. I smelled plenty of people but didn't catch even a whiff of Winkler. Then I started widening my search, heading east toward Oklahoma City. Time was ticking for me just as much as I figured it was ticking for Winkler, if he wasn't dead already. I drove past house after house, yard after yard, before getting into isolated farmhouses surrounded by wheat fields. Five o'clock came and went and I was still driving—only I was traveling mostly through wheat fields. I was just about to give up and head toward the house, hoping I had enough time to get there before sunrise when I caught a small glint with my headlights. Backing up in the middle of the narrow road between planted fields, I drove forward more slowly this time until I caught the glint again.

Shoving the van into park, I flung myself out the door to investigate. As bad as my luck had been for the past month, somebody decided to smile on me that night. It was the tail light of the Jaguar I'd seen. The car was buried in a deep ditch filled with brush and saplings, which nearly covered the car completely. Only a tiny bit of red plastic had been caught by my headlights. Winkler wasn't in the car but he'd been inside it, and there wasn't any scent of blood or anything else that might indicate he'd been killed. I did smell others around the car; I got a good whiff of them. There was also another scent there and it surprised me a little—*Mexican food.*

I followed the scents. They hung in the air as I crossed the road, walking into the wheat field. There was no fence around the field and the spring wheat was about a foot high and green, rustling around me in the early spring breeze. I found the footprints then—I could see them clearly. The ground was wet from rain the day before, the soil sucking at my shoes as I walked through it. When I caught the scent where the footprints ended, I nearly gave up hope right then and there. I smelled death and decay and almost sat down to cry. No time for that. I started digging. Something was buried there and I was pretty sure it was Winkler.

CHAPTER 6

$\mathcal{I}$f I remember correctly, it took ten years or more to dig the Panama Canal in the early 1900's. Had they hired vampires to do the digging, they might have gotten it done in a lot less time and the mosquitoes wouldn't have been a problem. My nails were blackened with soft, wet earth and the sides of my trench had caved in on me twice but I was moving so fast my hands were blurring before my face. That's when I heard the noise. I was even more grateful that I heard it before reaching the body lying atop the metal box Winkler's kidnappers had used as a coffin.

I recognized the body the minute I jerked it up, my hand twisting the collar of the shirt he wore. The head of the body lolled back as I examined it. It was a male security guard—the one that had been fired after having sex with his female co-worker. He flew out of his makeshift grave so high and so fast it was a good thing he was already dead—the ensuing fall to earth would have killed him anyway. The banging became louder inside the metal box; somebody was kicking the end, now. There was a heavy steel lid on it, locked with a padlock. I ripped the lock off easily, taking the hasp with it. The hinged lid was up and off next. I found Winkler folded up inside the cramped space with duct tape over his mouth and his hands and feet tied with heavy nylon cord.

Getting him out of that hellhole came first—I pulled the tape off his mouth once I had him upright in the wheat field. Cutting through the nylon cords was the next item on the agenda. I was thankful he was only half-conscious when I ripped those ropes apart like they were spider silk.

I wanted to weep as I saw the horizon pinken, but Winkler was beginning to show signs of lucidity, although he was still wobbling drunkenly. I was forced to hold him upright for a few seconds while I attempted to explain things. "Winkler, I need to find somebody who can take you back to the house," I peered into his dark eyes, hoping for swift understanding. Desperation almost made me hysterical and it was coming out in my voice. I'd never had much religion before that morning but I found a little bit of it, somehow, when I saw a farm tractor coming down the road. "Thank God," I muttered, hauling Winkler toward the middle of the paved, narrow lane.

I flagged the farmer down and ordered him, as strongly as I could, to drive the van and take Winkler to the address I gave him in Oklahoma City. I also commanded him to forget he ever saw me afterward. Winkler, still confused, blinked at me as I settled him into the passenger seat of the van before sending the farmer on his way.

Daylight was just about to hit me so I ran. The light blistered my skin before I ever reached the hole where Winkler had been buried. The blisters that were forming on my exposed skin began to blacken as I tossed the dead man inside the hole, and the pain I felt as my skin started melting is indescribable. I was shrieking from the agony as I shoved the dirt I'd removed from the site into the hole. Then, my arms black, my face most likely black and the rest of my body beginning to boil, I burrowed into the loose earth until every bit of me was covered. After that, I can't tell you what happened. I might have been dead, but wasn't I already?

* * *

When Winkler punched the code into the keypad outside the gate and let himself in, his entire staff—the ones that were still on their feet, anyway—all rushed him at once, demanding to know what had happened. Winkler was dazed and couldn't give coherent answers right away so Davis, Glen and Phil hauled him into the kitchen. Glen, who had some medical training, checked Winkler over and then started pouring fluids into him. "No soda, you need water and juice," Glen ordered. Winkler said something rude to Glen. Glen just laughed at his employer.

"Where the hell were you?" Phil demanded.

"Metal box buried in the middle of nowhere," Winkler choked a little on his orange juice, coughed a bit and then continued. "Lissa pulled me out of there. Don't know how she found me. Some dead guy was there, on top of the box."

"Where's Lissa now? Did she bring you back?" Davis asked urgently.

"Don't know. She stayed behind. Told the guy driving the van to drop me off here. So he dropped me off here and left." The van was still parked in front of the gate; the farmer had left it there and walked away.

"So, we don't know where she is?" Davis was a bit more concerned, now.

"Try calling her cell," Phil suggested. Davis pulled his cell out and hit Lissa's number on speed dial. There wasn't an answer.

"Fuck," Davis breathed, trying again. Still nothing.

"Now what?" Glen asked.

"She got me out of that hole and she seemed okay," Winkler was sipping more juice. "Is there anything to eat?" Davis herded the cook into the kitchen and she started making breakfast for all of them.

"Do you remember anything about where you were? What if those shitheads who buried you found her out there?" Davis was back to worrying about Lissa.

"I don't remember," Winkler rubbed his forehead.

"Stop bothering him. We'll worry about Lissa later," Glen growled. "She's a big girl. She can take care of herself." Davis almost growled at

Glen but held back. Phil got on the phone and managed to find a doctor willing to come to the house for a fee. The physician pronounced Winkler "In good condition but dehydrated," and charged a thousand dollars.

"I could have told you that," Glen muttered angrily after the doctor drove his Mercedes out of the driveway. They still hadn't heard anything concerning Lissa and they were all worried.

That was nothing compared to Gavin's anger and distress when he emerged from the guesthouse after darkness had fallen. Davis informed him that a Good Samaritan had left Winkler and the van in front of the house before disappearing. Davis also informed Gavin that Lissa was missing; she'd pulled Winkler from his underground tomb and sent him back with the unknown driver. "We can't reach her by cell and Winkler was still drugged enough that he has no idea where he was," Davis paced a little. Gavin looked thunderous.

"You didn't go looking for her?" he was growling, now.

"Where the hell were we supposed to start?" Davis raked a hand through his hair. "We have absolutely nothing to go on."

"We had nothing to go on last night as well," Gavin swore a little. "Lissa was the one who figured things out enough to go look."

"If she comes back, I don't know if I want her going off by herself like that again." Davis was allowing his anger free rein. Gavin's was mostly held in check. If he allowed his anger to surface, somebody might die.

"Keep trying her cell phone," Gavin ordered. "It's dark, now."

Davis gave Gavin a long look and pulled out his cell phone.

* * *

WE DON'T BREATHE when we sleep. If I'd tried, I would have suffocated there in the cold, wet soil. A dead man lay buried next to me—so close I touched his flesh when I scrambled out of my makeshift grave. My clothes and skin were covered in mud as I crawled out and I probably looked like a creature from one of those swamp movies. That didn't do much for my ego, let me tell you. Dirt and mud caked my hair, too.

Rain was falling as I stood at the edge of the wheat field, beating down on my back as I shoved the displaced dirt over my exit hole. The dead security guard could stay there and rot for all I cared. I figured he'd led the kidnappers straight to Winkler, handing out phone numbers and the address so they could lure him away from the house and then take him. The kidnappers had killed the former security guard for his trouble.

Now, all I had to do was clean myself up as best I could, find a ride into town and explain to Winkler and the others where I'd been all day. *No problem.* I walked across the road and then to the edge of the deep ditch where the Jaguar lay. Here was transportation, if it were on the road instead of in the ditch. I'd seen the keys; they were still in the ignition the night before. The farmer had come to get his tractor earlier, I imagined, it wasn't parked next to the wheat field where he'd left it.

I stared a little longer at the Jaguar. Was I a vampire or not? Time to find out how strong I was. I'd see if I could pull Winkler's Jaguar out of the ditch using my bare hands. Grabbing the back bumper, I heaved a little, lifting it right up. I decided that vampirism might have its perks—the jury was still out. Pulling it out of the ditch was a little harder; the soft ground sucked at the front wheels, creating deep ruts as I heaved and tugged on the vehicle. It took nearly five minutes to get it out of the ditch and onto the road, but I did it.

The Jaguar started right up, thankfully, but hunger was now gnawing at me. I'd ignored it at first, but my body had healed itself from the extreme sunburns I'd gotten and was now demanding to be fed as compensation for the daytime restoration. I checked my reflection in the rear-view mirror as I drove toward Oklahoma City. My mud-streaked face was frightful. Nobody was going to allow me to approach them like this. Nobody.

The hitchhiker, dressed in faded jeans, old boots and an unbuttoned flannel shirt over a ragged t-shirt was walking backward along the side of the road, his thumb out, a backpack slung over his shoulder. He'd do fine as a meal—if he consented to get into the car with me, that is. I slowed down and pulled over, rolling down the passenger window to talk to the boy.

"Wow, a Jag!" The kid couldn't have been more than nineteen, I thought, as he leaned down and peered appreciatively at the interior of Winkler's Jaguar. "Man, what happened to you?" He'd gotten a good look at me, his eyes finally adjusting to the dim interior of the car.

"Fell in the mud," I said. "Back in one of those wheat fields. You want a ride or not?" It never occurred to me at that moment why the boy might be hitchhiking after dark. My hunger was ruling my brain as well as my good sense. If I had any, that is.

"Yeah, I do," the kid hopped in and slammed the door. Loud noises hurt my ears nowadays. I disliked the kid already.

"Where to?" I asked. "I warn you, I'm not going past Oklahoma City."

"That's good enough," he said as I started to pull onto the deserted road. "Yeah, that's good enough," he repeated, yanking a knife from his jeans pocket and stabbing me in the ribs with it. The Jaguar screeched to a halt when I hit the brakes as hard as I could.

"All right, that's not really nice." My hand was over the kid's and jerking the knife out of my flesh in no time. His eyes were wide and frightened as I squeezed his hand, breaking bones. He released his grip on the knife while writhing and whining in his seat. Lowering my window, I flung the knife into the field on the opposite side of the road before turning back to the youth.

"I'm not even going to be gentle about this," I growled, jerking him toward me and sinking my fangs into his throat to drink. He was whimpering and had wet himself when I shoved him away from me. "Now," I said, angry compulsion in my voice, "you're not going to remember me or anything else about this. Get out and go home. And give up your life of crime while you're at it. You suck as a criminal."

The boy lurched out of the car, witlessly wandering away and leaving the passenger-side door open. "Fuck," I muttered, reaching over to close it. The wound in my side tugged and ached with the effort. The drive to Oklahoma City was almost calm and uneventful after that. I thought to check the knife wound while I sat at a traffic light later, but it looked to be closing up already. You should have seen the committee waiting on me, though, when I drove through the gate.

"Where the hell have you been?" Davis jerked the car door open and almost dragged me out of the car. I had to unbuckle the seat belt first before he had any success at it.

"Rolling around in the muck, what does it look like?" I was almost shouting at him. "That security guard we fired was in on this. They shot him and buried him right on top of the box they stuck Winkler in. I shoved him back into that hole and covered him up before working on getting the Jaguar out of the ditch."

"Why didn't you answer your cell?" that was Glen and he sounded really mad.

"I don't know." I pulled the cell phone out of my pocket. It was covered in muck just as I was, in addition to being completely dead. I handed it off to Glen so he could see for himself.

"Do we need to go out there?" Davis asked.

"Only if you want to show the police where the body is buried." I examined the driver's seat of the Jaguar; it was covered in mud. Gavin was there within seconds, examining it with me. Suddenly, gripping my arm in his hand, he hauled me toward the guesthouse.

"What the hell are you doing?" I was trying my best to pull away from him without exerting too much energy. It would certainly stir up unwanted interest if I threw him across the yard like I wanted.

"Tossing you in the shower," he said through clenched teeth.

"Good. Why didn't you tell me that? I can walk, you know. You don't have to drag me."

"Oh, I intend to help," he said.

"No you're not."

"I've seen everything you have before."

"I beg to differ. Unless you've sneaked in while I was sleeping." A horrible thought flitted across my brain. Had he? That made me pull harder against his hold. Gavin just found a better grip and forged on.

"I was speaking in female generalities."

"Well, you're still not helping," I informed him tartly.

"Do not be obstinate about this," he growled, hauling me up the stairs.

"I will be obstinate about it," I told him angrily, still struggling against his grip.

"Do not," he propelled me down the hallway toward my bedroom, "attempt to thwart me in this." He kicked open my bedroom door and pulled me inside. I tried to dig my heels in but my mud-caked shoes slid traitorously across the carpet. My shoulder met the tiled wall of the walk-in shower. Gavin was already turning on the taps and then reaching for my shirt. I should have just let him have his way. We ended up tussling in the shower instead and somehow my shirt and jeans got ripped until I let him have the shreds of each. They were pulled away and he was examining the thin cut that remained from my stab wound.

"What the hell happened?" Gavin asked, kneeling down to get a better look at my gash. The warm water poured down on both of us, soaking him (and me) in very little time.

"I picked up a hitchhiker," I mumbled as he poked the wound. "He stabbed me."

"No kidding." Gavin pulled the edges of the wound apart.

"Hey, that hurts!" I slapped him on the head. I guess vampires could feel pain—it hurt when the kid stabbed me and now Gavin's assistance didn't feel all that great either.

"What happened to the kid?" Gavin grabbed the soap and began cleaning the wound.

"I took his knife and threw it out the window, then told him to go home and give up his life of crime because he sucked at it."

"You don't say," Gavin was thoroughly washing the gash, now.

"I did say. You heard me, didn't you?" I wanted to slap his head again; he wasn't the gentlest nurse I'd ever had.

"How did you figure out where Winkler was?" Gavin was now cleaning my arms with a mesh sponge and body wash.

"Con. What Glen and Phil heard when they called Winkler's back-up cell. I took a wild guess and made a stab at Yukon. It was really lucky, too. I suck at *Wheel of Fortune* and *Jeopardy*, both."

"Yukon. You-con." Gavin tried it out for himself.

"Yeah. Lucky guess."

Gavin washed my hair, even, but let me do my breasts and between my legs, thank goodness. When he didn't try anything funny, I gave up and let it go. After years of visits to the gynecologist, I no longer needed that little paper sheet they let you drape over your lap. Why use it? They're just going to look anyway.

"Winkler wants to see Lissa!" Davis was pounding on what was left of my bedroom door. I was drying off while Gavin leaned against the vanity, his arms crossed over his chest, watching while I toweled myself dry. He'd knocked quite a bit off the bottom of my bedroom door, kicking it in earlier.

"I'll be out in a bit," I called.

"I don't care if it was luck." Winkler refused to listen to me. Ten thousand dollars cash in an envelope—that's what he handed me. A reward wasn't the reason I'd gone looking for him in the first place.

"You ought to care. If I'd guessed wrong, you'd still be there," I frowned at him. "I do have a proposition for you, though."

"What's that?" Winkler quirked a dark eyebrow at me.

"Take back half this money and let me have the next four or five nights to go hunting that scum."

"You think you can find them?"

"No idea. I'd like to try, though." I was already leafing through the hundred dollar bills inside the envelope, counting out five thousand.

"You know, I think I'm willing to let you try." Winkler was grinning at me suddenly. "Keep the money. It's yours." He waved a hand dismissively. "Take tonight off and rest up."

"Fine." The envelope went into my pocket. Gavin, Davis, Phil and Glen had all been there, listening to the conversation. Gavin was frowning, as usual, and he followed me out of the house when I left.

"What you did for him was worth five times that," he muttered beside me.

"Maybe you're used to the big bucks. I'm not," my voice was a little frosty. "Now, I think you've seen a little too much of me tonight. Go away."

"It was my pleasure," Gavin said and left, allowing me to make my way to the guesthouse alone.

"I'll just bet it was," I muttered at his retreating back. I heard his low chuckle as I started up the steps.

* * *

"Honored One, the secondary was kidnapped by enemies and there was very little information to be had to track him. Even his experienced staff failed to come up with any ideas or methods with which to locate him. The primary, however, managed not only to track him but dug him out of a field where he'd been buried inside a metal box. At great risk to herself, she sent him back to the residence and then more than likely slept in the soil—I smelled evidence of charred flesh as well as blood from a knife wound about her when she returned the following evening. I must say, there are not many among us who might have met with such swift success on a similar assignment.

G."

She'd been reading when he checked on her later during his meal break. Lissa glared at him when he peeked inside her bedroom door. Gavin had already asked Davis to have the door replaced; she didn't like being unable to close herself off from him and the others—he could see it in her eyes. Gavin sighed and left her with her book.

* * *

Taking my favorite van, (the farmer had left it parked out front when he dropped Winkler off) I drove off the property as soon as I'd taken a shower and dressed. Gavin was frowning at me when I left, so I briefly considered giving him the finger on my way out. I fought off the urge—he'd find a way to retaliate, I just knew it. Serge and Ed crossed my mind, too. I hadn't thought of them in days but now that I was going out to hunt someone myself, my old fear reared its ugly head.

People are creatures of habit. I certainly was. I went to the same kinds of movies. Had my favorite foods, went to the same restaurants and bookstores. I'd gotten a really good scent off Winkler's captors. At least some of them. There were two distinct scents inside the Jaguar, both of them fresh, along with Winkler's of course. And the security guard's body hadn't been transported inside the car; the scent of it wasn't there. That meant they had another car, truck or van following to take them away from the burial site.

The Mexican food? That was a plus. They'd been hungry before they took Winkler out to shut him up in a metal box. I knew what that box was, now—the metal toolbox that went on the back of a pickup. Since there had to be at least three kidnappers, I was more than likely looking for a club or extended cab.

I also knew where most of the Mexican restaurants in town were. The people I'd worked with at the courthouse loved Mexican and we'd sometimes go out on our lunch hour to whatever the popular place was at the moment. That night I drove by Ted's Café Escondido, Border Crossing, On the Border, Nino's, Cocina de Mino and several little hole-in-the-wall places. I didn't catch a scent at any of them. I even drove past the wheat field while more rain fell, watching as puddling water destroyed the footprints left behind. The ruts from the Jaguar were still there but since the police hadn't been brought in on Winkler's kidnapping, most people would think that someone had slid off the road and then managed to get their vehicle out again. It happened all the time in Oklahoma. Good Samaritans abounded usually and the odds of somebody coming along with a trailer hitch or tow bar to get you out of a mess were actually pretty good.

I fed while I was out, too, at one of the Mexican restaurants. Most likely, I was searching for a needle in a haystack but I wasn't willing to let those scum go. They hadn't been decent or honorable over what they'd done to Winkler. That metal toolbox was a makeshift coffin and if I hadn't gotten lucky he would have died—alone and frightened, I'm sure. Speaking from personal experience, I'd had it with people leaving you alone to die.

I also dropped by a twenty-four hour Walmart and bought more jeans. Gavin and the mud had ruined one pair and I was washing clothes every fourth day as it was. More tops found their way into the basket, too, along with additional underwear. I went out on a limb and bought cotton bikinis. Hey, I could wear that stuff now. If things had been different, I might have taken time to revel in the fact that I could now find pretty clothes that fit and looked good on me. Constant worry and watching your employer's back as well as your own will take those thoughts right out of your head.

"That was a bust," I said to Phil as I drove through the gate shortly before sunrise. I didn't take time to explain myself and he didn't bother to ask. I think we both knew I was grasping at straws.

A new door to my bedroom waited when I reached the guest-house. It was nice and thick, with (gasp) a lock on the inside. Not that I held any illusions about that—Gavin could probably kick this one in, too. That man was stronger than he looked and he looked pretty damn strong. His scent was more wonderful than anything I'd ever eaten, including freshly baked cookies. No, Gavin didn't smell like any food I'd ever tasted before, but that didn't keep me from wanting to sink my teeth into him anyway.

Dumping my Walmart bags into the chair at the side of the bed, I drifted into the bathroom and took a quick shower, washing away the smells and everything else I'd wandered through during the night. I used unscented soap but that even had a smell to me, making me wonder if every vampire's sense of smell was that keen. I had a pair of windows in my bedroom but the drapes were lined and I had rolled-up towels on the sills to help keep light from spilling in under the edge of the curtains. Any dim light that filtered over the top of the drapes didn't bother me; I was still alive, or as alive as any vampire could be, I suppose. I yawned a little while I combed out my hair and flopped into the bed afterward, asleep before I could cover up.

* * *

"WINKLER SAID I could come with you." That was Gavin, telling me he wanted to come along. I didn't want the distraction or the embarrassment.

"No," I said. This was my fourth night out, looking for the kidnappers. I was feeling inadequate enough as it was. I didn't need a witness.

"Tell me why." It sounded like an order, so I stood there beside the driver's side door of the van for a moment, considering my answer. Bumping my head against the glass of the window, I felt like crying instead.

"Because I feel like a fool," I said. "And you'll just say I told you so when I don't find anything."

"That could very well be true," Gavin's voice was soft at my ear. I hadn't heard him come up beside me—when had he done that? He'd been five feet away when I'd said no. His hand was on the back of my neck, stroking my nape with his thumb. Lazy circles were gently drawn on my skin as Gavin's breath fanned my temple. That might have made my knees give way in another life. That life was over, now. I didn't have time for this and it was dangerous in the extreme, on top of that. Did vampires get to have lovers? Once again, the *FVM* was missing in action. And it was never a good idea to date or bed anybody you worked with. That was trouble with a capital T.

"Gavin, get in the fucking van," I grumbled, jerking the door open.

"What are you looking for?" Gavin asked as we bounced over a speed bump. We were driving through yet another Mexican restaurant parking lot—On the Border, this time—the one on Northwest Expressway.

"Winkler was buried in one of those tool boxes that fit across the back of a pickup," I mumbled distractedly as I slowly drove past the row of vehicles up front. "And I smelled Mexican food inside Winkler's Jaguar but didn't find any evidence that the security guard had been in the car or the trunk. Obviously, there was another vehicle to pick up the one driving the Jag afterward, plus the toolbox had to be hauled in somehow, along with the dead guard. The only truck that can hold three or more people has to be a club or extended cab."

"So, you've put Mexican food together with a pickup that has a missing toolbox and extra seating?"

"I know. It's not much," I grumped. I sure as hell wasn't telling him about the scents of those men or the one associated with the dead body. I'd recognize that, sure enough.

"What's this?" I crept past a late model silver extended cab that looked like the toolbox had been removed recently. The truck was clean except for a bit of red dirt behind the cab where a toolbox might fit. I drove a little way past, found a space and parked the van. Gavin got out with me and followed along behind as I walked casually toward the truck. Glancing around quickly to see if anybody was watching, I slipped between the truck and the car parked next to it.

"This is it," I said, nodding in satisfaction. I'd gotten a good whiff of the dead body right away. Gavin blinked at me for a moment, his nostrils flaring a little in surprise. I was afraid he'd belittle me or refute my certainty.

"What are you going to do?" he asked instead.

"Convince our friends, here, to come back with me," I said. "Phil and Glen can have them, I think."

We waited more than half an hour and it was nearing eleven when three men walked out of the restaurant, heading straight for the truck. They'd all been drinking Margaritas; I could smell the tequila. Gavin ducked behind the car parked next to the truck, leaving me to handle the situation. Later, he and I might have a talk about chickening out. He'd insisted on coming, after all.

"Hi," I said, walking up to the three men. They'd reached the tailgate of the truck.

"Hey, look at this," one of them grinned as he placed an arm around my shoulders. I had to force myself not to shudder and gag at his touch. He was tall and heavy, wearing a stained t-shirt and jeans. Definitely not a neat eater. His brown hair was a little on the long side, too, and he wore a goatee. His friends both looked like construction workers, with close-fitting t-shirts showing off muscles and everything.

"Look at me, guys," I said, doing my best to sound sexy. Hell, I don't think I've ever been sexy. Mostly I just wanted to throw up. "You're all coming home with me, aren't you?" I tried to put as much of what I had into that command. All three of them nodded eagerly.

"Good. Come with me," I motioned for them to follow. Gavin was trailing the four of us, walking in front of the parked cars while the three men and I walked behind them. I loaded my three passengers into the back of the van; they were all smiling and sliding onto seats willingly. Gavin climbed into the driver's seat so I handed him the keys. He drove us to the house while I watched our three guests, all of whom were sitting in the back grinning foolishly at me.

Gavin and I got our prisoners seated inside the kitchen while we waited for Phil and Glen. "You're going to answer every question these gentlemen ask you and you're going to be honest with your answers," I informed the three as Phil and Glen walked into the kitchen. I didn't ask for names. I had no desire to know who they really were. Phil was grinning as he questioned the first of our captives so Gavin and I left him to it, walking out of the house quickly.

"I think we should go get their truck," I said, holding up the keys I'd filched from one of the men. They'd been in his hand when I'd stopped him in the restaurant parking lot.

"Sounds reasonable," Gavin agreed. He drove their truck back and I was happy to let him have that chore. The smell of decay inside it made me want to gag and hold my nose.

Winkler and Davis were in the kitchen when we returned, watching while Phil and Glen continued their questioning. Winkler drifted over to us when we walked inside. "I remember that one," he pointed to the messy eater. I wouldn't have picked any of them out of a crowd; there were no outstanding features or anything. I knew their smell, though. They were the ones, no doubt about that.

"How did they get you out of the house?" I hadn't asked until now.

"I uh, have a baby sister," Winkler admitted reluctantly. "She's in college and they told me they had her. They were asking for a ransom and for me to meet them alone. I fell right into that trap."

"Is she all right?" I asked. Winkler's dark eyes were watching Phil, Glen and Davis. They were asking the three if anyone else was involved.

"Yeah," Winkler answered without looking at me. "I couldn't get her on her cell after they called me, so I panicked. Turns out she was studying in the library with her cell switched off. She now has body-guards of her own."

"Better safe than sorry," I nodded.

"What do you intend to do with those three?" Gavin asked.

"Phil and Glen will take care of it," Winkler still wasn't meeting my eyes. I didn't know how I felt about that. I didn't say anything, though. Gavin handed the keys to the kidnappers' truck over to Winkler, who accepted them with a nod. "Why don't you go get a drink?" Winkler suggested. He wanted us out of the way while Phil, Glen and Davis did whatever it was they were going to do. I didn't want to hang around to find out what that was either, so getting the hell away sounded like a good idea.

"Come on," I grabbed Gavin's arm and pulled him out of the house. We drove the Volvo. It was the car the day staff used and not nearly as nice as the Jaguar, but I didn't want anything that smelled like those three men around me. Gavin didn't argue when I climbed into the driver's seat. We drove for a while, eventually parking in a little spot that overlooked Lake Hefner. It was March seventh, a Saturday and fairly calm if a little cold out as I watched gray water lap the lake's edge. Gavin sat silently beside me. For a while, anyway.

"What was your life like, before?" he asked. I went still with fear. "What life before?" I answered his question as evenly as I could with one of my own, keeping my eyes on the water. Gavin didn't reply. I might have given anything at that moment to be able to discuss my past freely with someone—perhaps ask for advice or even a little sympathy. That, as far as I knew, was impossible. I had a secret to guard, one that could get me killed if I breathed even a partial sentence of it. No matter how much I trusted or distrusted someone, they weren't going to pry that secret open. If I wanted to die, I knew how to do it now. I also knew how painful it was going to be but it would likely be over in a matter of minutes. I knew how quickly my skin had blackened and melted while an early morning sun spread fingers of light across an Oklahoma wheat field. From that point forward, I didn't think I would ever look at wheat fields the same way.

That's what I ended up saying instead. "You know, I'm never going to look at a wheat field the same again," I said. "I think I'm always going to see the dirt I was digging through after I heard Winkler kicking the end of the toolbox with his feet. If I hadn't seen a little bit of reflection off the Jaguar's tail light where it was buried in a ditch, I would never have found him and he'd likely be dead now."

"How did you get the car out of the ditch?" Gavin latched onto another portion of my story that would have to be explained away.

Lying isn't something I like doing, but I lied shamelessly to Gavin. "A farmer came along with a tow bar on his truck. He helped me get the car out after I told him I'd swerved to miss hitting a deer."

"I hope that mud pack you were wearing helped your skin," Gavin almost smiled.

"Hmmph," I grumbled. "I've never heard of Oklahoma's red dirt being good for much of anything in that department. Did you know they have a rattlesnake roundup every year in several Oklahoma towns?" I asked, deliberately changing the subject. "Sometimes I feel sorry for the rattlesnakes." I spared a glance for him, but he was watching the water now.

"Perhaps the snakes should mark their calendars and arrange to be out of town during those times," Gavin said, his mouth quirking a little as he turned toward me.

"Well, there's an untapped market," I retorted. "Snake calendars. With snake cell phones and MP-3 players after that. Of course they can only pay scale." Gavin just held his head, the joke was so bad. "Sorry," I apologized. "Didn't mean to give you a headache."

"Take me out to the wheat field," Gavin said suddenly. I studied his face briefly and blew out a breath. The mask was back in place.

"All right," I said, starting the Volvo and putting it in gear. We shouldn't have gone. I had to drive past the turn-off; the silver pickup was parked on the edge of the wheat field and Phil, Glen and Davis were all out there digging, with three bodies lined up beside the original gravesite. "Fuck," I muttered as we slowly drove past. I was hoping they hadn't seen us.

"Don't worry about it," Gavin said softly. I was shaking, I know.

Maybe he was used to this sort of thing but I sure as hell wasn't. When we drove into Yukon, Gavin asked me to pull over and he switched places with me. I think if I hadn't been vampire, I would have lost anything I'd eaten in the past few hours. As it was, I just hunkered down in my seat, pulled my knees up to my chest and stared out the window on the way home.

CHAPTER 7

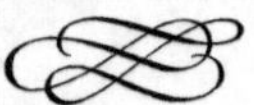

"*Honored One, the primary has performed past expectations. She found the three who kidnapped the secondary using what little she had at her disposal, including scent and deduction skills. I am amazed that she managed to solve that, yet remains ignorant of the fact that one of her own kind is never more than a few yards away most of the time. A fascinating paradox. Work has also slowed on the project. Will continue to keep you informed.*

G."

* * *

"PACK UP, baby sis wants to go on spring break." Those were the first words Winkler spoke when I walked into the main kitchen. Davis had been waiting on Gavin and me the minute we'd come away from the guesthouse, informing us that there was a meeting in the kitchen. Fortunately, I'd already sneaked out to feed.

"Where are we going?" Gavin's arms were crossed tightly over his chest.

"Port Aransas, Texas. One of the safer places for spring break, actually." Winkler was smiling. Maybe he could smile the day after having three men killed, but I couldn't. Yeah, I know they'd pretty much condemned him to death, but still. "We have to be at the airport in a couple of hours. The private jet will be there waiting for us."

Private jet. Winkler had a private jet. Maybe it was time for me to borrow somebody's computer and look him up on the internet. Instead, I grumbled the entire way to the guesthouse and even while I was throwing my meager supply of clothing into the roller bag.

"Stop complaining." Gavin stood in my half-open doorway, watching while I flung my six pairs of jeans into the bag. "Do you have any extra shampoo?"

Somehow, he must have known that I always buy in bulk. It saves future trips. Stalking into the bathroom, I pulled the full bottle from beneath the sink and brought it to him. "There," I said, plopping it into his hand. "Anything else? I have extra deodorant, conditioner and socks."

"No on all three counts," he replied, his beautiful brown eyes almost smiling. With Gavin, an almost-smile is as good as a guffaw from anyone else.

"Good," I muttered. "I don't like sharing my socks."

My trip on Winkler's private jet was probably going to come to mind every time I had to take a commercial flight from then on. The seats were wide and comfortable and nobody was crowded. No layover in Dallas, either—we'd flown straight to the Corpus Christi airport. Two security guards were there waiting on us with two of Winkler Security's ever-present SUVs. Winkler had left the add-on guards in Oklahoma City, hoping that continued activity there would indicate he was still in residence. If anybody left alive knew he'd been there, that is.

"You going out with us Tuesday night?" our security guard driver asked. Gavin, Davis and I had climbed into the same vehicle, but the driver was talking to Davis and not to us. Gavin had a few words with him and the other guard when we got off the plane but that was it. They could have been old friends, for all I knew.

"Yeah. Winkler already talked to Shirley." Davis was grinning at the guard. I had no idea who Shirley was and I found myself wondering if she was an old girlfriend or the proprietor of the local brothel. Those two choices seemed to encompass Winkler's relationships with women. Present company excepted, of course.

I also had a brand new envelope tucked away in my luggage, only this one held twenty-five thousand in cash. Winkler's reward to me for bringing in the three who'd tried to kill him. It felt like blood money to me, but it was money—ready cash in case I had to go on the run. The other thing he'd handed me (which shocked me completely), was a credit card with my name on it. It was an American Express employee card, through Winkler Security. Well, la-de-dah.

"So Davis doesn't have to keep giving you cash when you run errands for us." Winkler grinned as he said it, so I stopped myself from smacking him.

There was no condo waiting on us as the guard (whose name I learned was Todd) drove us out to Mustang Island. Oh, no. There was a beach house to end all beach houses. It had to be at least six thousand square feet with a detached garage and the inevitable guesthouse on top of that. Yeah, Gavin and I got that. "Come inside the house when you drop off your bags," Winkler ordered after we parked inside the spacious garage. "Sis is already here and I want you to meet her."

Gavin and I dutifully dropped our bags off in the large sitting area of the guesthouse, and he claimed the bedroom nearest the door, just like last time. It was larger than the one I was left with, but I wasn't about to argue. My bedroom had two twin beds in it; his had the queen. He was bigger than I was, I reasoned. I checked my windows plus the blinds and drapes that covered the windows. All appeared sufficient to block the light. My bedroom faced west, too, while Gavin had the east side. At least we had our own shower, just like last time.

Gavin was waiting for me at the bottom of the guesthouse steps after we'd settled in. Together we walked to the French doors at the back of the house. A wide, cedar plank deck that overlooked the waters of the gulf fronted those doors. The salt air on the barrier island was thick and almost tangible around us. Somehow, I knew there would be fog in the morning but I couldn't have said how I knew it. Gavin opened the door and motioned for me to go ahead of him. Winkler was there, a drink in his hand already, his sister peeking around his tall, muscular body.

"Lissa, this is my baby sis," Winkler said, pulling her around to introduce us. Her name was Whitney. Whitney Wynne Winkler. His name was William Wayne Winkler. And I thought my dad had a horrible sense of humor. Whitney took my hand and shook while I smiled at her. That warmed things up a little, I think. She was pretty, with the same shade of dark hair that Winkler had and stood about a foot shorter than her brother. Only Gavin was taller than Winkler, who topped six-three. That put Whitney just a little taller than I was and Davis, Phil, Glen and the two guards treated her like royalty.

Davis offered drinks and snacks to Gavin and me as we took seats inside the spacious family room. The others were engrossed in a Mavericks basketball game playing on the giant flat screen television mounted on the wall. Gavin asked for scotch and soda; I settled for a glass of wine. Alcohol has no effect on a vampire if they drink it straight. Mine had to be laced with blood and come directly from the source. In my limited experience, anyway. Gavin also had a quiet conversation with Whitney and she was smiling and laughing with him in no time. Go figure.

"Whitney wants to go shopping tomorrow evening at the mall in Corpus," Winkler informed me later. "I want you to go with her and Sam." Sam was the second guard that met us at the airport.

"All right," I nodded. Winkler and the rest of them went to bed around three; Gavin and I began our guard duty then. I enjoyed walking that perimeter—the ocean was beautiful and the sound of the water quite soothing.

The fog hung around all day and the weather was cooler than it normally was at this time of year. It served to hide me quite nicely when I rose the following evening and found a tourist to feed from. The young man tried to hug me as I drank from him. He even smelled nice—not covered up with suntan lotion or anything else—the scent was all him. I thanked him before telling him to forget me, sending him on his way down the beach.

That night was when I chose to wear the second outfit that Davis had brought to me in Dallas. I wore the short-sleeved plum top, along with the charcoal slacks and kitten heels. Winkler was appreciative of the clothing when I showed up inside the house a bit later. I'd passed Gavin on my way out the guesthouse door and noticed he was wearing a deep frown on his face, his arms crossed over his chest in obvious disapproval. Well, I was willing to let him take Whitney shopping while I stayed there and watched the house and the ocean.

Sam drove us in one of the SUVs. He and Whitney both sat in the front and kept up a teasing conversation during the entire drive into Corpus Christi. Sam was young, I thought, in his early twenties and quite a handsome kid. The blackest hair with eyes to match, coupled with a wolfish grin that came easily plus a great sense of humor. Whitney relaxed around him but always seemed a little tense around Phil, Glen and Davis. Maybe she was just sick of Winkler's bodyguards. I don't think it hurt any that Sam smelled three quarters human and one quarter warm puppy. Perhaps Whitney was responding to that, too. Phil always smelled like a wet dog to me. Could be his aftershave—how was I to know?

Padre Staples Mall is right off South Padre Island Drive and easy to find. We parked by Dillards and walked inside the mall, where I discovered quickly that Whitney was a shopaholic. Sam had to walk away while she rummaged through the lingerie section inside Dillards, talking about this bra as opposed to that one and loading the sales clerk down with underwear. "What do you think?" she held up a leopard-print bra in front of her small breasts, asking for my opinion.

"Well, that looks sexy," I said. "If that's your goal, mission accomplished."

Whitney's dimple showed in her cheek as she smiled at me. "I'll take it!" She bounced over to the clerk and added it to the growing pile. I hoped Winkler had as hefty a bank account as I imagined he might, he was going to need it. Whitney also picked out two pairs of panties that matched the leopard-print bra before turning to other colors. She spent fifteen hundred dollars on underwear in the first store alone.

Sam ran the bags out to the truck while Whitney and I ventured into the mall. Next came a small, exclusive dress shop where Whitney tried on dress after dress and then slacks and pretty blouses, most of which were silks or other expensive fabrics.

"I really want to look good tomorrow night when we go out," she dimpled again. I didn't ask her where she was going, I really didn't want to know. Wherever it was, it meant that Gavin and I got the night off to do as we pleased and I was looking forward to it. I'd already thought about climbing onto the roof of the beach house just to sit up there and watch the waters of the gulf. I'd only been to the beach twice before in my entire life and I'd never gotten to stay on the beach. Those hotels and condos were just too expensive for Don and me to afford.

Whitney spent another two thousand in the dress shop before going to look for shoes and handbags. An exclusive handbag shop got twelve hundred for two purses. The least expensive thing she bought was a pair of running shoes. We found heels, flats, sandals and flip-flops in Dillards on our way out. I could almost hear Winkler's credit card weeping pitifully from the abuse.

Whitney was hungry afterward, so we stopped at a seafood restaurant on the other side of the highway. She and Sam both ate like there was no tomorrow. I had no idea how she kept her pretty figure; they had appetizers, salads and three entrees between them. *Whitney must have the metabolism of a body-builder*, I mused while sipping my wine and watching the two of them eat and tease each other.

"Texas A&M, Corpus, is *not* the University of Texas," Whitney poked at Sam, who grinned and tried to tickle her. "*I* go to the University of Texas."

"Where they don't know a damn thing about agriculture," he shot back, tussling a little with her. "My dad owns most of the land south of here and we supply quite a bit of the U.S. with cotton and spinach," he grinned. "Come on, tell me you hate spinach." Whitney giggled as he successfully tickled her ribs.

"I hate spinach," she said, sitting up and straightening her long black hair. Sam laughed.

"We also grow avocados," Sam went on. "Tell me you don't like guacamole."

"I love guacamole," she offered a very pretty smile.

"See, there is something to love about me," he said.

Sam drove us home after that. Whitney was happily showing Winkler her purchases once we were inside the beach house. Except for the underwear, that is. That gave me the opportunity to slip out of the house. After changing into my normal uniform of jeans and athletic shoes, I took up my duty as guard. "Have fun?" Gavin grumbled as I passed him on my counter-clockwise walk around the perimeter.

"You have no idea," I rolled my eyes a little. He almost smiled. A good friend would have heard the tale of the bras and underwear, but Gavin wasn't a good friend. I didn't know what he was, truthfully, running hot and cold most of the time. He seldom showed any emotion, watching the rest of us covertly, at times. I didn't know what to make of that. As usual, I had to force Gavin out of my thoughts— that street went nowhere. While I worked my shift that night, I wondered if Winkler knew about the attraction between his sister and Sam. It was probably none of my business anyway, so I shrugged it off.

The following night off wasn't all mine to do as I pleased, I discovered. Winkler left a list of things to pick up at the grocery store in nearby Port Aransas, and the inside of the beach house looked like a hurricane had come through. The trip to the store came first, and (no surprise) the list was filled with snacks, junk food and sodas. Just as a practical joke, I threw in a couple bags of salad, fruit juice, bananas and apples, plus a few gourmet cheeses. I used to love Gruyere. A wedge went into the shopping cart. I also picked up ingredients to bake oatmeal cookies. At least those cookies had fiber in them.

I baked cookies later while I cleaned up the kitchen. With no cleaning staff in residence, things inside the beach house went down-hill as quickly as a loaded truck with no brakes. It was a beautiful kitchen, too, with granite countertops and island along with a very nice cooktop and double ovens. The cookies were done in no time. I let them cool before piling them on a platter and covering them with plastic wrap so the others would see what they were.

The kitchen was as clean as I could make it before starting on the living area and media room. There was popcorn between the sofa cushions, so I vacuumed the whole thing out. The rings on the glass coffee table were wiped off and I even dusted a little. No way was I touching the bedrooms, though. I figured those were in an even bigger mess. I did clean the main bathroom. It needed it already; it smelled like men.

Then I went to do my roof sitting. The peak of the roof was a good place to settle and watch a full moon rise over the gulf waters. The light cast a wide path over the ocean, which twinkled with the constant movement of the water. The sky above me was a deep, clear blue that nearly sparkled with crispness. Gavin didn't make a sound as he climbed onto the roof, sitting down about a foot away from me. My knees were drawn up to my chin while I sat there, my arms hugging my legs. Gavin didn't say anything as he settled nearby.

"Bored?" I finally asked to break the silence.

"Occasionally," he said. "Not now."

"I came up to watch the moon over the water," I said.

"I came up to watch, too."

My chin was now resting on my knees as I watched the water. Gavin had unwittingly disturbed my peace when he climbed up to join me. Now, instead of the soothing sound of the surf, Gavin's scent hung thick in the air. That unsettled me and eventually brought me to my feet. I dusted the back of my jeans and walked over to the edge of the roof, climbing down onto the frame of the wooden deck. That's how I'd climbed up to start with, so I decided to go down the same way. Gavin didn't follow.

* * *

"THOSE COOKIES WERE SO GOOD, I think Winkler ate half of them," Davis told me the following evening. "Does this mean you know how to cook? I mean for real?"

"Yeah, I know how to cook for real," I said. "Why?"

"Well, a meal might not go amiss, now and then," Davis was almost begging. "You know what a big deal it is for all of us to go out and eat."

I did know that. It was almost a circus, with Winkler surrounded by security at all times. That had to bother him. It would me.

"If you'll let me run to the store, I'll fix something tonight," I said. "In fact, I'll make Winkler a chicken-fried steak. Maybe the best he's ever had. At least it'll be authentic."

"Tell me what you want to drive," Davis was very interested now. There was a four-year-old Cadillac in the garage in addition to the two SUVs. I took the Cadillac and picked up everything I needed, along with enough chicken breasts and thighs to do fried chicken for them in a night or two.

Winkler got his chicken-fry, plus mashed potatoes and gravy, baby peas and Texas toast. I made chocolate pie for dessert. No, I can't taste it anymore, but I'd been cooking for nearly thirty years. I knew what I was doing. I did eat a little of the meal to make things look normal, but I had to get rid of it later, which was a shame. I had the memory of what it all had tasted like. It was a good thing I made three chocolate pies; Winkler ate half of one by himself. And he loved the chicken-fried steak.

"What do you do to the mashed potatoes?" he asked. Those were a specialty.

"A lot of butter and half-and-half, and then you whip them," I said.

"Do you know how to make egg custard pie?" Whitney asked, her eyes pleading.

"Yeah. My mother taught me," I said. "I use half-and-half in that, too, instead of milk. It makes it creamier."

"Will you make one for me? Please?" She was begging.

"Tomorrow," I laughed. "I'll do fried chicken and make a custard pie."

"Can you make enough for two extras, tomorrow?" Winkler asked. "We're expecting guests."

"I think so. Do they eat as much as you do?" I teased.

"Probably," he grinned. "Thanks for cleaning up, by the way. Phil wasn't looking forward to vacuuming."

"We probably need to clean some more if company's coming," I put my hands on my hips, just like my mother used to. Gavin was standing in a corner, snickering at my antics. "Are they spending the night?" I asked, glaring at Gavin. He schooled his face into a blank expression.

"No, not spending the night," Winkler said. Sam and Todd came into the house then and helped themselves to what remained of dinner. There wasn't anything left to throw out or put away when I loaded up the dishwasher the second time. I hauled out the mop, cleaned the kitchen floor and then did a little vacuuming after that.

"I think these guys were raised in a barn," I told Whitney later, making her laugh.

My rounds came next. Gavin and I passed each other three times before he said anything. "They'll expect those things from now on," he pointed out.

"I know." I sighed a little. "I don't mind cooking and cleaning. At least I know what I'm doing."

"You don't know what you're doing now?" The question and his gaze were almost gentle.

"I have no idea what I'm doing," I told him. "I've had to make this up as I go along. It's isn't like somebody handed me a manual, or anything." That was a double entendre but he didn't know that.

"And what if the manual doesn't exist?" he stepped a little closer and I felt his breath fan the hair at my temple.

"Then somebody screwed up," I said tartly. "If there isn't a manual, then somebody needs to write it or show up. What's that old saying—when the student is ready, the teacher appears? That's all idealistic bullshit." I watched his lips quirk a little.

"I'm not sure they meant a physical teacher," Gavin was smiling now.

"Then they need to say what they mean and stop talking in circles," I grumbled. We were standing in front of the house where we usually passed each other on our rounds. Gavin lifted his hand, just for a moment, as if he were about to touch my cheek and then thought better of it. That wasn't him and we were standing in front of the house, even though all the lights were out and everybody was probably asleep. I started walking again. After a few seconds, Gavin did, too. We didn't speak again the remainder of the night.

* * *

"Lissa, this is Weldon Harper and his son, Daryl," Winkler introduced his guests. Weldon Harper was tall and almost as broad across the shoulders as Gavin was. Dark-haired and eyed, he had rugged good looks and I imagined he might win the tough man competition should he ever decide to enter. His son Daryl looked very much like him. Maybe half an inch shorter, if that. Two others had come in as well—Shirley Walker and Daniel Carey. Here was the elusive Shirley Walker, and she didn't fit any of my expectations. Shirley was nearly six feet tall and looked like she could give Weldon Harper a good run for his money. Daniel Carey was tall and lean; he had to be at least six-six with a military bearing about him.

Thankfully, I had enough fried chicken. I'd asked Winkler if he wanted a sit-down dinner or if he wanted it buffet style. He opted for buffet style, so everybody helped themselves. Phil, Davis and Glen almost fell over each other, offering drinks to Weldon and his son. Sam was there as well, keeping his eyes on Whitney most of the night while everybody else pretty much ignored him and Todd.

It didn't take a genius to figure out that Weldon was important, although nobody ever said how or why and I knew enough not to ask. Whitney hugged me after she ate her first piece of custard pie and then had another slice. She might have eaten more than that but all four pies were gone by that time. "I'll make more, sometime," I promised. That got me another hug. Go figure. Female Vampire-Security Guard-Cook. I wondered how that would fit on a business card. That brought me to the thought about vampires in general. I knew Ed and Serge had come to the bar together. How did they know each other? How had they met? Was there a vampire network out there somewhere? Some way to connect? There was no way of telling.

The fog settled in again that night as I cleaned up the kitchen and left Winkler and his guests talking and laughing in the media room. Afterward, I went off to make my rounds in the mist. The fog thickened as the night wore on, bringing up something I'd forgotten. Was it a possibility, (it was, according to fiction and folklore) that vampires could turn to mist? I thought that it was likely just as ridiculous as a vampire turning into a bat. It might not hurt to try, though, just for fun, since I was surrounded by mist as I walked the perimeter.

When it was time for my nightly break, I walked out toward the water, standing there and concentrating. I know, I thought it was ridiculous, too. I was ready to give up on my concentration after a couple of minutes, but that's when I noticed the change. Looking down, I could no longer see my hands. Or my feet. *What the hell?* That shook me a little, causing my limbs to rematerialize. Taking a couple of deep, calming breaths, I decided to try again. I think it took roughly five minutes or so, but I felt light as a feather after that, discovering I could move around just by willing it. I floated over the house. Man, this was *something*. I wish I'd known about this before. I returned to the foggy beach and concentrated on becoming solid again. It took another five minutes. Okay, not good as a weapon if you wanted to jump somebody—it took too long. But if you wanted to slip inside somewhere, or had time to turn and then turn back again, it had possibilities. Too bad I didn't have any vamp friends with whom to discuss this. Or the *FVM,* to explain all the ramifications. Actually, I was too excited about the whole thing at the moment. I could turn to mist and *fly*.

"Who was visiting?" Gavin finally asked as we passed on one of our rounds.

"Some guy named Weldon Harper and his son Daryl," I said. I wasn't expecting his swift intake of breath. "What? Who is he?" I demanded, stopping short and staring at Gavin.

"It's better that you don't know," Gavin replied enigmatically. "For your own safety."

"Crap," I mumbled. "Was I in danger tonight?"

"No more so than you usually are," Gavin replied cryptically. "Don't ask any questions about him, Lissa. This is important." He gripped my shoulder—hard.

"All right," I huffed, pulling away from his grasp. His fingers digging into my skin hurt a little. We finished out our shift and I was more than glad to get a shower and climb into bed just as dawn was announcing its arrival.

"Are you going to cook for us tonight?" Whitney had a hopeful look in her eyes when I walked into the house the following evening.

"What do you want?" I asked. "I could run into Port Aransas to that little grocery store they have if you tell me what you'd like."

"Can you make chicken and dumplings? I haven't had that in three years," she was pouting a little.

"How old are you?" I asked.

"I just turned twenty, two months ago," she brightened up a little.

"Well then, as a belated birthday present, I'll make chicken and dumplings for you. Tell Winkler I went to the store," I said. Phil, Glen and Davis were all lounging around the kitchen and they heard me, so I guess that was good enough if she did forget to tell her brother.

Whitney got chicken and dumplings about an hour and a half later, plus peanut butter cookies. I don't know where she or any of those men, for that matter, puts all that food. They never gain an ounce. I'd gotten my meal in town, behind the post office. Just about anybody would have thought I was necking with the man and he certainly enjoyed it. "Where are Sam and Todd?" I asked while I picked up plates.

"Sam went home to spend a couple of days with his dad before going back to school," Whitney grumbled. "Todd works for Sam's dad, so he drove Sam to his dad's ranch."

"That was really good, Lissa," Winkler said, changing the subject. "You're spoiling us," he rubbed his stomach. "The cook we have in Dallas can't do chicken and dumplings like that."

"You can always look for another cook," I said and shut the door of the dishwasher, turning it on. "I'm off to trot around the property."

* * *

THAT WAS THURSDAY NIGHT. I was just getting out of bed Friday night when Davis came knocking on my door.

Gavin was already up and not looking happy about it, I noticed. He and Davis were standing outside when I opened my bedroom door. "What's going on?" I asked, confused. Davis was worried about something.

"Whitney's gone and we can't find her," Davis said, worry creasing his brow. "We found evidence that she walked out to the mailbox. That's what she told us she was going to do, but we found no trace of her when she didn't come back to the house. Winkler's about to tear the place apart. We're hoping you can help us out with this."

His eyes were begging me to be able to help them out with this. The truth was, I probably wouldn't have a better clue than they did about what had happened. "Did you find the mail or anything else she might have left behind?"

"There were a couple of flyers on the ground. Phil picked those up and brought them to the house," Davis said. "But we can't find anything unusual about them."

"Fuck," I muttered, running a hand through my hair. It hung three inches past my shoulders and was long enough to braid or pull up in a clip if I wanted. "Let me get dressed." I was still in my pajamas, my feet bare.

"All right, but hurry it up, willya?" Davis left the guesthouse.

"I suppose you're going to wait the usual twenty-four hours before doing anything?" I asked Gavin minutes later as I hastily stuffed a foot into one of my black athletic shoes. He shrugged as I ran out the door. Hot and cold. That was Gavin. It made me wonder if he cared about anything. The mail that Phil picked up was sitting on the kitchen island, so I held it to my nose and sniffed discreetly. Whitney's scent was fresh. Two other scents were Phil and possibly the mailman.

Winkler barreled into the room, ready to explode. No way did I want to stand in front of the man when he was like this and I was a vampire.

"Where does Sam live?" I asked, worried that Winkler might take the house and a few people apart. "You know Whitney has a crush on him."

"What?" Winkler thundered.

"They like each other, doofus. Have you checked with him?" It was possible—he had a cell, she had a cell. I assumed they'd exchanged numbers.

"Probably not a good idea to call the boss doofus when he's like this," Davis whispered in my ear.

"Gotcha," I said, allowing Davis to back me away from Winkler, who now appeared to be growling.

"Sam lives between Alice and Freer," Glen said, punching a number into his cell phone. With my hearing, I could hear it ringing from where I was standing. The conversation came in loud and clear, too.

"Hello," a man answered, and it wasn't the Sam I knew.

"This is Glen Danford," Glen said. "Is Sam Jr. there?"

"I wondered when you'd call," the voice said. "I'm afraid Whitney and Sam managed to get a marriage license three days ago. They got married this afternoon and only called a few minutes ago to let me know. They're on their way here now."

"Oh, lord," I muttered. Winkler went crazy.

"Get out of the house, get out of the house," Davis had a hard grip on my upper arm and was dragging me out the French doors and onto the deck as Winkler raged inside the house. "Go down the beach, go somewhere. Just get the hell away from here. I'll call when it's safe," Davis almost flung me down the steps leading to the beach.

I ran. Not as fast as I could go, mind you, but pretty fast, anyway. While I ran, my brain worked furiously. I figured Sam might be in trouble if Winkler caught up with him anytime soon. Sam was a good kid and I didn't want anything happening to him. Skidding to a stop on the sandy beach, I turned on a dime and trotted toward the garage, punching numbers into my cell phone as I went.

I knew Sam's last name and hoped he was listed in the phone book. It took a few minutes to call information on my cell phone, since the reception on the beach sucked. Seconds ticked away while I waited for an answer. After getting an operator, I asked if there was a listing for Sam Sheridan.

"Junior or Senior?"

"Uh, Senior, I guess," I replied. "Is the address the same for both?"

"Yes." The operator rattled off the number and the address, which was somewhere off highway 44. I thanked the woman and hung up.

"Where are you going?" Gavin demanded when I raced inside the guesthouse to grab my purse. No sense driving without a license, even if it was bogus.

"To prevent a murder, I hope," I said and ran downstairs to the garage. One of the SUVs was missing; Winkler was on his way already.

"What happened?" Gavin was beside me in a blink.

"Sam and Whitney got married this afternoon," I said, jerking the door to the Cadillac open. I hoped it had gas in it.

"Christ," Gavin muttered, running a hand through nearly black hair. "Lissa, you don't need to get in the middle of this." Was that concern in his brown eyes? Couldn't be. They were hooded immediately.

"That kid doesn't deserve to die and don't stand there and tell me Whitney didn't participate in this," I snapped at him. He could've volunteered to help me, but then this was Gavin, the man who stood on the sidelines and watched everybody else worry. "Winkler just needs to calm down enough to see sense," I said.

"And if Winkler doesn't calm down, you could end up dead!" Gavin was almost shouting, now. Well, here was emotion—it was just the wrong kind.

"You know what?" I looked at him steadily over the car door. "I'm already dead." I slid into the Cadillac, starting it up and driving off, leaving Gavin standing in the garage, cursing loudly.

The Cadillac had built-in GPS; I'd never have found the place without the gadget telling me how to get there. Winkler, Phil, Glen and Davis had gotten there ahead of me—I could see the SUV parked in the driveway of the large farmhouse while all four of them fretted and paced behind the vehicle. They never saw me as I drove slowly past the lane leading to the Sheridan home. I watched in shock as Phil lifted up the rifle he was carrying, firing it at the house. Okay, things were already serious. All four men ducked behind the SUV when return gunfire came from the house. It was time for strategy.

I left the car about a quarter of a mile down the road and ran back. There were a few trees around the house suitable to hide my presence, so I sneaked in behind one of those. The gunshots were sporadic; I don't think anybody wanted the police to show up. There was some shouting back and forth, though, and more than a little creative cursing going on. Blocking all of that out of my mind, I concentrated instead on turning to mist.

A window on the second floor was open a couple of inches. The night was nearly perfect, with a light breeze rustling the trees and the surrounding cotton crop as I misted through the small space the open window provided. It would be infinitely more enjoyable if bullets weren't flying. I couldn't hear anybody upstairs so I floated halfway down the steps. Sam was there at the bottom of the landing, holding a sobbing Whitney. Sam Sr. was gripping a rifle and kneeling next to one of the front windows. For a moment, flashbacks to hundreds of old westerns skipped through my mind, along with visions of gun-wielding cowboy heroes that never seemed to run out of bullets.

It took the full five minutes to turn back to myself and Whitney almost shrieked when I slipped down the rest of the steps, coming to a stop next to her and Sam.

"Calm down, both of you," I said, holding my hands out in a placating gesture. Sam Sr. was now pointing his rifle at me, but lowered it when Sam explained that I was a friend.

"Why are you here?" Whitney was still sobbing.

"Whitney, if we aren't careful, somebody is going to die over this," I told her. "Maybe more than one somebody. If you want to avoid that, you need to walk out of this house with me, right now. Your brother needs to calm down—enough that you can talk some sense to him, anyway." I wiped tears off her face with a thumb. "You have to be the grown-up here, I think."

"Will was going to sell me to Weldon Harper's son," Whitney was back to weeping. "I don't want him. I don't."

"I know that, honey. But you have to say that to your brother. I don't think he wants to hurt you. He was shocked when he found out you cared about Sam." Whitney blinked as I explained this to her and more tears fell. Sam was trying to get his arms around her again while Sam Sr. went back to his window.

"Will you walk out with me?" Whitney's voice quavered. She'd made a decision.

"I said I would," I nodded.

"We're coming out!" I shouted, "Whitney and I!" I was slowly opening the front door so they wouldn't shoot first and ask questions later. I was also shielding Whitney's body with my own as much as I could. I had no idea what reaction a vampire's body would have if it sustained bullet wounds. Yeah, I was shaking when I walked out the door.

"Winkler, we're coming out," I called again, watching him, Phil, Glen and Davis closely. They were all standing there, rifles at the ready, as Whitney and I walked across the wide front porch and then down the steps leading to Sam's home. I think we would have been all right and Winkler might have calmed down as soon as he got his hands on Whitney, but Sam, thinking Whitney was walking away from him for good, ran after us shouting her name. It took every bit of speed I had to shove my body in front of his, and I felt all three bullets enter my back when they shot me.

CHAPTER 8

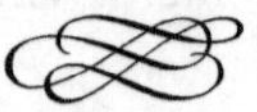

I must have been in and out of consciousness and had no idea how I came to be where I was. I thought I heard Gavin shouting at one point, followed by more blackness and then horrible pain around my back, as if someone were digging around in it. More yelling came, followed by something cold in my mouth and after that, nothing.

I was a little stiff when I woke but I did wake—alone and inside my guesthouse bedroom. Well, that was it for me. I didn't care who it was that shot me. They'd been trying to shoot Sam instead of talking about it first. I didn't need this. I sat up slowly, swinging my legs over the side of the bed. I felt achy, experiencing a bit of sharp pain around my back. Vampires heal extraordinarily fast, I suppose. I'd certainly healed quickly from the burns I'd gotten in a wheat field one fateful morning. Dragging myself to the closet, I pulled my bag out and with much effort and hefting, I lifted it onto the bed. Wishing I could move faster than the snail's pace I was going at right then, I dumped clothing inside the suitcase, not caring if it was folded properly or not. After the clothes, I tossed in my toiletries and the envelope of cash I had. No way was I giving any of that back now. The fuckers had shot me. I intended to call a cab on my cell phone and then throw the phone at the house as hard as I could when I left. Surely I could get a plane ticket—one that would land me somewhere else before dawn arrived.

"What the fuck are you doing?" Gavin was standing in my doorway, staring at my nearly packed suitcase. I was tossing my bottle of shampoo in the bag when he appeared.

"Getting the hell out of here," I snapped. "No way I'm working for somebody who's that trigger happy."

"And just where do you intend to go?" Gavin glared at me.

"Just about anywhere," I said. "As long as they speak English there and don't shoot at me." I glared right back at Gavin.

"Lissa, listen to me. You can't go."

I zipped my bag closed and set it on the floor. "Why the hell not?" I asked.

"Because Winkler won't let you, that's why," Gavin said. "Do you think he didn't run a background check on you when you went to work for him? He's in the security business, Lissa. He knows your ID is fake." He now wore a slight frown and his arms were crossed over his chest while he watched the fear come over me.

"Oh, dear God." I slumped onto the bed, dropping my head in my hands. "Why did he hire me, then?" I looked up at Gavin. I was having trouble keeping the quaver out of my voice. Tears were threatening and I had no desire for Gavin to see that.

"Because you could be useful to him and he had a way to blackmail you, didn't he?" Gavin said.

"So, all he has to do if I don't obey his every whim is threaten me?"

"Or worse. Don't get me wrong, most of the time he's a reasonable man. Other times, well, you know what happened last night."

"Yeah." My back was throbbing from what happened last night. "Is Sam still alive?" I was shivering, now.

"Yes. Very much so. And still married to Whitney, it seems. Flaring tempers almost turned that whole thing into a bloodbath last night. You were the one standing in the middle of it all."

"Lucky me," I retorted. "I hope he never wants a meal cooked by me again. The asshole."

"Lissa, he didn't shoot you. Phil did. All three times."

"Great. My least favorite asshole." I got off the bed and paced a little, hugging myself tightly. "Prick. Jerk. Motherfucker." I wasn't sure I had enough obscenities to cover what I thought of Phil. Turning back to Gavin, I examined his face. It had become just as shuttered as it usually was. "Why are you bothering to tell me this? Why do you care?"

"Lissa, don't." Gavin turned away from me.

"So, I'm supposed to stay and pretend nothing happened? Like I wasn't shot, getting his sister back for him? Like I didn't stop Phil from murdering Sam? Because that's what happened. When Sam ran out the door, it was all I could do to jump in front of him before the bullets started flying."

"I think Sam's father is grateful," Gavin said, his back to me, still.

"Yeah? That does me a lot of good." I picked up my suitcase and flung it through the closet door. "Get out," I said. "Right now, I don't think I want to talk to anybody, including you. Does Mr. High and Mighty Winkler expect me to guard the perimeter, tonight? I'll drag myself to work if I have to. And thanks for waiting to tell me he could blackmail me any damn time he wanted. Get out!" I flung an arm out, knocking a vase of silk flowers off the chest beside the door. That must have done it for me. I threw everything I could get my hands on, smashing it against the wall. Some of it went through the sheetrock, I threw it so hard. I was weeping and cursing while things broke inside my bedroom that night.

* * *

"She's a little upset," Gavin informed Winkler. "I told her she had to stay and she started throwing things. It'll stop when she runs out of things to throw. I hope you didn't have anything important in there."

"Fuck," Winkler sighed and walked into the kitchen. "I can't let her go—fuck."

"Phil should stay as far away from her as he can get," Gavin observed dryly.

"You think I didn't tell him that already? I'd be dead if not for her. Hell, Sam or Whitney might be dead if not for her. And I still don't know how she tracked those three assassins. I can't let her go."

"Your second in command ruined this, you know. Now she hates you just as much as she hates him. You've seen how fiercely she protects someone she cares for. You may have removed yourself from that equation."

"I know. Fuck."

"When do you expect her to go back to work?"

"I don't know. What is it, Saturday?" Winkler was pacing in the kitchen.

"Yes. Saturday evening."

"Then put her back to work on Wednesday if she's up to it. If not, let me know. Do you think she'll accept payment as compensation?" Winkler looked at Gavin.

"I may be very wrong, but I don't think she'll accept anything from you right now."

"I know that, too."

Gavin let himself into the guesthouse as quietly as he could, but silence was all he heard from Lissa's bedroom until he heard the sob. And it was followed by another. "No, Lissa," Gavin whispered. "No."

* * *

GAVIN SLIPPED a note under my door, telling me that I wasn't to go back to work until Wednesday. Great. Perfect. I still wanted to run away, but Winkler could call holy hell down on me. No way could any normal person get over three gunshot wounds to the back that quickly. *No way.* He knew what I was. It was likely that Gavin and the others did, too. Fucking perfect. I'd made myself a hostage. Tied myself up with a ribbon and handed myself right over to them. Now there wasn't any telling what I might be asked to do. I still had one option, as painful as that might turn out to be. At least I'd be dead at the end of it and beyond their reach. And I still had to feed myself, on top of it all. It's not as if you can go to the counter in 7-Eleven and buy a pint of blood.

"Where have you been?" Gavin started in on me the minute I got back from having dinner.

"You know what I am so I don't have to mince words anymore," I snapped angrily. "I have to eat, you know."

"Lissa, there are other ways. Come here. Winkler had this brought in for you."

I didn't want to "come here", but Gavin repeated his request so I followed him into the kitchen. He opened the refrigerator door and I stared at shelves filled with bagged blood.

"Money can get you anything," I said angrily, slamming the refrigerator door so hard it rocked a little.

"Don't try to heat it, it will kill the nutrients and make you ill," Gavin said. "You have to drink it cold."

"So, just pour it in a glass and add a stalk of celery?" I asked sarcastically.

"If it makes you feel better, go ahead. And you won't upset me if I see you drinking it," he added.

"Yeah, figures," I grumbled. "Gavin—the man that nothing bothers."

"Lissa, not everyone is your enemy."

"No? Point out somebody who isn't," I flung out an arm as I turned and stalked back to my bedroom.

I ran out of books to read on Sunday, so I took the keys to the Cadillac. Somebody had found it and driven it home. I didn't even ask or tell anybody where I was going, which meant there was the usual committee waiting on me when I got back.

"I went to Barnes and Noble. Vampires read. Get over it," I said, holding my bag of books up when I got out of the car. Fortunately, Phil wasn't a member of the welcoming party. I'd have thrown the hardcovers at his head if he'd been there. I wouldn't have missed, either. As it was, Gavin, Winkler, Davis and Glen were all there. Whitney had gone back to school—Gavin said that Todd had taken her to Austin while Sam had gone back to school in Corpus Christi. They were going to see each other on weekends until the end of the semester. Sam and Todd had been the bodyguards Winkler had assigned to Whitney, and that's how the two had gotten together in the first place. Winkler might be a genius, but that didn't prevent him from having blind spots. I thought about throwing books at him, too.

"What will make you not angry with us?" Winkler asked as I brushed past him, heading toward the guesthouse stairs.

"Nothing comes to mind," I said and ran up the steps.

Gavin told me later that Winkler decided to stay in Port Aransas for a while. He wanted to be closer to Whitney and Port A was a compromise. A crew drove all his equipment down on Tuesday afternoon, and then helped set it up for him in one of the extra bedrooms inside the house.

I also had a letter in the mail from Whitney. I found it on the kitchen table when I rose on Wednesday.

"Lissa," the letter began, *"I am so sorry for what happened to you. My brother says you won't even talk to him now and Sam feels responsible. We were so afraid Will was going to send me off to Daryl Harper that we had to do something. I should have known better. I'm sorry.*

Whitney"

I had to dig through several drawers in the guesthouse before I found paper and a pen to write an answer. *"Whitney,"* I wrote back, *"I would never have come after you if I hadn't been scared to death that your brother was going to kill somebody. I had no idea Phil would turn out to be more trigger happy than your brother. I can't say whether I appreciate it all that much or not. Don't worry about me. Study hard. I hope things work out well for you and Sam—Lissa."*

"Here," I slapped the folded note in front of Winkler before I went to work. "You'd more than likely read it anyway before it got mailed so I'm saving you the trouble of steaming it open. Please see that it gets to your sister." My back ached a little as I walked the perimeter afterward. I didn't speak to Gavin at all while we worked and he barely looked at me when we passed one another. I saw Glen when he relieved us in the morning, but Phil wasn't anywhere around. I hadn't seen him since he shot me, and that was more than fine.

Winkler was sitting on the end of my bed when I woke Thursday night. "Very nice," I said angrily. "Just walk right in when I can't defend myself. Is this your way of making me feel special?"

"Lissa, I just came to apologize. For everything." Winkler picked at the comforter that I'd kicked to the foot of the bed. "No," he held up a hand, "I can't let you go. You're important. You've done more for me in the past few weeks than most people have during years of employment. I can't let that walk away, Lissa. I understand that an irresponsible vampire turned you and left you out in the cold. There's nothing I can do about that. What I can offer, though, is as much safety as I can during the day when you sleep. I always have guards around me, Lissa, and they'll guard you, too, just as you do me at night."

"And just how many of them do you intend to tell about what I am?" I demanded. "All of them? If so, you might as well stake me right now or cut off my head."

"Lissa, the only ones who know are the ones who are here now. Me, Phil, Glen, Davis and Gavin. That's it."

"Phil," I snorted. "Did he take shooting lessons from Dick Cheney?"

Winkler ducked his head to hide the smile. "Lissa, he's been reprimanded."

"That ought to improve our relationship," I said tartly.

"He's doing his best to stay out of your way," Winkler went on. "Lissa, we miss you. Glen, Davis and I. I can't speak for Phil."

"Yeah? I spoiled all his fun by living over it, I'm sure. Who dug the bullets out, by the way? I vaguely remember somebody digging around in my back. It wasn't a pleasant experience."

"Gavin did that," Winkler said, rising from my bed. "And he shouted at us the entire time." Winkler walked out of my bedroom.

"Fuck," I said and slid off the bed.

The waves were washing up just a few feet from where I sat on the beach, digging my toes into the sand during my break later. There was the barest sliver of moon overhead, but with my enhanced eyesight, I could see clearly. Gavin came to sit beside me.

"So," he said. "Care to tell me now about your life before?"

"Not really, no," I said, refusing to look at him.

"I can do research and find out for myself."

"No doubt," I snapped in irritation.

"Actually, I already did," he told me. "The Lissa is correct—you were Lissa Beth Workman, who disappeared on January fourth. Haven't been a vampire long, have you, Lissa Beth?"

"Nope. Died on the same day as my husband, but you probably know that already," I said. "Did you know I was a bar bet?"

"A bar bet?" Gavin didn't understand. Neither did I.

"Those two who turned me? I found the cocktail napkin they wrote the wager on in the cellar where I woke up. One was agreeing to pay a million pounds if I took less than nine days to turn. Isn't that great? Those two must have been a barrel of laughs. And now they're out there somewhere, searching for me so they can make me very, very, dead. Too bad they don't know Phil. So far he and the sun in a wheat field almost did me in."

"You were burned." He didn't make it a question.

"Yeah. I figure that if things become unbearable, that's my ticket out. I know how painful it is, now. And how quickly it can happen. I was able to dig into the ground and cover myself up in that field. Next time it'll be on purpose and I'll stand in the middle of a concrete road to do it. Poof." I fluttered my fingers.

"You almost sacrificed yourself to dig Winkler out of that field."

"Yeah. Stupid, huh?"

"Lissa?"

"What, Gavin?" I turned to look at him, then.

"Don't talk about walking into the sun to me. Ever again." He stood and stalked away.

* * *

"WE'RE GOING to the movies and that's that." Winkler had gathered us inside the beach house. Phil was there but I was doing my best not to look at him. Why was Winkler doing this to me? He didn't need more than three or four people and now he was taking Glen, Phil, Davis, a new hire named Leon, and then Gavin and me.

"Calm down," Gavin whispered in my ear. I wanted to slug him.

Winkler picked the film, of course. We all piled into both SUVs and went to the movies. At least it wasn't a horror flick. I hate those things. They sling buckets of fake blood around and slice off body parts made of animals or something. I don't find that entertaining. It was an action/adventure and almost as bad—it still had fake blood and improvised body parts in it. I just turned my head while that was happening. Gavin, who sat next to me, started stroking my spine until his fingers were at the small of my back and then he made slow circles there. I shivered. Nobody had touched me that way in a long, long time. Don had heart problems and with the medication and everything, the risk was too great. It had been more than seven years since I'd had sex. I missed it at first, before resigning myself to the fact that that part of my life was over. Gavin was trying to wake something that should be left sleeping. I gently removed his hand and he didn't try again.

Winkler wanted to eat afterward, so we ended up at Outback Steakhouse.

"Why didn't you just order an entire cow?" I asked Winkler. There was enough beef on the table to assemble a cow, I figured.

"Can you survive on beef blood?" Phil chewed a huge chunk of steak.

"I have no idea. Can cows have orgasms if a vampire bites them?" Gavin snickered beside me.

"Is that what happens?" Glen was now interested.

"I leave everybody with a smile on their face," I said.

"You're kidding?" Davis said in disbelief.

"Not kidding. And no, I'm not about to let you find out in person."

"Do we need to have this discussion now?" Winkler cut into his steak.

"Hop Along started it," I nodded at Phil. "You know, I went to a restaurant in San Francisco, once," I went on. "And they brought out this huge, live lobster on a tray so everybody could stare at him and decide if that's what they wanted for dinner. My husband, God rest his soul, stood up and shouted *Let my people go*! Of course the restaurant asked us to leave."

"You were married?" Davis asked.

"I was, for twenty-three years. He died the same day I did."

"I knew that already," Winkler said.

"Lissa, enough," Gavin admonished.

"All right. If I leave now, I can be home in a few minutes. Let me out, Gavin." I bumped my hip against his so he'd let me out of the booth.

"No. You will sit there and be polite," he informed me. "I don't know what has gotten into you."

"Me either," I muttered sullenly.

"Lissa, you should be more circumspect. You never know who may be listening," Gavin lectured me later after we drove home.

"I know," I mumbled, ashamed. "It's just that there hasn't been anyone to talk to about any of this, nobody to tell me what's right or wrong and I've had to hold it inside me all this time. It hasn't been easy and there are still times I want to scream my lungs out because I'm so angry. I didn't ask for this, Gavin. And now, my brother-in-law and his wife have everything that was mine that I worked for—everything I put together and held together, even when my husband was too sick to work anymore. I'm here because Winkler still wants to use me, there are two out there who want to kill me, possibly three—Phil would still like to take me down, I figure. I have nobody who wants to be friends because they like me or anything. I'm a useful tool, Gavin. That's what I am." He didn't say anything or argue with any of my statements. *Swell.* I walked away from him to make my rounds. Any other guard would need a flashlight to do what I did. I didn't need one. Useful tool, indeed.

* * *

"You cannot allow this!" Gavin was shouting again.

"It's already done," Winkler said, resignation in his voice. "He called this morning. The arrangements have already been made. She'll be back in two weeks."

"Tell me why you agreed to this." Gavin was growling, now.

"I don't have a choice. I take orders from him, in a manner of speaking. I have to abide by that."

"This is untenable," Gavin stalked out the French doors.

"Lissa, Winkler wants to see you," Gavin announced when he walked inside the guesthouse.

* * *

"What does he want?" I asked. "Cookies?"

"I wish it were cookies," he said. "Go. Find out for yourself."

"What is it?" I asked, the minute I made my way inside the beach house.

Winkler was sitting at the kitchen table when I walked in. He looked a little rumpled, to be honest. "Lissa let me start out by saying that if I had a choice in the matter, I would have said no. As it is, Weldon Harper is an important man and I have to follow his orders. He will be flying you to North Dakota where he lives and you will provide security for him as a personal bodyguard. You must do this, Lissa. You must guard him and his son, if he desires, as zealously as you ever guarded Whitney or me. Do you understand?"

"Does he know about me?" I swallowed nervously.

"He knows. He knew when he was here. He hasn't become powerful by being stupid, Lissa. We will ship blood with you. If you run out, he will provide for you. All right?"

"No, it's not all right," I huffed. "But since you're pulling the strings attached to your little vampire puppet, I suppose I have to go."

"Lissa, you know that's not what you are," Winkler raked fingers through his hair. He was sitting at the table near the kitchen and turned his dark eyes up to me. "Life isn't fair, Lissa. Ever. Do I wish it were better for you? Yes. I do. But wishes don't go very far, do they?"

"Where and when?" I asked. He'd given his permission. I had to go.

"I have to take you to the airport tomorrow evening. The private jet will fly you to Grand Forks. Someone will be there to pick you up."

"Fine," I grumbled and walked away.

* * *

"Honored One, they are sending her to act as bodyguard to Weldon Harper. I know you recognize that name. She called herself a puppet to the secondary. He disagreed with her but that statement is not far from the mark. Things should have been different for her. She should have had a solicitous sire. She has nothing. She might count the taking of her life in the end as a blessing.
   G."

* * *

"Lissa, he said only two weeks. That's not forever," Winkler told me as I jerked my rolling bag across airport tarmac. Winkler walked beside me, carrying a second bag as we made our way toward his private jet. I was getting the whole thing to myself this time, except for the pilot and co-pilot. He'd also loaded me up with more clothing, including a warm coat—the weather in North Dakota was still cold and unpredictable.

"Why should you justify yourself to me?" I snapped. I was owned and I knew it.

"Lissa," I held myself stiffly as he pulled me into his arms and held me, kissing the top of my head. "Lissa, don't. Just go." He turned me loose and pointed me toward the jet. I carried my own bags up the steps. They were as light as a feather to my vampire strength. The co-pilot shut the door behind me and we took off shortly after that.

Daryl Harper was there to meet me when the plane landed, and there was snow on the ground so I needed the coat. Not because I was truly cold, but because I would stand out. I shrugged into it. Driving north out of Grand Forks, Daryl turned west onto a gravel road after a while and then traveled another ten or fifteen miles. We were in the middle of nowhere when we stopped, except for the huge log house that stood there. Smoke curled up from the chimney, giving off the smell of a fragrant wood fire inside. Daryl and I hadn't talked much on the trip. I'd considered asking questions about the scenery and the nearby cities before thinking better of it. Why the hell did they need a bodyguard? Were they getting attacked by grizzlies?

"Dad?" Daryl called, the minute we stepped inside the house. At least it was warm inside and well insulated.

Weldon Harper came out of the kitchen, a cup of coffee in his hands. "Here's the little vampire, now," he said. I wanted to tell him that not long ago I'd been human and hadn't believed vampires existed. Now I was getting the second-class citizen treatment.

"Yes. Your vampire is here. At your service, and all that. Last time I cooked for you. What do you want now?"

"Gets right to the point," Weldon nodded at me. "We're having a meeting of sorts in a couple of days. There'll be lots of people here, setting up tents and the like right outside. You and Daryl will be going out with me. You only at night, of course, just to be an extra set of eyes and ears and to help out if somebody decides they want a piece of me."

"You think that might be an issue?" I asked. "They're your guests."

"Yes. They are, aren't they?" Weldon smiled at me.

Daryl showed me to a bedroom. The windows had been boarded up and heavy curtains hung over them. At least they'd made preparations for a vampire to sleep there. Daryl also brought in a mini-fridge along with my cooler of blood. I immediately transferred the blood over to the fridge. No sense wasting the stuff—there wasn't a plethora of warm bodies walking around to feed from if it became necessary. The bedroom was a twelve by twelve square with a single bed, a nightstand and a chair plus a small closet off in the corner adjacent to the door. The nearest bathroom was down the hall and I figured we were too far away from civilization to have city water and sewer. It had to be on a well and a septic tank. The bed was covered by a hand-made quilt in creams, browns and yellows, sewn in a fan pattern. A hand-woven Navajo rug covered the wood floor at the side of the bed and there was a deer's head hanging on the wall. *Ugh*.

I still had some books to read from my last visit to the bookstore. Pulling one out of my suitcase after unpacking everything else, I settled down to read. Weldon and Daryl went to bed around three; I heard them padding down the hall at the time. Nothing disturbed us during the night—I was reading with one ear open and never heard anything other than the wind and perhaps a coyote or two.

Beds don't matter much to me anymore. Not to sleep in, anyway. Dawn comes and I'm unconscious, it's as simple as that. No way to tell then if the mattress is lumpy or if the pillow's too thin. There wasn't a lock on my bedroom door, either. Nothing to keep anybody from walking right in and shoving a stake through my heart, or to stop them from carrying me out to the bright sunlight and dumping me in the yard just to watch me burn. Yeah, I'm full of cheerful thoughts, nowadays.

"Look who's up." Weldon sounded almost happy as I came out of my bedroom for the first time in sixteen hours.

"You're not one of those triple-P persons, are you?" I frowned at him.

"Triple-P?"

"Perpetually Perky People. They make me want to tear my hair out. I've worked with five during my lifetime. I'm pretty sure they ought to pass a law against them or something."

Weldon grinned. "I'd ask if you wanted coffee, but I know better," he said.

"Good. I'm going out for a bit," I said, pulling on my coat.

"It's snowing a little," Daryl was shoving a huge log into the fire-place. Actually, I was wondering if I'd freeze if I turned to mist while the temperature was freezing. Maybe I'd give it a try. I'd thaw in the spring, just in time to get fried by spring sunshine.

"I'm still going out. Need any trees uprooted or anything?"

"She's funny," Weldon said, pointing at me with his coffee cup.

Fat flakes of snow were falling when I stepped outside the door and it was cold, no doubt about that. I heard water running off in the distance and I figured there was a river nearby. I took off in that direction. The banks of the Red River (not to be confused with the Red River that separates Texas and Oklahoma, this was the Red River North) had some ice around the edges, but the middle was a strong flowing current when I found it. That's where I concentrated on turning to mist. I didn't freeze. Who knew? I floated over the tops of trees, saw the log home off in the distance and then the river, winding its way toward Canada. The night was still and cold while snowflakes continued to fall around me. Honestly, if there'd been a good supply of blood nearby, I might have considered settling there, it was so peaceful. Far off to the south, I could see the lights of Grand Forks. I didn't turn back to myself until I was around a hundred yards from the cabin, kicking the snow off my shoes before going inside. I'd only been gone about an hour or so.

"I don't suppose you'd consider making cookies or a pie or something?" Daryl looked a bit wistful.

"What do you have to cook with?" I asked. He'd get cookies if he had the right ingredients. He hadn't done anything (yet) to piss me off.

Daryl led me into the kitchen. At least it looked like it belonged in the twentieth century. Maybe not the twenty-first, but we were in the middle of nowhere. I found sugar, both white and brown, butter and flour. Somebody knew how to shop for groceries, here. Winkler? I think he'd have problems recognizing a loaf of bread.

"Do you have peanut butter?" I asked, digging through a cabinet.

"Yeah." Daryl found a large jar inside a cabinet.

"Do you like peanut butter cookies?"

"Yes." He was smiling.

"Good. We'll have that." Daryl sat down at the small table inside the kitchen and watched while I put his peanut butter cookies together. I heard Weldon inside a room not far away, talking on the phone. I didn't listen in.

Daryl was busy eating a plate full of peanut butter cookies when Weldon emerged. He grabbed a handful for himself and poured out a glass of milk to go with them. "I heard you won't cook for Winkler anymore," Weldon said.

"Well, Phil shot me in the back and then Winkler blackmailed me. Go figure," I said, wiping my hands on a kitchen towel. I'd just finished washing the dishes by hand. No dishwasher here, thank you very much.

"You don't have legitimate ID," Weldon reminded me.

"Even if I did still have my own license, the photograph doesn't look like me anymore. Not even a good facelift would accomplish what happened to me. Besides, the assholes who turned me stole my purse. What was I supposed to do? Go off to the police and say hi, I'm a new vampire. Can you please help get my purse back from the two vampires who killed me?"

"I have absolutely no advice for a new vampire," Weldon said. "Sorry. You haven't lost your talent in the kitchen, though." He stuffed another cookie in his mouth.

"That's me. Old stand in front of you and take bullets and then whip out a batch of cookies Lissa. What can I say? I'm multi-talented."

"That was Winkler on the phone earlier, asking how you were," Weldon informed me. "I asked him if he wanted to talk to you. He sounded like you might not be willing."

"He might be right," I said. "I'm going to go read, now. Let me know if you need something guarded or Bigfoot tracked." I went off to my room.

"For a leech, she's really pretty, dad," Daryl said. I heard him all the way through my bedroom door.

CHAPTER 9

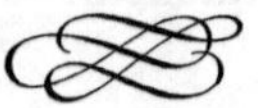

$\mathcal{P}$eople started arriving before dawn the following morning, driving vans, SUVs, trucks, RVs and rental cars. One vehicle had tires on it taller than I was. Eventually I stood in Weldon's front yard and watched all of them drive through, stopping in this spot or that and either hauling out a tent or going outside briefly to relieve themselves before climbing back into their van or whatever. Weldon came out a little while before sunrise with a cup of coffee in his hands to watch with me. "Must be some meeting," I said, as more vehicles drove past. It looked like most of Weldon's guests were male.

"It is," he nodded, sipping from his coffee cup. "Be ready to work when you get up later."

"Oh, sure. Do I have to watch all of them take a piss?"

"Not unless you want to, or I tell you to." He grinned at me.

"Well, have fun." I patted his arm and went inside so the sun wouldn't catch me again.

* * *

WINKLER PREPARED me for the great outdoors before I left Corpus Christi. I was now the proud owner of hiking boots in a chocolate brown and I wore them now, along with jeans, a sweater, and my down jacket. The murmurs started as soon as Weldon, Daryl and I walked through the sea of tents. Campfires were going almost everywhere and people were eating, talking, laughing, grumbling, and as soon as I walked past them, whispering. About me. Somehow, the moment I came anywhere near them, they knew what I was. I heard everything from *vamp* to *leech*, and quite a few other derogatory terms that I didn't recognize. If I'd been able to flush, I would have. I suppose I no longer had the blood supply or the circulation to do it. Again, the missing *FVM* came to mind.

"Do they think I don't hear?" I asked Daryl, after hearing *fucking vampire* for perhaps the fiftieth time.

"They don't have enough experience around your kind," Daryl replied softly.

"They're not getting cookies," I snipped. Daryl chuckled.

There had to be at least five hundred people there, perhaps more, making the area surrounding Weldon's cabin extremely crowded. "Grand Master, I'm the Packmaster from Des Moines," a man came forward and offered his hand to Weldon.

"The one who took Corwin down?"

"Yes." Weldon took the man's hand and shook it.

"I liked Corwin, he was very effective," Weldon said. "See that you do justice to his Pack."

"Yes, Grand Master," the man almost bowed and got the hell out of the way. My head was spinning suddenly and my suspicions were confirmed when a huge wolf bounded past.

"Fuck," I muttered. Here I was, surrounded by something else that I'd thought myth—*werewolves*. And not only that, I was serving as bodyguard to the fucking *Grand Master*. How lucky was I? Winkler, Phil, Davis and Glen? All had to be werewolves, too. And Whitney. And Sam. And who knew who else? Was that what Gavin was? Is that how they could tell what I was? By the smell? "Jesus Christ," I said.

"What?" Daryl jerked to a halt beside me.

"Nothing. Winkler's a dead man," I said.

"Dad might object to that. Winkler's the Dallas Packmaster, you know. And Phil's his Second."

"They may both be dead," I retorted. "Your dad can object all he wants. Is Winkler coming, too?"

"No, he and dad had their meeting when we were in Corpus Christi," Daryl said. Weldon was greeting other werewolves and ignoring us. I was dutifully glancing around us, watching for anything suspicious while Daryl and I talked.

We walked through the whole, huge camp that night—Weldon talking to this one or that, seeing old friends and new faces. I continued to hear the comments regarding his vampire bodyguard, but I tuned them out after a while. What was I supposed to do? Challenge five hundred werewolves? No wonder Phil always smelled like a wet dog. That's exactly what he was. Winkler had a different smell to him, as did Davis and Glen, but I always thought it was the differences in people. Come to think of it, Gavin didn't smell like any of them. He just smelled good to me and I couldn't explain it.

Weldon settled down at a campfire after a while to have coffee and a sandwich with somebody while Daryl and I stood guard. The man Weldon was eating with looked old; he had gray in his hair while everyone else I'd seen looked younger. Except for this man, nobody looked more than forty.

"That's Thomas Williams," Daryl whispered to me after a while. "He's the oldest Packmaster we have. Dad figures he'll get challenged before next year's meet, so this is a goodbye meeting."

"Dear God," I muttered while scanning our surroundings. "How old is he?"

"Almost two hundred," Daryl said. "Usually they don't live past a hundred and fifty—as a Packmaster, anyway," he added. "We can live to around two-ten, two-fifteen, otherwise."

I didn't want to ask him what the life expectancy of a Grand Master was. No way. We made it back to the house about an hour before dawn. Weldon had called in some other security and now there were two new werewolves waiting beside the door. "This is Emmett and this is Kipp," Weldon introduced the two dark-haired werewolves. "From the Fargo Pack. They'll be extra daytime security."

"Don't call her a leech or you won't get cookies," Daryl offered.

"She makes good cookies," Weldon agreed.

Emmett and Kipp stayed outside, Weldon, Daryl and I went inside. "We'll be having a hunt in two days," Weldon informed me before I headed off to bed. "It's a way to blow off steam before the meetings begin. Daryl will be running with me, so you can stay here and bake cookies or do whatever you want," he grinned. "Emmett and Kipp will guard the house."

"Watch out, Bambi," I said dryly.

"Exactly," Weldon laughed.

Emmett and Kipp got chocolate chip cookies before we went out on patrol the following evening—somebody had made a run to the store. The kitchen was filled with all kinds of food and the fridge was stocked up, too. Weldon placed six cookies in a sandwich bag and took them with him. I'd made a double batch since I knew Weldon and Daryl could polish off a batch by themselves. Weldon stopped by a tent and handed the cookies off to a man there. Well, *werewolf* would be a better description.

"You learned to bake?" the werewolf teased Weldon as he accepted the bag. He had dark hair, brown eyes and an easy smile.

"Nope. Lissa here baked them. Don't worry, Daryl and I have already eaten a dozen apiece. They're safe."

"A vampire that knows how to bake and is willing to do so?" the man was smiling at me.

"Hey, I've only been vampire for less than three months. I've been baking cookies for thirty years." I probably shouldn't have opened my mouth, but I did.

"Lissa, this is Martin Walters, the Fresno Packmaster," Weldon introduced me. Martin Walters held out his hand first, so I took it and shook.

"Nice to meet you," I said. He bit into a cookie.

"These are good," he nodded at me. "Want to sit?" he turned to Weldon and pulled out a campstool for the Grand Master. Weldon sat.

Emmett and Kipp left us after a while. They needed to sleep—they'd been guarding all day. It was Daryl's and my turn, now. Another werewolf walked up, causing Daryl to growl low in his throat.

"Just passing by," the man held up his hands and went on his way.

"Look out for that one," Daryl told me as I watched the man walk away. I would. I had his scent, now.

"What's the deal?" I asked.

"That's Lester Briggs. He opposed dad when he and the Head of the Vampire Council hammered out the Peace Agreement between the Vamps and the Wolves. It's been in place for about twenty years, now. Before, it was all-out war. Some of the Wolves don't like the peace—they still want to kill you guys. The truth is, we were headed for extinction, vampires *and* werewolves. Our numbers are down to about a third of what they were before. The peace is going to allow everybody to rebuild the races."

"Holy cow," I said. "Was it really that bad?"

"Yeah. Trust me."

"Daryl, how old are you?" He looked to me like he was in his twenties.

"Forty-eight," He grinned.

"Geez Louise, you're older than I am, but not by much," I said.

"Dad told me you were forty-seven," Daryl said quietly. "Here comes Bart Orford, he's one of Lester's supporters and runs the Wichita Pack. Lester is the Santa Fe Packmaster."

"Did you say there's a Vampire Council?"

"Based in London, but they have eyes and ears everywhere," Daryl shivered a little. "And they have Enforcers and Assassins. If any vampire gets out of line or goes rogue, they don't last long."

Great. Something else to worry over. I made a mental note to ask Daryl later if he could tell me what constituted a rogue or what stepping out of line entailed. The terms *Enforcer* and *Assassin* weren't something that set my mind at ease, actually.

Weldon talked to Martin Walters for about an hour and had coffee and cookies with him before getting up to go pay other visits. Again, we walked until close to dawn and stopped many times, just like the night before. I noticed that we didn't stop to talk to Lester Briggs or Bart Orford, although we passed both their RVs. I saw somebody in Lester's vehicle peeking out the window as we went by.

"You know, Daryl," I said when we'd walked maybe five minutes after passing the RVs, "I want to check something. Give me a minute, will you?" Weldon had found someone else to talk to, so Daryl just nodded. "I'll be right back," I said, taking off to the left and going through rows of tents. Daryl might fidget before I got back, but I wanted to make sure there wasn't any funny business going on. Finding a tree in a dark area, I went up it in a flash and turned to mist as quickly as I could. Someday I was going to have to time myself, just to see how long it took.

I misted to the two RVs, hovering around them and listening.

"They'll expect us to raise the question," I heard someone say.

"During the meeting," somebody else agreed.

"I think we've got enough support, don't you?"

"We will have."

That was the most I got and it was pretty inane, actually. I figured they wanted to raise the whole issue of the Peace Agreement and whether enough of the werewolves wanted it or not. I had no idea if this was a democracy or even something close. I also didn't figure Daryl or Weldon would be happy to answer my questions about werewolf politics. I misted back to the tree, turned to myself and went to find Daryl.

"Anything worthwhile?" Daryl asked when I got back. Weldon was still at the same spot, talking.

"They were just saying they intended to raise the question during the meeting and that they thought they were going to have enough support."

Daryl sniffed. "No way. At least two thirds of the Packmasters are on dad's side. The peace is stable. On the vamps' side as well."

"Good. We don't need war to break out again, just as I'm surrounded by five hundred werewolves."

Daryl grinned over that. "Who'd make cookies?" he asked.

"Not me, if they rip me to shreds," I replied with a shrug.

We made it to the house before dawn and Emmett and Kipp were yawning and having coffee when we walked up. Not wasting any time, I went straight to my bedroom, grabbed my pajamas and the robe Winkler had bought for me and went to get a shower before I passed out.

Emmett and Kipp were the only ones around when I got up the evening of the hunt. I'd had my blood already; it was impossible for me to finish off a pint. Usually I got about two-thirds of one down and put the rest back in the fridge. My skin was prickling for some reason when I walked into the living area and I couldn't really say why. "Have they started the hunt?" I asked Emmett, who'd come in to warm up, leaving Kipp alone outside for a couple of minutes.

"Not yet, they're probably out there disrobing and seeing who has the biggest dick," Emmett laughed. "These hunts are all about power. When a normal pack hunts on the full moon, we just dump our clothes as fast as possible and start running. When we force the change to hunt, it's all a show."

"You all get naked together?" I was blinking in astonishment at Emmett.

"Yeah. It's not a big deal if it's the full moon. We have to make the change and we're itching to do it. We don't even look at the females if there are any. I heard females are kind of scarce in the vamp community, too."

"Well, who knows about that?" I mumbled. "Do you know where they're going?"

"East of here is all I know. Me? I wouldn't want in on that for a truckload of money. Sometimes they get so involved in showing each other up that they come back injured. All of them want to be the one to bring down the deer or the bear or whatever."

I was still blinking up at Emmett. "Okay," I said. "I think I'll go out for some air. Don't wait up."

"Just be careful," he said.

"Oh, I intend to," I replied, walking out the door.

Turning to mist a few minutes later, I sailed high over the treetops until I found the multitude of werewolves, all disrobing and placing their clothing into piles. I sure hoped they were going to be able to sort it all out later. Weldon and Daryl were there at the front and I didn't see a flabby body anywhere in the crowd. Looks like the wolves get plenty of exercise. They must have an outrageous metabolism, too, to be able to eat like they do.

I hovered around a stand of pines waiting for things to get started, trying to pick Lester and Bart out of the crowd. I couldn't really see them and after a while, it wouldn't have mattered anyway. The werewolves started to change and it went in a huge ripple. One minute there'd be a man standing there, the next a huge wolf. There was an ocean of black, gray and russet-colored fur across the clearing. Weldon, who was a huge black wolf, lifted his head and howled. The entire sea of werewolves took off at a run.

Weldon didn't know it, but I misted over him and Daryl that night as they ran at the head of what was likely the biggest pack ever. They scented something after a while and went after it, scrambling over rocks, around felled trees, forcing their way through snowdrifts and wading through small streams. They have stamina, that's for sure. Weldon and Daryl were ahead of the pack by several seconds when they shifted direction, veering away from a stand of trees and following whatever scent they'd picked up, I suppose. From my high vantage point, I saw about twenty others separate from the pack and cut across a second stand of trees in an effort to meet up with Weldon. At least that's what I thought they intended to do. I was very wrong.

Weldon was running all out, Daryl at his tail, when a large wolf from the breakaway group ran right into him, bowling him over. You know, sometimes I wonder why I don't have any good sense. More than likely, I should have just let things go. But I couldn't. Weldon hadn't mistreated me. In fact, he'd been pretty civil—nice, even. Call me an idiot—I was calling myself one. I dived downward at an angle and was almost fully turned by the time I hit the ground.

Daryl and Weldon were fighting for their lives—snapping, snarling and biting. They had three Wolves down already and those three weren't getting up again. There were still seventeen to be reckoned with and they were all trying to rush Weldon and his son at once. I wondered where the rest of the pack was. Turning my head, I saw them, all sitting off in the distance like they were waiting for the outcome.

That pissed me off. Nobody was helping and there were more than enough to help. I waded into the pack of slavering wolves that was attacking Weldon and Daryl. I can't say how many bites I got getting to Weldon, but it was a few. I was smashing ribs and breaking necks as I went through those wolves. Some of them I flung so far into the surrounding field they landed with a yelp and didn't get up again. Weldon and Daryl were still fighting when we got down to about three of the attackers. Those three backed off a little. Weldon was still growling at them and Daryl was doing the same. I thought it was over. It should have been over. Except that it wasn't.

Another ten werewolves separated from the larger pack, approaching the three of us. The three wolves that had backed off circled around to join the ten new ones. *Time for a new strategy.* Weldon had a deep gash on his left hip; somebody had done his best to rip the Grand Master's leg off. He was the main target, so that left Daryl in better shape. "Daryl," I said, looking down into his golden wolf eyes, "when I get your dad, I want you to run as fast as you can right into that inert pile of shit that looks like a pack, over there," I nodded toward the main body of werewolves that seemed content to do nothing. "If some of these shitheads follow you in, it'll turn into a free-for-all. At least some of the others might get pissed and start fighting and you could get lost in the scuffle."

"Weldon," I turned to the Grand Master of the werewolves who was bleeding sluggishly from the hip wound, "I'm sorry to treat the Grand Master this way, but right now I don't think there's any help for it."

I lifted his wolf body up and flung him over my shoulder. He wasn't heavy to me, just bulky, and I hoped that his body wouldn't get in my way when I ran. I was about to see if a vampire could outrun a werewolf. I took off in a blur and most of the thirteen came after me. I was jumping over logs, across streams, running up boulders, through outcroppings and wading through snow faster than even I thought possible. Weldon was grunting after a while and somewhere, I couldn't really tell you where, he turned into a man. I now gripped a naked man over my shoulders and I was running out of steam. The bites I'd gotten were burning almost as badly as the burns from the sun. I was going to have to stop soon and rest a little.

I didn't want to set Weldon down anywhere; the Wolves chasing us would be able to pick up his scent. At the moment, they were only following mine. We reached a stand of trees when the idea hit me. "Weldon, are you still alive?" I asked softly. I could hear the wolves following us off in the distance.

"I'm good," he mumbled.

"Great. Hang on, we're going vertical." It was difficult, climbing a tall pine tree with a fully-grown man over my shoulder, but I did it. I hope I never have to do it again. "You think you can hold on here so I can lead them away?" Weldon had his arm wrapped around the trunk of the tree and his skin appeared a little gray as he sat there on the rough bark of a thick tree limb. His hip was still bloody although it did seem to have stopped bleeding. Haggard best described how Weldon looked as he shuddered slightly and gripped the trunk of the pine.

"I'll be fine," he murmured, staring at me with those black eyes of his. He was a handsome man, even wounded.

"Good, because I'm getting down, now. Hopefully they'll chase after me, thinking I've still got you. Stay quiet, alright?"

Weldon was about twenty feet above the ground in a huge pine and pretty well hidden. I just hoped his scent wouldn't drift to the ground. "You don't have to tell me to be quiet," he grimaced.

I climbed down quickly, landing at the spot where I'd started climbing. Scuffling around a little, I took off running again—the Wolves had almost caught up with me while I'd gotten Weldon settled in the tree. I found the river after running for nearly half an hour. Not knowing how long those Wolves could run or track me, I gambled a little more. They'd followed me without stopping at Weldon's tree, after all. I waded into the ice-coated edge of the river, hoping to make my pursuers think I'd gone into the frigid water. Standing there in the bone-freezing river, I shivered and turned my body to mist.

The point of the river where I turned to mist had to be at least ten miles from where I'd left Weldon, but as mist I can move as fast as my mind can, almost, and I was back at his tree in no time. He was still sitting there on his limb, his body covered with bites and rips, his eyes closed in pain and breathing with difficulty.

"Did you think I wouldn't come back for you?" I asked softly, materializing on the limb next to his. "And since I'll never have grandkids," I grunted as I hefted him over my shoulder again, preparing to make the descent, "you'll have to tell yours about how you got rescued from a tree by a cookie baking vampire."

Coming down with him was a lot slower than going up but I managed it, loping off toward the cabin as soon as I hit the ground. Weldon grunted painfully from his spot over my shoulder, so I apologized to him for making the trip so rough. We made it back to Emmett and Kipp about half an hour later. I was wiped and Weldon wasn't in any shape to do anything except get medical attention. "Get him in bed and clean up those wounds," I ordered the two werewolves, who stood staring at both of us as if we were a bad dream come to life. I wished I knew if Daryl were still alive, but there wasn't any way I could go and check. Unfortunately, my nightmare was only beginning.

Emmett and Kipp hauled Weldon into his bedroom and started working on him. It looked like they knew basic first aid, at least. I figured they knew better than I did what a werewolf might need, so I started to go into the bathroom and clean out my own bites. That's when I heard the howling. Somebody, I had no idea who, was heading toward the cabin and he didn't sound friendly.

I made my stand at the front door of Weldon's log house. I'd quickly piled as many thick logs from the woodpile in front of the door as I could, but that wouldn't keep attackers from going through the windows. All that stood between what was coming and the three werewolves inside the house was me. Sending up a silent prayer, I dumped my down jacket off to the side so I'd have freedom of movement, rolled up the sleeves to my sweater and watched the pack of fifteen come after me at a run.

CHAPTER 10

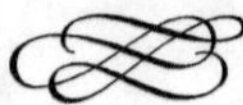

They hit me like a storm and again I was punching and breaking, tossing and fighting. There were so many bites after a while—so much of my flesh ripped away—I didn't know what was left of my body. I'd managed to take down nine of them but there were six left and they were still coming after me. I don't know how much longer I might have been able to stand and take the beating before they took me down when Daryl, Martin Walters and Thomas Williams showed up.

Daryl still had some fight left in him, thank goodness, and Martin was ripping into the enemy so viciously I knew right away how he kept his spot as Packmaster. Thomas Williams was putting everything he had into the fight; he managed to take down two of the attackers before one of the remaining wolves ripped out his throat. Martin managed to get that one while Daryl took down the last wolf.

My clothes were in shreds and my breathing shallow and labored as I slumped down before the pile of logs I'd placed in front of the door. My body felt as if acid had been poured over it and I was nearly numb from the pain.

"Dad?" That was Daryl's first word.

"Inside. Emmett and Kipp working on him," I wheezed.

Martin moved me to the side and he and Daryl removed the logs so they could get into the house. I was left sitting in front of the cabin, a bloody mess and unable to move.

* * *

"WEREWOLF SALIVA HAS this effect on vampires," I heard the words from a strange voice and scent. I didn't know where I was; everything looked dark to me. And the pain? My body was on fire.

"Surprised she's not dead yet," another fragment floated past. I wanted to know if Weldon was all right, but that thought, along with my consciousness, drifted away.

I woke up a little when they moved me and somebody was dripping blood from a bag into my mouth. "Go ahead and swallow," a voice urged. I wanted to cry but there wasn't anything left in my body to produce tears. I wanted to move, but my body felt paralyzed. The pain wasn't going away. I wished I was dead and then remembered that I already was.

"She's opening her eyes," someone said. My ears felt like they were stuffed with cotton, deadening the sound. I blinked, there was light, but I couldn't bring anything into focus. "Lissa? Can you hear me?" I thought it might be Daryl, but I didn't know for sure. Blackness came again.

* * *

DARYL CARRIED Lissa up the steps to Winkler's jet. He was flying back with her and turning her over to Winkler. What was left of her, anyway. Weldon had been stiff for a few days but held the meetings as if nothing had happened, although he did cut them short by three days. Lester, Bart, and about thirty-five others had died in the attempted coup, including Thomas Williams, who'd fought and died to keep Weldon alive.

Weldon buried Thomas on his North Dakota property, and many of the werewolves carried large stones from the river to cover his grave. Weldon gave the eulogy, naming Thomas a hero. Lissa, though, she probably wasn't going to make it. At least that's what the werewolf physician said when they brought him in from Chicago. Winkler demanded that she be brought back to Texas. If she were dying then he'd see to her comfort beforehand. Weldon didn't want to move her, told Winkler that he'd see to her and he and Winkler held a shouting match over the phone. Winkler won out eventually, sending his jet to pick her up.

Martin Walters sat down at Lissa's bedside before she was taken away and took her hand. "I wanted to explain to you, before they took you away," he said softly. "Thomas and I came to help there at the last, because we have children. Thomas's kids are grown, but mine—I have a daughter who's four and a son who is two. I didn't want them growing up in a world where they have to watch their backs if they smell vampire. None of us kept the peace the other night. You did." Martin patted her hand and stood up to go.

"Lissa, I wish you'd wake up," Daryl whispered softly in her ear as he settled her into the seat and buckled the seatbelt around her. Winkler was growling when Daryl came off the plane carrying Lissa's body wrapped in a blanket. "You have to be careful, the wounds drip fluid and won't heal," Daryl said, handing the bundle over to Winkler. Gavin stood off to the side, an unreadable expression on his face.

"What the hell did they do to her?" Winkler asked, finally controlling his anger.

"The doc says that werewolf bites do this to vampires," Daryl said. "Their skin tries to heal itself, locking the saliva inside. It acts as a poison in their system. It should have been cleaned out right away and it wasn't. She has bites and rips everywhere. I know dad told you she saved him, but she killed herself doing it. She accounted for at least twenty of the thirty-seven who tried to take dad down."

The night sky was overcast as Davis drove Winkler and Gavin back to the beach house. Winkler held onto Lissa the entire way, growling at the others if they got too close and he and Gavin lifted the blanket from Lissa's body when they got her inside. Winkler carried her into the main house instead of her guesthouse bedroom and made sure the room was as dark as he could make it.

"What did they do to you?" Winkler said as he and Gavin pulled the blanket away. They'd dressed Lissa in some sort of loose gown to send her back and it was soaked in a yellowish fluid. Gavin felt ill, staring at the weeping wounds.

"Send somebody out to buy as many bottles of peroxide as they can find," Gavin turned to Davis and Glen, who were peeking over Winkler's shoulder.

"How many do you need?" Davis asked.

"Enough to fill a bathtub to about six inches, at least," Gavin said. "And buy scrubbing brushes. The stiffer the brush, the better."

"What are you going to do?" Winkler looked at Gavin.

"Attempt to do what those fools should have done to start with. All those bites need to be reopened and cleaned out. She won't survive like this and that's the only chance we have. If it kills her, well, she'd die anyway." Gavin looked both angry and determined.

"Christ," Winkler muttered. "All right," he waved at Davis and Glen. "Go clean out everybody's supply of peroxide and get back here as quick as you can." Davis and Glen took off. Every pharmacy, grocery and discount store had their shelves emptied of peroxide that night. Davis and Glen had to make four trips to the car to bring it all in. Gavin made sure the bathtub was watertight before pouring the peroxide into it.

"This is going to hurt," he told the unconscious Lissa. "I apologize beforehand."

"She looks like shit," Phil stuck his head inside the bathroom door.

"And you may, too, if you don't get the hell out of here," Winkler was up and growling. Phil disappeared.

Gavin started on Lissa's legs first, scrubbing with one of several brushes that Davis and Glen had bought and rinsing the scrubbed skin often. When he made his way to her thighs, she started whimpering.

"Just hold on, baby," Winkler was kneeling at one end of the tub, stroking Lissa's hair. Gavin worked on her throughout the night, getting the last bit of skin on top of her head shortly before dawn. Lissa moaned and thrashed while he did her ribs and the area around her breasts. Winkler was crooning to her when that happened. Gavin let the peroxide run out of the tub afterward and then bathed her carefully, using the mildest soap he could find.

"There, now," Winkler had Lissa out of the tub and wrapped in a towel as soon as the bath was over. Leaving her naked, they placed her in the bed and covered her up.

"Now, we wait," Gavin said, rolling shirtsleeves down his arms. "Don't disturb her during the day. Her body has to heal if it can. If not, well," he didn't finish the sentence.

* * *

THEY TOLD me later that I'd been unconscious for nearly two weeks, and that Gavin had scrubbed out the saliva that my body was attempting to lock inside skin and tissue. If I had known how toxic werewolf saliva was, I might not have stood there and fought with them on that cold North Dakota night. But what's done is done. There's no way to take it back, now. What I did know, for the first time in days, was whose arms were around me when I woke up completely. It was his arms, and his scent, and he left me as soon as he knew I was waking. *Gavin*.

I was stiff, too. Stiffer than my arthritis had ever made me. Gavin had already gone out the door to start work that night, so I limped and scuffled my way down the steps of the guesthouse. I didn't know then that I had slept for three days and nights inside the beach house before Gavin talked Winkler into placing me inside my bedroom. Someone had also unpacked my clothing, washed what needed washing and folded and hung all of it. My suitcases were empty and inside my closet.

"You should have called us, someone would have come to get you," Winkler was frowning as I walked through the French doors.

"I need to get myself around," I said, my voice sounding as rough as sandpaper.

"Sit down," Winkler pulled a chair out for me at the dining table. He'd been having a sandwich when I walked in.

"All right," I heaved myself into the chair, sighing heavily when I stopped forcing myself to move.

"Daryl's coming tomorrow just to see for himself and to take a report to the Grand Master," Winkler watched my face. I'd seen it myself just a few minutes before when I'd painfully showered and combed out my hair. There were red lines everywhere, covering my body, top to bottom. There were even telltale indentations in my scalp, indicating the bites I'd gotten there.

"I want to send a message to Thomas Williams' children, if they're still alive," I rasped.

"You met Thomas?" Winkler sounded surprised.

"I watched him die," I said. "That last batch of werewolves would have killed me if Daryl, Martin Walters and Thomas Williams hadn't shown up. Thomas was killed after taking two of them down. And if it's possible, I'd like to send a thank you to Martin as well."

"I think that can be arranged," Winkler told me. "Thomas' son is Packmaster now. He was Thomas' Second and has successfully fought off the challenge."

"He was probably pissed. I know I would be."

Winkler left for a few minutes, going to the bedroom he used as his workspace and coming back carrying a laptop. "You know how to use a computer?" he asked. I just glared at him.

Thomas Williams Junior's e-mail address was already pulled up, the cursor blinking, waiting for me to write a message. My brain had slowed along with my body, so it took a while to think of something to write. This is what I wrote:

I am sorry for your loss. I had the privilege of fighting alongside your father, as well as the sadness of watching him die. He killed two Packmasters before a third took him down and he died with more than dignity. He died for your future and the future of every werewolf child. It is my hope that you honor him and remind your Pack how fortunate they were to have him as a leader. I wish you fond memories and brighter days.

-Lissa.

Winkler was reading over my shoulder as I typed and he didn't object when I hit send. Then I wrote the note to Martin Walters after Winkler pulled up his e-mail address.

Mr. Walters, I thank you for your timely rescue and for your words afterward. I was barely conscious when you said them and in much pain, but I appreciate them more for those very reasons. It is my hope that your children truly do grow up in a world where there is no danger from the source you mentioned. Every child should have the opportunity to grow and prosper in a hate-free environment. My best wishes go out to you for your continued health and well-being.

-Lissa.

"I think you missed your calling as a diplomat," Winkler said after I hit send on the second message.

"I have some questions for you," I told Winkler. He sat down beside me after returning his laptop to the bedroom, his dark eyes focused on my face.

"What do you want to know?" he asked.

"Daryl said something about a Vampire Council," I said. "And he mentioned Enforcers and Assassins. He talked a little about rogue vampires, Winkler. What constitutes a rogue? What happens to them?"

Winkler looked more uncomfortable than I'd ever seen him look. "Lissa, I really don't want to answer those questions," he said, raking fingers through his hair and then covering his face briefly with both hands.

"I think you owe me those answers. Or the Grand Master does."

"Yes, we both owe you those answers." Winkler removed his hands and studied my face before answering. "Every vampire that is successfully turned is registered with the Council by their sire, and their sire teaches them for a period of five years before they are considered a separate entity, able to go out and thrive on their own." Winkler watched me carefully as I digested this information. "Until that five year period is over, the sire is held responsible for his child's actions," he added, gauging my reaction to his words.

"And if the *sire*," I pronounced the word with distaste, "fails to register his child?"

"If the Council learns of it, they bring the sire in on charges and the child is considered rogue in most cases. Perhaps if the child is captured quickly, and fostered out with another vampire..."

My heart no longer beats, so it cannot increase its pace. What happens to me when I become terrified is this: my skin quivers—over my entire body, almost. This time, in addition to the quivering, I wanted to cry. "How quickly is quickly?" My voice was quavering, too.

"Perhaps a day or two. The new vampire will be feeding off the population, with no instruction or training. Many of the newly turned, or so I have heard, kill their donors if they are not taught to take blood properly. The killing of humans threatens the exposure of the race, just as it is with the wolves. In both cases the killers are deemed rogue and someone is sent to destroy them."

"I'm a rogue." I got up from my seat and wobbled toward the French doors. Winkler didn't try to follow me. "I didn't kill any of the ones I fed from, but I guess that doesn't make a difference, does it?" I put my hand on the door handle and walked out of the beach house.

It was hard, but I managed to drag myself to the top of the guest-house, which was taller than the beach house by at least six feet. The same word kept slowly revolving in my brain—*rogue*. I was a rogue. Did the Council know about me, yet? Were Ed and Serge still out there, desperate to find me so they wouldn't be brought in on charges? I wondered what their punishment would be for the charges brought against them. More needed information from the missing *FVM*.

"Little girl, what are you doing on top of this roof?" Gavin seated himself beside me. I hadn't even heard him make the climb.

"What are *you* doing on top of this roof?" I asked coolly. If I'd wanted company I'd have asked for it, but I didn't tell him that.

"I asked you first."

"Well, if you must know, I'm wallowing in self-pity. There. Happy now?" I kept my eyes straight ahead, watching the waxing gibbous moon rise over the gulf waters. Another full moon would come soon. It made me wonder if Winkler and his bunch would run with the Corpus Christi Pack or fly back to Dallas for the evening. Shirley Walker was the Packmaster here in Corpus Christi. I'd seen her at the meeting in North Dakota; we just pretended we didn't know each other. I also recalled that she hadn't come to the Grand Master's defense.

"How are you feeling, other than sorry for yourself?" Gavin asked.

"Are you asking out of politeness or because you want to know?" I answered his question with one of my own.

"You're prickly tonight," he said.

"Winkler just informed me that according to his knowledge of vampire law, I'm a rogue. How about that? I'm entitled to a little self-pity."

"Winkler is a werewolf. And while he may be better versed than the average werewolf in the racial laws and politics of the vampire race, he may not know everything."

"Honey, I wish I believed that," I muttered. "And I'm stiff all over, thank you for asking."

"It may take a while for the poison to completely leave your system," Gavin rose and stretched a little. "I must go back to work." He walked over to the side of the roof and let himself down to the stair rail below.

* * *

"HONORED ONE, the Grand Master lives because of her efforts, although she was poisoned by the bites of many in his defense. I can only imagine that she is a formidable fighter already, as I was told she took down at least twenty Packmasters, receiving grievous wounds in the process. Only now is she making a recovery, which is practically a miracle.

G"

* * *

"LISSA, THIS IS KATHY JO GREENE." Winkler brought the woman into the guesthouse the following evening. She was a werewolf; I could

140

now tell the subtle differences between a human and a werewolf in human form by scent.

"I'm a nurse at the hospital in Corpus," Kathy Jo approached and held out her hand. She was around five-six and slender, with long, straight dark hair. She was pretty, too. I shook her hand, wondering why Winkler had brought her in.

"Kathy Jo knows how to give massages," Winkler was grinning at me, answering my silent question. "You're moving pretty stiff there, so we thought we'd see if a massage helped."

I wanted to roll my eyes but thought better of it. Kathy Jo didn't deserve my sarcasm. I didn't even know her yet. She had lotion and a variety of massage oils in the bag she'd brought with her and asked me to get undressed.

"Winkler," I nodded toward the door.

"I saw every bit of what you have already," he was still grinning.

"I wasn't awake to lodge a protest when you saw it," I pointed out.

"Werewolves lose their modesty pretty fast," Kathy Jo informed me as she pushed me toward the bed. "Now get undressed."

"Not a werewolf, and I'm sure you noticed that already," I said. The good news was that my red lines were fading to pale pink now and barely visible. I was hoping they'd disappear, at least before the Council's Enforcers or Assassins came to call. I wanted to look my best when I died for the last time.

"I did notice. Doesn't bother me a bit," Kathy Jo smiled. "I met some very nice vampires about three years ago. Worked with them a little, too. You don't scare me. Besides, Winkler told me you almost made the ultimate sacrifice for the Grand Master. I don't know of any other vampire who'd do that."

I was hoping fervently that she didn't correspond daily with any of those vampires or I was dead meat. Or ash, or whatever it was I'd be when the Council got done with me.

"Your secret's safe," Winkler assured me as Kathy Jo pulled my top over my head.

"Your body is somewhat the same, but your cells are denser and more closely packed so your skin is harder to pierce," Kathy Jo informed me as she rubbed knots and sore muscles. "I'm hoping that by stimulating the muscles, the poison still in your system will drain out of it faster. Someone told me that your body reacts to werewolf saliva in the same way that a human body produces histamines in reaction to something it's allergic to. Did you know that your tears— a vampire's tears, that is, are almost clear blood serum and not water?"

"Wow," I said.

"A vampire's tears would likely taste good to another vampire," she told me.

"Good information to have," I said, my voice a little wobbly as she worked on my shoulders. Winkler leaned against the wall while I received my massage, apparently enjoying the show.

I did feel better after Kathy Jo was done with me and I thanked her for the help. What I didn't know was that Daryl had arrived and was waiting inside the beach house for Winkler and me. Kathy Jo came in with us so she was introduced to Daryl. If I'd ever seen a case of love at first sight, I think I saw it then. Daryl was fawning all over Kathy Jo, who I learned was a widow. Her husband had been killed three years earlier, after they'd been married six months. I knew that pain, all right. Daryl looked me over, seemed quite happy with my apparent health and promptly took Kathy Jo out to dinner.

"Well, there you go," Winkler muttered as Daryl and Kathy Jo walked out the door together. "Shirley was all over the males down here, forcing them to back off so Kathy Jo could make up her mind on her next mate. And there I thought Daryl and Whitney would be good together."

"Daryl's too old for Whitney," I looked at Winkler. "She's still young and she needs that youth that Sam has."

"Do you know how old I am?" he asked, his eyes searching my face.

"No. Daryl told me he was forty-eight."

"I'm eighty-four," Winkler said, shocking me a little. "Whitney was a late-life baby for my mother. My father was the Dallas Packmaster before me. Do you know what that means?"

I went perfectly still. The term *challenge* came to me then and I knew this was going to be bad. "You had to challenge your own father?" My voice was barely a whisper.

"He demanded it," Winkler paced a little, his hands doing a nervous rake through his hair. "And he didn't even fight that hard. He was old —nearly a hundred and sixty and that's old for a Packmaster. Phil was just about to challenge him and dad was worried about Whitney and me. My baby sister was eleven at the time. We were all concerned that Phil would take her if he took the Pack. I wasn't about to let that happen so I took down my own father. Mom killed herself three days later with a bottle of pills."

"Geez, Winkler, that's awful," I said. "Sit down honey. Maybe you should have gotten Kathy Jo to give you that rub instead of me." I almost had to push Winkler into a seat at the breakfast table.

"Lissa, I know I have you over a barrel, not only because you don't have legitimate ID but now you know I could turn you over to the Council at any time." Winkler stared up at me. "The truth is, you're the best thing that's happened around here in a long while. Phil's a devoted Second now, just as he was for dad. And Davis and Glen would make good Seconds in any Pack. Phil would have taken over, Lissa, if you hadn't found me in the wheat field that night. I would have run out of air. The kidnappers drugged me when they caught me —shot me with a tranquilizer that would have brought down an elephant. Werewolf metabolism is fast so the drug didn't kill me, but lack of air would have. Phil would be in charge of the Dallas Pack and he would have forced Whitney to marry him. It would be his right as Packmaster."

"Winkler, look at me," I sat back down, taking his hand. "Phil doesn't need to be in charge of anything. There's something wrong with him and I'm not saying that because he shot me in the back three times. I thought that before then. And I would have killed him myself before I'd let him have Whitney."

Winkler blinked a few times before nodding—he appreciated the fact that I'd have protected his sister. But Winkler was werewolf, through and through. "Phil has been a good Second, Lissa," he defended Phil for that. "I disciplined him after he shot you while trying to hit Sam. He expected the discipline and accepted it. That whole incident was too soon after the full moon. Our tempers and emotions flare that entire week."

"Must be hard to deal with, at times," I said.

"It is. We don't schedule anything important during that week if we can help it."

"It was quite the surprise when I figured out what all of you were," I muttered. "And right in the middle of five hundred werewolves on top of that. Daryl thought it was funny."

"Lissa, I'm sorry we put you through that. But Weldon Harper is still alive, thanks to you."

"Yeah, how about that," I said. "It's not every day I carry naked men up and down tall pines, just so we can avoid a pack of rabid Wolves."

"Is that what you did?" Winkler laughed.

"Yeah. When I carried him down to get him home, I told him he was obligated to tell his grandchildren how he was rescued from a tree by a cookie baking vampire."

"You know, most vampires I've met are secretive and reserved and I've yet to meet one with a sense of humor, except for you. Maybe it's good that you're rogue, Lissa. They didn't spoil you."

"Yeah. That's me all right. Lissa Hood, the outlaw vampire."

"Are you still mad at me?" he asked, more seriously.

"A little. Maybe more than a little. Too many people knew things and they weren't sharing. I've made this up as I went along. If I'd known what werewolf saliva would do to me, I might not have fought so hard to stay alive. That was worse than burning in the sun after I dug you out of that field."

"Lissa, I'm sorry," Winkler took my hand that covered his and kissed it.

"Don't be sorry. I think I've been sorry enough for both of us. Self-pity is now a regular destination," I said, taking my hand back.

"I don't expect you to go back to work until you feel like it," Winkler said, lifting his arms over his head and stretching a little. "Leon's helping Gavin at night and James is holding the fort in Oklahoma City, still. Both are werewolves, in case you didn't know."

"I figured it out," I shrugged. "I think I'd like to go into Corpus Christi tomorrow evening. I need more books," I said. "And I'd like to go by myself. Don't worry; your little puppet should be safe."

"Lissa, I wish you'd stop calling yourself that."

"What else should I call myself? Willing captive? Voluntary suicide? The stupid twit who's waiting for the Vampire Council to catch up with her?"

"You're not stupid, Lissa. Don't say that to me again."

"You and Gavin. 'Don't walk into the sun, Lissa. Don't call yourself stupid, Lissa'." I mimicked both of them as I walked out the French doors.

* * *

I HAD a pile of books on the café table inside Barnes and Noble, sipping hot tea and flipping through some of the hardcovers to make sure I really wanted to buy them. The weather was a little stormy outside, too. It was the eleventh of April, prime time for unstable conditions. The Cadillac was sitting in the parking lot so I hoped it wouldn't hail and dent it up. Spring weather in tornado alley is always unpredictable—it's just a fact of life.

"Mind if I sit?" A man walked up with a stack of books in his arms. All the other tables were taken so I slid my books out of the way to give him space. "Thanks. I'll be right back, I need coffee," he said and went off to stand in line at the counter. He was back in less than five minutes, sitting down and doing the same thing I was doing—flipping through his books to see if he wanted them. I sipped my tea while I kept going through my books, reading beginnings as well as the flaps in some cases. Money deserts me swiftly inside a bookstore if I'm not careful.

"I read that one," the man pointed at the front of my book. "It was so good I read it twice."

"Wow. That's a recommendation," I said. "Do you read this author?"

"No, not normally," he told me. "I think I've read one other by her. I liked it, too."

"I'll give it a try," I said, putting it in the keep pile.

"Do you live here?" he asked.

"I'm a temporary resident," I said. I wasn't sure I wanted to get sucked into a conversation with this guy, even though he was attractive. He was also young—looked to be around thirty-five or so and that wasn't a plus in my book.

"I'm just here for vacation," he said. "I took a whole six weeks. Actually, my boss made me use some of my time since I had too much vacation built up."

"Yeah? What do you do?" I asked.

"I work for the government," he said. "My boss thinks I'm about to get burned out so he sent me out the door and told me not to come back for six weeks."

"And what did you think about that?" I couldn't help it; I was beginning to like this man.

"I think I called him a name," he said as he sipped his coffee with a smile.

"Oops."

"Yeah. So here I am. Forced vacation."

"Poor thing."

"Am I whining?"

"I think I like it," I said, smiling for the first time in days.

"You're welcome to whine back if you feel like it," he said. "Any chance I might run into you on the beach sometime in the next few weeks?"

"Probably not. I work nights and sleep days," I said.

"A night job?"

"Security," I said. "You know—the kind that carries flashlights." He laughed.

"Tony Hancock," he held out his hand.

"Lissa Haddon," I took his hand and shook.

"Lissa? For real?"

"Yeah. Everybody thinks its Melissa, but it's not. I blame my parents."

"Mine almost named me John Hancock instead of Tony

Hancock." He had dimples. I love dimples. He also had black hair and gray eyes. I usually didn't see that combination outside of Irish actors.

"Having John Hancock for a name might be unconstitutional," I said, grinning helplessly at Tony.

"Nah, I think they made an amendment," he replied.

"You know, it's nice when the entire country goes out of its way for you."

"You know it. And my boss didn't even fire me, when I called him a dick."

"And his name's not Richard, is it?"

"No. It isn't."

"He must like you," I said. I was smiling again. The most I'd smiled in a long time. His eyes were almost dancing with humor.

"He says he doesn't, but then I don't get fired, so what do you make of that?" he said.

"I think he likes you, or your work, or both," I said. "And he's a liar on top of that."

Tony laughed out loud. "Come on. Let's pay for our books and then go find a drink somewhere."

"You're kidding?"

"Not. Come on." He had my arm in his hand, almost dragging me toward the register. He'd picked up my books, too.

"Your car or mine?" he asked after we'd paid.

"The last time I picked up a male, he stabbed me," I said. "So you drive. That way I can slap a knot on your head if you get out of hand."

"Fair enough. If I ask, will you slap a knot anyway?"

"No, and don't misbehave, I don't want to hit you."

"Did somebody really stab you?" He was serious, suddenly.

"Yes, he did. I threw him out of the car and had to go get the wound cleaned out. That wasn't fun." We walked toward his rental. The weather had let up and the clouds were blowing away as Tony unlocked the doors of his compact SUV. He even opened the door for me. The rental was nearly new and smelled it as I slid inside and buckled up.

"There's a bar and restaurant in Port Aransas, are you hungry?" he asked, sliding into the driver's seat.

"No, not really," I said. "I'll just have a drink. You can eat if you want."

"Good enough," Tony said and off we went. The restaurant was called Victoria's. It had a nice bar and tables lined up along wide, plate glass windows overlooking the water. Boats were coming in and going out, although it was long past nightfall. Port Aransas is a sleepy fishing village most of the time; it just turns into a Mecca for college kids on summer weekends and during spring break. Tony ordered fish caught locally, along with a pile of coleslaw and French-fries. I asked for a bloody Mary while he had a beer.

"So, you do security?" he asked while he ate.

"Yeah. Patrol the building, secure the perimeter, boring stuff."

"Ever have any excitement?"

"Not since two guards got fired for having sex on the job."

Tony laughed again. "I don't think I've ever run into that one before. Have you ever gotten hurt, doing what you do?"

"Only when I was moonlighting," I said. I didn't want to go into detail with that. That was dangerous territory. "Where are you from, since this is vacation?"

"Virginia," he said. "I know, I'm a long way from home, but somebody told me Florida would be coast to coast college kids when I left and recommended this place as a little quieter."

"It is, unless you go down by the main beach," I said. "Are you staying in town or farther down the beach?"

"Staying at the Aransas Queen," he said. That was a condo about half a mile from Winkler's beach house. It was one of the nicer ones on the beach, too.

"Do you like it?" I asked.

"It's nice," he said. The waiter came by and Tony asked for a club soda. "Driving, you know," he told the young man, who asked if I wanted another bloody Mary.

"No, I'll take a club soda, too, with lime, please."

"I don't suppose you'd be interested in coming by my place for a while?" Tony asked as we walked out of the restaurant later.

"Not tonight," I said. I figured Gavin and Winkler would be having a cow as it was. I shouldn't have to answer to either one of them for every minute of my time, but that's how things were. Tony drove me back to the Cadillac. Barnes and Noble had been closed for nearly half an hour by that time and they stay open late.

"Nice car," he said when we pulled up.

"It's not mine, it's borrowed," I said.

"Can I get a kiss or do you not do that on a first date?" Tony was smiling as he opened my door.

"Is this a date? Good lord, I had no idea." I patted his cheek. "Maybe next time. I did enjoy it, though. I don't think I've laughed in a while," I told him. "Thanks."

"You're welcome," he said, leaning in faster than I expected and kissing me anyway. It wasn't forced, he only kissed me lightly, but I was still shocked. I hadn't kissed any man except Don (aside from the quick peck I'd gotten from Winkler at a basketball game) for more than twenty-three years and didn't really know what to do. Tony didn't push it; he just took my keys, opened the Cadillac for me and got me inside. "Here's my card and this is my cell number," he pulled a pen out of a pocket and wrote a number on the back of the card. "Now, I'll wait until you get away," he said, closing my door.

I started the car and pulled away, leaving him standing in the parking lot, staring after me. I didn't look at his card until I got back to the beach house and parked the Cadillac in the garage. The hair almost stood up on my head when I did look. It read *Anthony Hancock, Director, Joint NSA and Homeland Security Departments*, listing an address in Washington, D.C.

"Holy fuck," I muttered, shoving the card in my jeans pocket. Clutching my bag of books, I left the garage and trotted up the guesthouse stairs.

CHAPTER 11

The shower felt good. I felt guilty about washing Tony's scent off my body, but there wasn't any way I wanted a nosy werewolf asking if I'd been meeting somebody. And I liked Tony. Even if he might be bigger and badder than some of the werewolves I knew. Freaking NSA *and* Homeland Security. Crap. If he was the Director, who the hell was his boss? I was brushing my teeth when Gavin walked in.

"I just wanted to make sure you got back," he said. He could tell just by checking if the Cadillac was in the garage, but I wasn't going to point that out to him.

I wiped my mouth with a towel and looked at him instead. "I got some good books, I think. You might want to borrow one of them. It's by that author you like."

"Which one?"

"Conner Phelps."

"I'll borrow it," he nodded. "What did you do tonight, little vampire?"

"I had a drink with a man. I didn't bite him and he managed to kiss me once, despite my best efforts." I wasn't about to lie. Why should he care what I did? "And I don't know how I feel about being called *little vampire.* That hasn't been part of my life for very long. It doesn't define me, I don't think. Is that what you think? That's all I am? A bloodsucker?"

"It wasn't my intention to upset you," he said. "Did you enjoy your time with this man?" Gavin leaned his shoulder comfortably against my bathroom door.

"He made me laugh. I haven't done that in a long time," I said. "I'll likely never see him again. Is it wrong to want to feel normal, now and then? You know what I was afraid of, tonight, when I went out for drinks? That you and Winkler would ask for an accounting of my time. Is that any way to live? I used to have a life. I used to get to make decisions for myself." I tossed my hand towel onto the sink.

"I have tomorrow off. Perhaps you will come out with me," he said, shocking the hell out of me.

"Where were you thinking about going? I don't do tractor pulls or greyhound races." That seemed to encompass the local offerings. Besides movies and dinner, that is.

"Little girl, I do not do either of those things." Gavin actually smiled at me. That might have been as rare as a blue moon.

* * *

THE PINK TOP was sleeveless silk and fit like a glove. It was also one of those that came to the top of your pants or skirt, as long as you were standing upright and perfectly still. Otherwise, it showed the barest hint of midriff, now and then. I'd never worn it or the short, black skirt. I wore both for my outing with Gavin, thinking I must be out of my mind to accept his invitation. I also had low heels I hadn't worn before, bought in a moment of weakness at the mall in Oklahoma City. My feet didn't bother me anymore so I could wear heels as much as I liked. That in itself was a blessing.

My hair was French braided again, too. Still no jewelry, though. I didn't want to spend any money on it—who knew if I'd need the cash I had for something desperate someday?

Gavin wore a suit, something I hadn't seen him in until then and he wore it as if he were used to it. He looked really good in it, too. The white of his shirt contrasted with his skin color, which was several shades darker than mine—like he had European roots or something.

"You look quite nice," he said as we walked down the steps to the guesthouse together.

"You still haven't told me where we're going," I said.

"It will be a surprise," he said, handing me into the passenger seat of one of the SUVs.

It certainly was a surprise; Gavin took me to a wedding reception. "Do you know the couple?" I asked as we pulled into the parking lot of a nice hotel.

"I do not," he said. "You have no idea how difficult it is to find a place to dance in this city. That sort of thing doesn't exist as a regular venue. Therefore, we are attending a reception where there is a live band."

Gavin likes to dance. No way would I have ever guessed that in a million years. No way. I was glad I had heels on since he's so much taller than I am. He dances well and leads nicely. We toasted the bride and groom with champagne, just like everyone else and the last dance we danced before Gavin pulled me away was to *The Dream*, one of David Sanborn's best pieces. The band had a great saxophone player and he did a wonderful job. Gavin pulled me close against him as the music wound its way through the ballroom. When I stole a glance at Gavin's face, his eyes were closed and my hand was held tightly inside his, snug against his chest.

Gavin loaded me into the SUV as the reception was breaking up, and took me driving. We ended up at a Park Ranger's station where we had to pay to drive onto Padre Island National Seashore. The truck went into four-wheel drive and we drove down the wild, natural beach for nearly an hour, leaving everyone and everything behind. Gavin parked the truck on the sand, slipped his suit coat off, rolled up his shirtsleeves and then removed his shoes and socks. We were getting out. I slipped my shoes off too and opened my door.

The water was beautiful—washing up there on the beach in the moonlight. The moon was close to full and cast a nice trail over the gulf.

"Come," he said and lifted me onto the hood of the SUV before hopping up to sit beside me.

"I only got to see the ocean a few times in my life," I said, "before now."

"Your husband was ill, wasn't he?"

"He was. He was born with a heart defect and had problems all his life. That's not what killed him, though," I said.

"I investigated that. He died of complications from a procedure."

"Yes, he did. I went to a bar to get drunk for the first time in my life when they turned off the machines. And here I am, a bloodsucking vampire."

"Lissa, as you told me quite eloquently last evening, that does not define what you are."

"I don't feel like that's what I am." I sighed. "I miss the sunlight, Gavin. Those bright, sunny days with fluffy clouds floating in a blue sky. I can only see that in movies and photographs, now. And food? I used to love to eat. That's why I'm a good cook. No way was I going to waste something by cooking it badly." I swung my legs out in front of me, over the side of the hood.

"You have beautiful ankles," Gavin said. That stopped me in my tracks. Nobody had ever looked at my ankles before.

"I think I'll take a walk, now," I said, slipping off the SUV.

"I made you uncomfortable," Gavin was beside me in seconds.

"Nobody ever found anything about me attractive, before," I said. "So it's just a shock, that's all."

There were a few jellyfish washed up on the beach, so we stepped around them. "Is there anything you like about being vampire?" Gavin asked as we walked. The sand was soft under my feet—I was digging my toes into it from time to time.

"I like not having to go to the bathroom," I said. That made him laugh.

"Of all things, to pick that one," he squeezed my shoulders.

"You have to admit that you never have to leave a movie in the middle, just to run down the hall," I said. "That's definitely a plus. I like the way I can smell things, now. Like Winkler's scent. That's what I was depending on when I went looking for him the night he was kidnapped. It was just a fluke that I found the Jaguar instead. I definitely smelled the decay around the truck those kidnappers used. I got the scent off the dead security guard. It was all over the truck. That's how I knew it was the right one. And then I recognized the scent of two of those men when they came out of the restaurant. Their smell was inside the Jaguar."

"You have a sensitive nose, then," Gavin said. He still had an arm draped loosely over my shoulder.

"If I'd known those schmucks were werewolves, I would have forced them to go with me when I went looking for Winkler that night. We might have found him sooner. But I was afraid to give myself away."

"You must always protect yourself, no matter what," Gavin said, his voice and his gaze gentle.

"Where were you and your good advice when I was wading into an angry pack of werewolves?" I asked.

"Doing what Winkler was doing and worrying over you," he said.

"Well, that doesn't make me uncomfortable or anything," I muttered.

"Lissa," Gavin stopped and turned me to face him, both hands on my shoulders. A finger went under my chin, tilting my head up so my eyes would meet his. "You have no control over how others may feel about you, most of the time. If they know what you are, they will either love you or despise you. That is the way of what you are. Unless you deliberately go out of your way to make enemies, that is, and that is not a part of you. Some believe that vampires are a darkness, but there is a light in you."

"I have so many vampire acquaintances to compare myself to," I grumbled, looking away.

"Lissa, do not regret that, I beg you." Gavin's hands moved to cup my face, bringing my gaze back to his. And then he leaned down to kiss me. I remember shivering from the intense pleasure of his mouth upon mine, but I have no idea what happened next because I fainted.

I woke later, buckled up in the passenger seat of the SUV while Gavin drove toward the beach house. "What happened?" I felt a little woozy.

"You fainted, little girl. I am driving you home now."

"Wow. I'm sorry." I rubbed my forehead.

"It was probably too soon and after a long night," Gavin said. "You are still recovering from your ordeal. We will not repeat this."

What was he saying? That we weren't ever going out again? I thought he'd had a good time. Maybe he didn't like his dates fainting on him or something, which brought me back to reality. This was Gavin we were talking about. Hot and cold Gavin. No surprise. I should have seen it coming. I didn't speak to him the rest of the way home.

GAVIN CURSED HIMSELF. Never. Never again. He'd drank from her. He couldn't deny the scent of her any longer and he'd held her tightly against him while her body shivered and convulsed in climax. He'd been forced to place compulsion when she woke after fainting. Sweet little Lissa. He was going to kill her at Wlodek's command when all was said and done and he was treating her like this. He hated himself at that moment.

"WHITNEY AND SAM are coming to Dallas for the full moon. They'll run with my Pack," Winkler informed me. The full moon was on the sixteenth of April, and here it was the thirteenth. "We'll leave tomorrow and fly up. I have some business to take care of while I'm there anyway."

"Are we staying there or coming back here?" Gavin asked.

"We'll be coming back, so pack light."

We'd tentatively agreed that I would go back on duty the nineteenth. According to Winkler, we'd be back in Corpus Christi by then. Gavin had barely spoken two words to me after we'd come back from our date. All sorts of doubts gnawed at me, driving me crazy with worry. What had I done? I couldn't put my finger on any single thing, so I'd come to the conclusion that he hadn't enjoyed himself at all. Well, better to find out now, I guess. I was reading later while Gavin was out on patrol, when my cell phone rang. Thinking Winkler wanted something, I answered without checking the ID. "Hello?" I said.

"You're a hard woman to find." Somehow, Tony had found my cell phone number.

"What makes you say that?" I asked, mentally gulping. *The man had tracked me down.*

"When you didn't call me back, I had to try to find you."

"You know, I'm not even going to ask how you did that," I said. "I'm sure it involves aliens and a time machine."

"Now it's my turn to ask how you knew that," he laughed. "Lissa, I really want to see you again. I promise I'll leave the aliens at home."

After my failed experiment with Gavin, I thought seeing Tony again might be fun. "I might have the eighteenth open," I said. "That's a Saturday night. I'll be in Dallas until then."

"Work taking you there?"

"In a way."

"How about meeting me at the bookstore at eight?"

"Sounds good." I was going to suggest meeting there myself.

"See you there and please don't be late. I'll get an anxiety attack if you're not there on time."

"You get anxiety attacks?"

"Where you're concerned. Why do you think I tracked you down? I couldn't stand it anymore."

"You know, I may bring a therapist with me. I think you need help."

"I just need to see you. That'll do the trick, I promise."

"All right. Don't have an aneurysm. I'll do my best to be there on time."

"I'm crossing aneurysm off my to-do list," Tony chuckled.

"See that you do," I said, and hung up.

The flight from Corpus Christi to Dallas didn't take very long and there were four security guards waiting at the airport when we arrived, herding us around and loading us into even more SUVs. Winkler must have gotten a substantial quantity discount on those things. The wall around the house had been fixed after the blast that knocked part of it down in early February, and painted to match the rest already. Gavin and I were in the same vehicle as Davis but it was Davis who was sitting next to me.

"You gonna make us dinner, or cookies?" He sounded wistful as we made the trip from the airport. Smiling at him, I shrugged a little at his question. I hadn't had that many conversations with Davis since I'd come back from North Dakota and I sort of missed those a little.

"I'll think about it," I said.

Gavin and I had the second story guesthouse again, but we weren't speaking to each other much. Whatever I'd done, it had been a doozy, or maybe he just didn't appreciate his dates passing out on him. I still couldn't explain that. I also had no plans to tell him that I had a date with Tony on Saturday night. If he wanted to play twenty questions when I got back, I might consider telling him to fuck off.

Whitney and Sam were already at the house when we arrived and Whitney ran out the front door of Winkler's mansion to hug me. Sam was a little slower to arrive, but he hugged me too and said his dad wanted to send some sort of thank you. He just didn't know how to go about it.

"Tell him that seeing you alive is the best thanks I could have," I told Sam, patting his shoulder. "Tell him he's welcome."

I also baked cookies for the people in the house that night. Oatmeal *and* chocolate chip, and both kinds were gone in two blinks. Gavin went straight to the guesthouse and didn't join the others. He wasn't expected to work until the following evening, so I figured he was reading or watching television. Whitney wanted to show off the ring Sam bought for her and talk about the problems they faced, going to different schools and not seeing much of each other. I just told her it was a temporary thing, that summer was coming up and neither one of them was going to be in school forever.

Winkler slipped silently behind me, wrapped his arms around my shoulders and kissed my cheek lightly while I put cookies out to cool. We would have to have a talk, Winkler and I. A werewolf-vampire relationship just seemed doomed from the start. There was also the matter of a bit of blackmail between us. And after getting poisoned by werewolf saliva and nearly dying over it, having a relationship with one of them didn't seem like a good idea. Plus, he was able to reproduce. I wasn't. He probably needed to find a nice female werewolf somewhere and settle down to have puppies. At least I hadn't seen him go off to a bar to pick up a floozy lately. That brought up a question.

"Davis," I said quietly after a while. Davis was still in the kitchen getting a bottle of water out of the fridge.

"What, Lissa?" he straightened up—he'd been bending over to get his water off a lower shelf.

"Are werewolves susceptible to diseases? I mean, I worried every time Winkler brought home a girl from a bar."

Davis grinned. "Nope. Somehow, our system burns right through that stuff. So if his protection fails, he won't get sick."

"Can werewolves have children with humans?"

Davis shut the door to the fridge and opened his bottle of water, drinking a little then replacing the cap before answering my question. "Yeah. But none of them will be werewolves," he said. "Werewolves can only be born to a mated pair of werewolves. Sad but true. That's why Winkler is very careful about that sort of thing. He doesn't want any unscheduled children."

"In my understanding, there's only one way to make vampires," I said. "And it doesn't involve reproduction in the traditional sense."

"Yeah. I know that, too."

"Winkler needs to find someone suitable," I said.

"Yeah."

My life was just chock full of cheerfulness lately. I finished cleaning up the kitchen and went out the door, heading toward the guesthouse. Gavin must have been in his bedroom, he wasn't in the living area or the kitchen. Just as well, I didn't want to see him anyway.

* * *

"Honored One, I received information tonight that indicates the project is more than 75% percent completed and security is being increased. Primary is nearly healed and will return to work soon.

G."

* * *

Whitney wanted to go shopping in Dallas on the night of the fifteenth, so Winkler asked Glen and me to accompany her and Sam. The Galleria was her mall of choice and Sam was buying as well. Apparently, a new spring wardrobe was in the offing, to go with the old spring wardrobe Whitney had purchased a few weeks before. I'd never had that kind of money in my life and wondered what it felt like to spend it with abandon. We stopped at a jewelry store the very last thing as the mall was about to close. I think we had maybe fifteen minutes.

"Winkler said to buy you something here," Whitney was smiling at me. I just stood there like a dimwitted fool for a minute.

"No." I said. "Winkler doesn't need to buy me jewelry. Nobody needs to buy me jewelry. No." I flung out an arm and left the store, walking quickly into the mall. What was he doing? I was just about to explode from the duality of our relationship. He owned me, he'd blackmailed me, and he punctuated that with hugs, kisses and an offer to buy jewelry. I wasn't having it. What was I? A favored slave or something? A lapdog kept on a leash, wearing a diamond collar and told to sit, stay and roll over?

"Lissa, what's wrong?" Whitney trotted up beside me with Sam and Glen right behind. She didn't know. Of course she didn't. Well, Winkler could keep secrets from his sister if he wanted.

"I just don't want any jewelry. I earn a salary. That's sufficient." Whitney tried to coax me at first, but the mall was closing and I was walking toward the parking garage. We made it home without mishap and I didn't talk to anyone the whole time. Glen was driving and I sat up front with him while Whitney and Sam sat in the back.

"You upset Whitney." Those were the first words out of Winkler's mouth when he barged into my bedroom without knocking. I was huddled against the headboard of the bed, my knees under my chin, my arms around my legs, trying to come to grips with my life and my position and status within that life.

"Tell her I'm sorry. That wasn't my intention." I blinked up at Winkler. He looked ready to explode.

"Lissa, why? I offer to buy something you might want and you fling it away."

Whitney wasn't the only one upset, I could tell. "Sorry, Winkler. I just wasn't in the mood."

Winkler growled. I remembered then that it was the night before the full moon and the Wolves were a little touchy. "Winkler," I tried again. "We'll talk about this soon, okay? It was just such a shock and they were already making announcements to close the mall."

Winkler stared at me for a moment and then sighed. "Trust Whitney to leave it until the last minute," he said. "We'll talk about it later." He left my bedroom, closing the door behind him.

Four security guards drove Winkler, Phil, Davis, Glen, Leon, Whitney and Sam inside two SUVs the evening of the full moon. They were going to someone's ranch north of Dallas, where the run was scheduled. The human guards were instructed to drop them off and they all thought Winkler and Co. were invited to a barbeque. The SUVs and the drivers were coming back to the house until called for. Gavin was in charge of the guards while everyone else was gone and since I was a little bored and still upset over the whole jewelry fiasco, I decided to go to the roof and sit. There wasn't a good way to get up there without the guards seeing and freaking, so I turned to mist inside my bedroom, floated out of the guesthouse and up to the roof of the three-story house. The SUVs were driving through the front gate and I was about to turn back to myself when I caught movement a little way down the street.

If my blood hadn't been cool already, it would have chilled then. A semi was parked behind some of the nearby businesses, which wouldn't normally have caused any stir; trucks unloaded and loaded from there all the time. Now it was after hours, very dark, and all those businesses were closed. There were people swarming around the truck like termites and I watched in horror as they unloaded a vehicle that looked as if a tank and a hummer had a baby. That baby had a nasty-looking rocket launcher attached.

If I'd had a voice, I'd have screamed my lungs out. I didn't and the swarm was now driving their vehicle straight for Winkler's walls. The termites? They all had assault rifles. They were trotting alongside the attack vehicle, too.

Gavin, Gavin, Gavin, Gavin—if I could have expressed myself verbally, I would have been sobbing out his name. I sent it out mentally instead, as if he could hear me, somehow. Angling off the roof as mist, I swooped downward, flying toward the small army as swiftly as I could. As it was in North Dakota, I realized it would take precious minutes to change to myself—minutes I didn't have. Gavin wasn't the only one behind the walls surrounding Winkler's mansion. There were at least a dozen security guards there as well, many of whom had families who might never see their loved ones again.

I settled somewhere behind the attackers, who were making their way to the wall swiftly. I figured they intended to blast their way through the wall first and then open fire on whomever and whatever they found inside it.

Lissa? Gavin's voice dropped into my mind, a note of surprise accompanying it. Did vampires have telepathy? Could they send and receive thoughts? I didn't have time to ponder that. *Gavin, they're about to blast the wall down! North side!* That was the best I could do while attempting to materialize at the same time. The attackers were nearly at the wall and preparing to shoot when I became myself.

The man at the rear of the small army had his gun yanked out of his hands and the stock of it smashing against his head in less than a blink. The ones in front of him turned toward me but I was already doing the same to them. It had taken too long for me to become solid, however. The rocket launcher fired and a gaping hole was blasted in the wall with a resounding boom, sending bricks and debris flying and bouncing across Winkler's manicured lawn. The attacking termites up front were shooting now, while answering gunfire was erupting right back at them. If I'd stopped to think about it, I would have realized that staying where I was placed me in just as much jeopardy as the termites. Bullets were flying all around me.

I was still punching and smashing as I watched the vehicle (which was armored heavily against rifle attacks), drive through the blasted opening and into Winkler's yard. Chaos erupted around me as the attackers realized that something was moving among them so quickly they couldn't put their hands on it. I grabbed one man's gun and caved his face in with the butt of it before flinging the rifle toward the man operating the rocket launcher. He stood behind a shield of some sort, preparing to fire the weapon at Winkler's house. I have no idea how hard I threw the gun but it was enough to separate the man's head from his body. The head rolled far into the yard as the body slumped over where it stood.

More gunfire erupted and I felt something sting my right shoulder, but that didn't slow me down at all. Sirens sounded nearby; the police were coming. I kicked one man in the stomach and sent him sailing. Somebody else was now climbing toward the rocket launcher. I jumped at least twenty feet, landing right behind him and tossing him far into the yard. He didn't get up. Then, just to make sure of things, I wrapped my arms around the barrel of the launcher and bent it downward. No way was it going to shoot again. The sirens were now shrieking in the alley behind us—*time to get the hell out of there.* I had no idea where Gavin was, whether he'd heard me or if I'd imagined his voice inside my head earlier. I leapt off the vehicle and the termites, what was left of them, were now shouting and scattering. Taking off at a run, I blazed toward the back wall as fast as I could go. No way was I going to hang around and answer questions for the police. That would be disastrous, as well as exposing my face on national news programs. Definitely didn't need *that*.

Climbing high into one of the trees in the neighbor's back yard, I sat there for a while, waiting for the anthill to settle down. Winkler and the others came home a little after dawn, but I'd misted into my guesthouse bedroom by that time. The police had already searched it and the perimeter was secured. I was out like a light.

WINKLER WANTED to grumble as he was forced to make a statement for the media the morning following the attack, although he had no desire to do so. The house was still intact but police tape was everywhere and officers, detectives and even the FBI were on the scene. Three of Winkler's security guards had been killed and he'd already released their names to the media. The authorities were still trying to sort out whom the attackers were and how they'd managed to do what they'd done. Twenty-three of those were dead, some from blows to the head. Three others who'd survived were babbling incoherently and no sense could be gotten from any of them.

Whitney and Sam were closely guarded inside the media room—Glen and Phil were seeing to that while Davis stood beside Winkler in April sunlight as he answered a few questions for reporters. "My security team performed above expectations," Winkler took the opportunity to promote his business as cameras clicked all around him and video was recorded.

"I hear that the barrel of the rocket launcher was bent," one reporter said.

"We think they ran into a portion of the wall with it, possibly bringing down some of the concrete when they did so. You can see the rubble lying all over my yard," Winkler was smiling slightly.

"How do you feel about all this?" another reporter asked.

"Lucky. Very, very lucky. That I had such well-trained personnel, who acted bravely and efficiently in the face of these terrorists."

"You consider them terrorists?"

"They caused me to feel terror. Wouldn't they you?" Winkler asked. Winkler had to deal with police and the FBI for the remainder of the day and then had to call in workmen to place a temporary patch over the hole in his wall. When he was finally alone just before sunset, he sighed and went to see about Whitney and the others. Winkler was exhausted but refused to allow anyone to see it.

"We haven't been able to check on Lissa; too many cops crawling around," Davis grumbled.

"Then come with me now," Winkler took off at a trot toward the front door, Davis following close behind.

* * *

MY SHOULDER HURT. I noticed it was hurting before I could unglue my eyes and open them at sundown. "Lie still or I'll tie you down," Gavin was growling. He was digging in my shoulder, stabbing into it with something. My eyes popped wide open then. "Never go to sleep with a bullet inside your body, your tissue will heal around it," Gavin gritted, probing my shoulder with tweezers that looked about a foot long. Of course, they were right next to my face and they looked huge from that distance.

"Ow," I said as he stabbed into me.

"Shut up and let me do this," he grunted. "There." He pulled those things out of me, showing me the slug that had been embedded in my shoulder.

"Lovely," I muttered ungratefully, staring at the bloody piece of metal.

Gavin dumped half a bottle of peroxide into the wound next, getting me and my bed wet. That's when I discovered I was naked. "Hey," I swatted at him, trying to get him away from me. Who knows how long he'd been there, digging around? Winkler and Davis walked in right about then, so they enjoyed the show, too.

"I had to make sure you hadn't been hit anywhere else," Gavin said, getting off the bed. "You'll heal now and not have a slug inside your body forever."

"Lucky me," I mumbled, grabbing the sheet from the bed and trying to wrap myself in it.

* * *

"Honored One, she is capable of mindspeech. She sent a warning to me that lodged inside my head somehow, but my attempts to send back to her were unsuccessful. I am sorry to disappoint in that way. I am sure you have seen the news reports by now and have drawn the conclusion that she was responsible for thwarting the attack for the most part. I only caught a few glimpses of her as she fought off nearly thirty attackers, but she was moving so swiftly even I could not follow her movements at times. None of the three who survived required more than a small amount of compulsion.

G."

* * *

"Charles!" Charles came trotting into Wlodek's study.

"Yes, Honored One?"

"Charles, get Susila on the phone," Wlodek was up and pacing behind his desk.

"Right away, sir."

"And Charles."

"Sir?"

"Pull out the records, all of them, on all the females, past and present, living and deceased."

"Of course, sir." Charles rushed away to do as he was bid.

* * *

"I'M SENDING you out of here tonight. You and Gavin. We don't need the authorities finding out the two of you didn't get questioned with the others, now do we?" Winkler was tossing clothing at me.

"Do I have time for a bath?"

"No!" Winkler and Davis exploded at the same time.

"Okay, okay, sheesh," I said, grabbing the underwear, bra, jeans and t-shirt Winkler had flung at me and running into the bathroom to get dressed. I barely had time to run a comb through my hair before he was rushing me out the door. He hadn't had any sleep at all, I knew, and it was the day after the full moon. No sense in trying to argue with him.

He and Davis practically tossed me into a security van. The vans didn't have windows on the sides and only two darkened ones in the back. Gavin sat on the middle seat with me, completely silent, his eyes hooded. I only looked at him briefly before turning away. I suppose I should have thanked him for digging the bullet out of me, but he'd started while I was still unconscious and I hadn't given him permission.

The driver had to make sure we weren't followed before driving us to the airport, and from there we were herded into the private jet, taking off in a matter of minutes. Todd was there to meet us in Corpus and dropped us off at the beach house. Gavin had the key so he let us both in. I hadn't even had time to eat that evening, so I went to the fridge, pulled out a bag of blood and took it to my bedroom.

I had a message on my cell when I remembered to turn it on— from Tony. I called him back.

"Hey, beautiful," he said, his voice all warm and sexy. I wasn't sure I was up to the sexy part.

"Hey, yourself," I said. "I just got back from Dallas and I'm a little pooped. What's up?"

"I just wanted to talk to you," he said. "Make sure we were still on for tomorrow night."

"We're still on unless something untoward happens."

"What might happen?"

"Well, you never know. A satellite could come hurtling in from space and crash into the house. Or a herd of wild bovines could come for dinner. You can't ever tell about these things."

"Wild bovines?"

"Maybe horses or goats, then."

"Lissa, you are truly unique. I'll see you at eight tomorrow."

"Sure thing. Bye."

I ended the call and tossed the phone onto the bed.

CHAPTER 12

Tony was waiting for me at the table we'd first shared when I made my way inside the bookstore. I was five minutes early, too. Didn't want him to have an anxiety attack. He was flipping through a magazine when I sat down, but closed it the minute I got there and gave me a beautiful smile. "So, what are we doing?" I asked. I had on the blue top and black slacks I'd worn to the basketball game, and my hair was held back with a clip.

"You look really nice," he complimented me.

"So do you. But you probably get that a lot," I said.

"Mostly from people I don't want to talk to," he agreed. "Let's go to Landry's; it's on Ocean Drive and we can see the water from our table." He stood and took my elbow.

"Are we taking yours or mine?" I asked. I'd borrowed the Cadillac again. Gavin had glared at me when I walked out the door, too. Winkler and the others had come in sometime during the day but they were resting. They hadn't had much sleep since the attack and were a little snarly as a result.

"Let's take mine, that way there's no argument over who's driving," Tony grinned, leading me toward his rental.

"Do you often have arguments over who's driving?" I asked as I slipped my seatbelt on.

"You have no idea. My dog wants to drive all the time. I tell him when he gets a car, he can drive."

"Does he have a license?"

"He's studying the manual."

"Sounds like an insurance nightmare." I settled back in my seat while Tony drove us out of the parking lot.

I ordered the least amount of food I could—a small salad and a bowl of gumbo, picking at it for the most part. What I enjoyed most was talking to Tony. He laughed. Actually laughed—a lot. It was heavenly to sit across from somebody who not only wanted to talk to me but wanted to see me smile and make me laugh, too. He tried to get me to order dessert but I refused. I was already going to have to bring up what I'd ingested, so I excused myself to go to the ladies' room and do just that. I had a small purse with me and there was a tiny bottle of mouthwash inside it just for situations such as this. Waiting until I was the only one inside the bathroom, I quickly brought up everything I'd eaten and flushed it away, rinsing my mouth with the mouthwash afterward. I felt better when I went back to the table. Tony had already paid the check, so we left.

We drove to one of the public beaches on Mustang Island. Tony had gotten a parking permit so we walked down the beach for a ways. I'd left my shoes in the car so I could feel the sand beneath my feet. Tony had jeans and athletic shoes on and went walking like that. After a while, his arm came around me and I didn't try to move away.

"How's your condo holding up?" I asked as we walked along. "Do you have cheese puffs between the sofa cushions yet?"

"How did you know about that?" he teased, squeezing my shoulder.

"It was either that or popcorn," I said. "Cheese puffs stain better. I've heard hotels and condos are asking for a deposit if you come in with a bag of cheese puffs."

"They should just buy furniture to match cheese puffs," he said in mock indignation.

"That's my general rule if you're going to eat spaghetti," I said. You have to wear something that matches the sauce you're about to eat. Red for marinara, cream for Alfredo."

"Why didn't I think of that?" he grinned.

"I'm thinking about writing a book. Don't steal my ideas."

"I'd rather steal this," he said, leaning down to kiss me. Okay, that was a little hot. As in, *he's nibbling on my lower lip* hot. And then giving me a little tongue and he tasted way too good for his own good. I had to push him away; my fangs were threatening to pop out.

"Sorry, I'm just not used to holding my breath that long," I apologized. I hadn't had that problem before, my fangs always behaved themselves. Always. Now, they wanted to nibble and nip on him. That couldn't be. Could never be.

"For the length of time it lasted, that was something," he breathed and kissed my neck. His arms were around me too, which was really nice. I let my forehead sink against his chest, relaxing for the first time in a very long time.

He tried to convince me to come to his condo, but I wasn't ready for that. I didn't know if I would ever be ready for that. Thanks, *FVM*.

We kissed a little more in the parking lot when he dropped me off near the Cadillac, and then I drove home. Tony wanted a commitment for another date, but I told him I didn't know when my next day off was, and I didn't.

Gavin didn't say a word when I walked into our apartment. Maybe he couldn't tell I'd been near another man, but Winkler certainly could and it was a good bet that if I'd had sex, (heaven forbid) he sure as hell would have known about that. I took a shower and hung up my clothes, promising myself I'd have them cleaned as soon as possible.

My job commenced the following evening and instead of having to work with Leon, Gavin passed me on his rounds. Maybe I was dreaming, but I imagined that he wanted to growl and pounce every time he walked by. Glen let me know that Winkler wanted to see me when he and Phil took over around five the next morning. Winkler was having breakfast and a cup of coffee with Davis when I walked inside the beach house.

"Lissa," Winkler pointed me toward a seat at the end of the breakfast table. I sat. "Lissa," he repeated, "it doesn't take a genius to figure out that you came up behind those fuckers and took out most of them before they ever made it to the wall. While I appreciate that, things like the bent rocket launcher don't go unnoticed. We had to explain that away, Lissa."

"I know." I hung my head a little. It was stupid. I just hadn't known what else to do at the moment.

"And Gavin tells me you're dating someone. That you've seen him twice, now." Winkler buttered a roll and bit into it.

Great. Now Gavin was spying on me and reporting it. "Do you pay him extra, just to keep tabs on me? Is that what you do?" I was standing and furious in the space of a heartbeat. "I keep your fucking house from getting blown to bits, and try to keep as many of those bumbling things you call security guards from getting killed and what do I get? I get reprimanded. And then, on top of everything else, *Carnac* out there is spying on me when I decide to go out and talk to somebody who doesn't mind smiling once in a while. Somebody who isn't blackmailing me, or threatening me, or who thinks I'm a blood-sucking leech. Is there something wrong with that? I don't bite him, for fuck's sake! I pretend to eat dinner, or sip a drink and we talk. Suddenly, I'm a whore? Well, Mr. I pick my women up in bars, you can take this out of my salary." I lifted the chair I'd been sitting in, twisting the metal frame into a pretzel. Tossing it in the floor, I stalked out the French door, slamming it so hard I broke two of the small glass panes.

Gavin was standing inside the guesthouse door when I came inside. Angrily I shoved him aside and nearly ran for my bedroom. I slammed that door, too. Fortunately it didn't break. My blood serum tears were falling when I slumped in the floor between the two twin beds. I always slept in the one closest to the door, giving me a clear path in case I needed to leave in a hurry. Don used to have a saying: *No good deed goes unpunished.* I was learning all about that—in spades. I heard shuffling outside my door but it went away after a few seconds. Just as well, dawn arrived and I didn't even have time to crawl into bed. I dropped over, right there in the floor.

"Shirley Walker is coming for dinner tomorrow, so Winkler wants you to cook," Davis was the one sent to inform me the following evening.

"What does he want?" I didn't slow my angry trek around the property and Davis had to trot just to keep up.

"He doesn't care, just something good."

"Shirley Walker," I turned to look at Davis as I walked, "never lifted a finger when the Grand Master was attacked. Neither did the rest of them, except Martin Walters and Thomas Williams. I don't think much of Shirley right now. She and Winkler might get a bowl of oatmeal." I jerked my gaze away and focused on the path again.

Davis coughed a little. "That's uh, just the way things are," he said. "When a challenge is made, if it's not the Second that's challenging, well, that's the only one who's allowed to interfere. Granted, the challenger and his second are supposed to be the only ones fighting."

"You guys have some fucked up rules," I snapped. "What would happen if Weldon had lost and Lester Briggs had won? You'd be at war right now with the vampires. Is that what you want? For things to go back to that? Sometimes, you have to stand up and defend what you believe in. Fucking wolves," I muttered.

"Hey, now," Davis said. "I've never heard you talk like that."

"That's because I've never held your race in such contempt before. Do you know how many times I heard the phrase *leech, bloodsucker* or *fucking vampire* while Weldon walked through those werewolves? Do you? It's sort of hard to keep a smile plastered on your face while that's going on."

"I've never thought of you in those terms."

"I know." I slowed down and patted Davis on the arm. "I'm sorry. That remark wasn't aimed at you."

"Can you make lasagna? That's one of my favorites." We were back to the meal.

"I know how to make lasagna," I said. "I just need to buy the ingredients ahead of time. It takes a while to make it properly."

"Then go now. The store is still open in Port A and I'll watch things until you get back."

"All right," I sighed. "Thanks, Davis."

The Cadillac was almost out of gas so I filled it up while I was in town and then bought what I needed to make lasagna, garlic bread and a nice salad. Everything was in the fridge before I went back to guard the perimeter. Winkler silently watched as I put things away, his expression betraying a desire to say something. Wisely, he didn't and I certainly wasn't about to start a conversation.

"You'll get your lasagna," I told Davis when I took over guard duty again.

"Winkler's just a little jealous," Davis said before he walked away. "He can't stand it that somebody else is interested." Davis waved as he strode toward the house.

The lasagna was perfect. I baked a huge pan and every bit of it disappeared. Shirley Walker didn't say a word to me as I set dinner on the table for her and Winkler. Phil, Glen and Davis ate with them. Leon was out working my shift while I cooked and cleaned up.

I never said a word to any of them and went out right after I finished with the kitchen. Gavin still looked like a thundercloud whenever we passed on our rounds and almost growled at me a time or two. Well, he could go to hell. He'd had his chance. He still smelled like heaven on earth to me but that couldn't be everything. There were other things one might want in a love interest and speaking once in a while constituted a big part of that.

Winkler didn't let me have a day off for two solid weeks and I figured Tony was probably getting ready to go home soon, if he hadn't already. Tony left me voicemail right at the two-week mark.

"Hi, this is Tony," he said. "I, uh, was waiting on you to call, this time. C'mon. Throw me a lifesaver or something. I'm drowning, here. I have to go home soon and I really wanted to see you before I left."

I'd just gotten up and showered before going to work when Davis shoved his head inside my bedroom door. "Winkler says you guys have the day off tomorrow," he said.

"Thanks," I sighed. Davis waited to see if I had anything else to say and when I didn't, he left. Gavin was still in silent movie mode; I heard Davis telling him the same thing out in the hall. Gavin mumbled something and I ignored it, tapping Tony's number on my phone instead.

"Thank God," Tony said the minute he answered his phone.

"Tony, I've worked two weeks straight without a day off. There wasn't any way I could come out with you."

"I'm sorry. I've just been going crazy here. Please tell me you have tonight off."

"I don't, but I have tomorrow night."

"That'll have to do. Can I pick you up?"

"It's better if I meet you in the usual place," I sighed. "What time?"

"Seven?" He sounded hopeful.

"No. Eight," I said. "That's as quick as I can get there."

"All right, eight then," he grumbled. "I'll be there early, just in case."

"Honey, didn't anybody ever tell you to play hard to get?" I asked.

"No, but they did tell me that absence makes the heart grow fonder. I'm counting on that one."

"I'll bring you a life saver and hatched chickens," I said, hanging up.

"Going out, again?" Gavin growled at me as I walked to the fridge to get my blood.

"What's it to you? Or is Winkler paying you by the piece? I'm sure you'll go running right to him with this bit of information." I bit the top off the unit of blood and started drinking. "You know what?" I stopped sipping for a moment, "Just send him to me and I'll tell him myself." I went back to my bedroom, drinking my dinner.

* * *

"I HAVE to leave in two days." Tony was depressed.

"And you're the guy who didn't want to take a vacation," I said, teasing him a little.

"Please tell me you'll see me before I go."

"Tony, I can't. I have work to do."

"What's so important that you can't call in sick?" he demanded. "Everybody gets sick leave."

"I don't," I said.

"Who the hell do you work for? I'll call them up and tell them I'm from the IRS or something."

"You will not, now stop that right now."

"Come on. Tell me who you work for." He took my hand across the table.

"Do you really work for the government? Is that card for real that you gave me?" I asked. Tony's thumb was making slow circles on my hand. It felt nice, actually.

"It's for real," he said. "Why? You working for drug smugglers or something?"

"No. I work for Winkler Security," I said. "I work as a bodyguard for William Winkler. I don't get days off unless he says so."

Tony drew in a breath when I said that. "Holy shit," he muttered. "Were you in Dallas when those terrorists hit? Jesus Christ, Lissa." His gray eyes were actually concerned. I appreciated that.

"Yeah, I was there," I said. "Tonight is all we have, Tony." I put my best compulsion on him. "You won't go searching into my background. You'll just remember that we had a good time and leave it at that." I got up and leaned down to kiss him. "You're a great kisser, Tony. Thanks for dinner." I walked out of the restaurant. It was an Italian place not far from the bookstore so I didn't have any trouble getting back to the car. My sniffles had almost cleared up by that time. We had no future, Tony and I. Either he'd go looking into my background and start asking questions or ask me to come visit or something, and neither of those things were good things. Winkler wouldn't let me go. We were joined at the hip, he and I, and Tony had no place in any of that. It was a real shame. I would have enjoyed spending a lot of my time with someone who could make me laugh. In a perfect world, maybe I could have been the person to convince Tony to take a vacation now and then. With me. My world had never been perfect, but now it was as far from perfect as it could possibly get.

"Well?" Gavin was growling again.

"He leaves in two days, so I broke it off. He doesn't need to remember me or anything about me. I can't have a relationship, Gavin. You already figured that out, didn't you? Once was enough, wasn't it? Not worth it, was it, Gavin?" I walked down the hall to my bedroom and slipped inside. I intended to read, if I could see through my tears.

Things settled into a routine after that. May rolled around and Whitney and Sam got out of school for the summer. Sam was going to help his dad with the farming, so Whitney spent a lot of time at his dad's place. They'd come up for the day now and then, mostly on Sundays, and I'd cook for them. Winkler showed me an e-mail I'd gotten from Martin Walters, saying I was welcome in Fresno any time. That was nice, I thought. A written note came from Thomas Williams, Jr.

"Thank you for your kind words," it read. *"I don't believe I have ever heard of any werewolf receiving condolences from a vampire before and that has made them all the more special to my family and me. The Grand Master has explained that my father wasn't the only one who went down that night. I am grateful for your life and for my father's as well. He lived a good, happy life for the most part and died with honor. That is all that any of us can hope for.*

Sincerely,

Thomas Williams, Jr."

Well, maybe I was the first vampire to get a note like that from a werewolf. It was nice either way and I stuffed it in my underwear drawer. Isn't that where things like that go? Special notes, maybe a photograph or two? I thought of Tony, and wondered if I should have taken a photograph of him. He had such nice eyes and a wonderful smile. It probably wasn't a good idea to torture myself with that sort of thing anyway.

Winkler knew, whether Gavin told him or not, that the man I'd dated a whole three times was a thing of the past—he'd only been there on vacation, after all. Winkler tried to hug me a time or two, but I'd just slip out of his embrace. There were three words I was waiting to hear from him and they weren't the three words most women wanted to hear from a man. Oh, no. I was waiting for *you can go,* and not *I love you.* The three I waited for wouldn't be coming. Who knows, I'd probably stay for a while if I knew I was free to go if I wanted.

Winkler wasn't going to take that chance. He had somebody willing to fight for him and he wasn't giving it up.

I also received a wedding invitation from Daryl Harper and Kathy Jo Greene. They were planning a wedding the end of May on Weldon Harper's property. What do you know about that? Maybe I'd be the first vampire ever invited to a werewolf wedding. Winkler and company received invitations, too. They were all planning to attend so it looked like I'd be going.

Whitney came to the beach house primed for shopping before we flew to North Dakota, so Winkler requested that I go with her. I took money with me since I needed something nice to wear and bought three outfits. We were only staying five days but Whitney in her usual manner bought everything she saw that she wanted. I sneaked into a jewelry store while she and Sam were looking at shoes and bought two pairs of earrings for myself. Nothing fancy, just one pair in platinum and one in gold—simple hoops that would go with just about anything.

The plane ride was a bit bumpy over Kansas. There was some weather but we got out of it quickly and landed in Grand Forks close to schedule. It was around two-thirty in the morning and there were two wolves waiting with vans to take all of us to Weldon's place. I was getting to stay inside the house along with Winkler and Whitney, and tents and RVs were set up for the others. I was also surprised to learn that Gavin had a sleeping bag in the corner of my bedroom. I suppose it was to keep the vamp from going on the rampage or something. The most I'd done was twist one of Winkler's chairs into a pretzel. Of course, there was the matter of roughly twenty werewolves that I'd killed, but who was counting? The Grand Master was still alive because of that.

Kathy Jo Greene was positively glowing and I knew, even if nobody else did, that she was pregnant already. Daryl was pretty darned happy, so I guess he knew it too.

Shirley Walker came in since she was Kathy Jo's Packmaster, and the night before the wedding she held a ceremony, turning Kathy Jo over to Daryl's pack. Winkler came up beside me, whispering that it was something they did when a female went to another pack. She received the Packmaster's blessings, as it were. Weldon, as the new official Packmaster so to speak, accepted Kathy Jo and then gave her over to Daryl. It was actually a nice ceremony. I had no idea what vampire protocol was, or if there was anything even close.

When the pre-wedding ceremony was over and everybody was having drinks and snacks, Winkler came to sit beside me. We were in chairs outside and it was cool out but not unbearably so. "Winkler, what happened to all those werewolves that attacked Weldon?" I'd been unconscious afterward with no idea what had happened.

"Buried on-site, usually. If they die in wolf form, they normally don't change back," Winkler said. "Their families are notified that they attempted an unsuccessful challenge."

"Holy cow," I said softly. "Where's your dad?"

"On a ranch in Texas," he said. "Mom's buried next to him. The family that owns the ranch gave permission."

"Werewolves, too?"

"Yeah."

"Winkler, I'm sorry for that part of your life," I said. And I was. That had to suck, big time. "What happens to the widows of the Packmasters that got killed?"

"The new Packmasters have the option of taking them, if they're not married already. Sometimes that works out. Sometimes not."

"Sounds a little brutal to me," I said.

"It's to perpetuate the species. Female werewolves can bear young until they're at least a hundred and fifty. If the mate was human, they're excluded from the Pack. They take whatever they have of value and move away if they're able. Sometimes the Pack puts funds together to accomplish that.

"Why do they do that?" I asked.

"To prevent retaliation. Humans don't see things the same way werewolves do at times. I've heard tales of humans taking a gun to a run area on the full moon and just shooting indiscriminately."

"There certainly are a few differences in the species, aren't there," I said.

"Yeah. Same for the vamps, obviously."

"I'm still waiting for the Vampire Manual to be carried at B&N," I said.

"You'll be waiting for that forever," he informed me dryly. "They guard that information better than Fort Knox. It's all oral tradition, passed on from sire to child."

"You're just a fountain of cheerful information," I retorted.

"Sorry to burst your bubble and all," he said.

"You could have strung it out a little, maybe said there *might* be a manual, someday, when the unicorns and fairies come out of hiding."

"Don't make fun of unicorns," Shirley Walker came to sit down nearby.

"Have you seen one?" Winkler was teasing her. Personally, I wouldn't want to tease Shirley. She looked like she could stop a speeding bus with one hand.

"Now, why would I tell you that?" Shirley smiled. "What I will say is that sometimes there really are more things in heaven and earth." She accepted a cup of coffee from someone and sipped it.

"Three months ago, I would have told you that vampires and were-wolves didn't exist. That they were a myth," I said. "Funny, isn't it, how your convictions can sometimes bite you in the ass?"

Weldon came over and sat down next. He already had a cup of coffee in his hand. "Little vampire," he said, "I've thought and thought, trying to come up with some way to repay you for what you did for me. I'm not even sure how you did half of it, but that doesn't make me any less grateful. What I have is this." He pulled a slip of paper out of his pocket and handed it to me.

"What's this?" I asked.

"A phone number," he said. "I suggest you memorize it. If there's ever anything the werewolf nation can do for you, call that number. We'll do our best to answer the call for help."

"All right," I said. I looked at the number, hoped it would stick in my mind and then handed the paper back to Weldon. Chances were I'd never need it. I'd either be stuck with Winkler or the Council, Ed or Serge would find me and it wouldn't do me any good at all then. "Thank you," I said to Weldon.

"Well, thank you is inadequate, on my part, anyway. I appreciate what you did. And I will honor you, as long as I live."

"Nobody's ever offered to do that before," I smiled at him.

"And I will tell my grandchild I was rescued from a tree by a cookie baking vampire," he grinned.

"See that you do," I laughed.

CHAPTER 13

The wedding was held as soon as the sun was down and fireflies winked here and there during the ceremony, lending an ethereal quality to the service. Kathy Jo wore a beautiful, ivory gown and Daryl, dressed handsomely in a tux, was grinning the entire time. Weldon stood up with his son and Martin Walters came in for the wedding with his wife and two children. I got to hold his youngest, Martin Walters, Jr., but they called him Mack. He was dark-haired with black eyes, just like his father. His daughter was at the shy stage, hiding behind her father's legs and refusing to come out.

Somebody was there acting as DJ for the reception and there were a few couples dancing. I remembered a night when Gavin and I had crashed a reception and danced with that crowd. I liked that Gavin. Now he was surly at the best of times and there was no talking to him. He'd been absent during most of the stay in North Dakota, off to who knew where, but he continued to guard at night just like always, sleeping in his corner during the day. He didn't disturb my sleep, but then nobody could.

"You look lovely." Davis was there, a cup of punch in his hands. Somebody had spiked it a little; I could smell the alcohol from yards away.

"Davis, don't say anything you can't take back tomorrow," I smiled at him.

"Come and dance with me," Winkler walked over and took my arm.

"Winkler, there's been several women ogling you all night, you should dance with them," I said.

"I want to dance with you," he insisted.

"Fine," I sighed. We waited until the current song ended and the DJ started something else. It was *Shameless,* by Garth Brooks. The thought crossed my mind briefly while we were dancing that Winkler had almost died in a wheat field on the outskirts of Garth Brooks' hometown. It made me wonder if he appreciated the irony of it all. I also wondered where Gavin had gotten off to. He could have danced with just about anyone there. They all looked at him—when he wasn't watching, anyway. He was so tall and handsome (when he wasn't scowling, that is), and his wide shoulders alone would make most women swoon—even werewolf women. Winkler tried to get me to dance with him again, but I begged off so he took Whitney for a round and then Kathy Jo.

Weldon was the one who came and insisted I dance one more time, so I danced with the Grand Master of the werewolves. Held against his warmer than average body while we danced, I wondered how many women had the honor of dancing with Weldon. Probably none of them vampire, that was a safe bet. The party broke up around four and people went off to find beds while I took my shoes off and ran toward the river. There was no ice now, although the water was still freezing. I wondered if I could jump the river if I took a run at it, but wasn't willing to take the risk. Sitting down on the bank instead, I mulled over the last five months of my life and wondered how different it might have been if I'd still been human, or if I'd had a sire who'd taken responsibility for me. I was quite shocked when Gavin came to sit beside me after a bit.

"You missed the dancing," I said. "There were plenty of women looking for you."

"I wasn't looking for them."

"Man, I made you swear off women altogether, didn't I?" I said.

He didn't answer my question, asking one of his own, instead. "What are you doing out here?" he asked.

"Thinking. I was just wondering how my life would have been different," I said. "If I hadn't been turned. I guess I'd be at home after working a full day, having something small for dinner and watching the news before going to bed. And I was wondering how my life might have been different if somebody turned me that gave a damn, instead of betting on the outcome."

"No speculation on that one?" he asked.

"I have nothing to base it on," I told him.

"I will do it for you," he said almost gently. "Your sire would have watched carefully, to make sure you were making the turn instead of dying a final death. He would have a ready supply of blood nearby when you did wake, and he would have fed you the very first time. Then he would fill your nights with the teachings that you needed to learn and take you out and show you how to take blood properly from a donor. Your vampire father would be your shield and protection for several years, until you were ready to stand on your own. He would have seen to your financial well-being, making sure you had a safe place to live. And he would always be available in case you needed help of any kind. You would have been his child, for as long as he lived."

"Well, that's really nice," I said. "You make it sound good instead of horrible. I'll think of that instead of the image I have of being abandoned."

"You should not have been," Gavin said, rising. "You should go back soon." He walked away. As long as I live, I may never figure out that man. I got up, carrying my shoes in my hand and headed to the cabin. Gavin came in behind me, just as I was getting into bed. He climbed into his sleeping bag and I turned out the light.

* * *

THE NIGHT in Corpus Christi was rainy when we got back, with water standing in little puddles around the tarmac when we got off the plane. I got my own bags off the plane even though Davis offered to take them for me. I wasn't helpless or weak anymore. I was vampire and a lot stronger than I looked. It didn't rain often there on the beach, but Gavin and I made our rounds in the rain that evening. Whitney and Sam spent the night—they were planning on going to Sam's home in the morning. My hair was plastered to my head when Phil and Glen took over and I probably looked like a drowned rat. That's what my mother used to say, anyway. Gavin was completely soaked as well. I went straight to the shower and turned the water as hot as I could stand it. Even I felt chilled after all that cold rain. Gavin must have done the same thing; he was toweling off and wearing dry pajama bottoms when I came out to grab one of my partial bags of blood. I was feeling a little hungry for some reason, so I drank it on the way to my bedroom. Gavin, as usual, didn't even blink as he watched.

The weather turned really hot in June, but the beach was always ten to fifteen degrees cooler on Mustang Island than it was inland. The days were longer, too, so I woke later in the evening. The summer solstice came and I didn't wake until long after eight on that day. That must be a weird day for vampires. A short night and a long sleep.

I cooked for Winkler and the others too, on that night. They wanted pork chops, so I stuffed some for them. Winkler was as happy that night as I'd ever seen for some reason, and he hadn't even gone to find a hooker. Not that I knew of, anyway.

Cleaning up the kitchen afterward wasn't all that bad. It was done quickly, so I made my way out the door to help Gavin. At least he wasn't as surly as he'd been before and I couldn't figure that out—the man was more mercurial than the planet or the god. There are insects that sing almost constantly throughout the summer on the beaches along the Gulf Coast and they were making their noise, now. Sometimes it was nearly deafening to my ears. We occasionally heard the random car drive past on highway 361; vacationers coming home from a bar or teens that had been necking over on the ship channel. Otherwise, our guard duty was peaceful and uninterrupted.

Three days later Davis was there the moment I woke, asking me to cook dinner again. "Winkler wants to celebrate a little," he said, so I checked the fridge for something I could fix. Winkler had sent someone after cube steak, which meant he wanted a chicken-fry. That's exactly what he got, with all the trimmings. He uncorked a couple bottles of wine, too, pouring out for everybody. "I have an announcement," he said, lifting his glass. "I finished the program, today. The preliminary tests are very good. I think we have a winner." Everybody clapped and Winkler even handed a glass of wine to me so I could toast with the others.

"Congratulations," I said, clinking my glass against his. He was nearly vibrating, he was so happy. He hugged me, too, and didn't stop there, kissing me a couple of times. I made the excuse that I had to go clean the kitchen, so his fellow werewolves expressed their appreciation and they all loaded into one of the SUVs and took off toward a bar.

They probably should have taken Gavin or me with them, as they were all plastered when they got back and I wondered how steady their driving had been on the road home. I also wondered what kind of shape Phil and Glen would be in to stand guard when morning came. That's why I went ahead and looked through Winkler's book that he kept on the bar with phone numbers in it.

"Sam, he's drunk and the others are, too. Do you think there's any way we can get somebody else up here to stay for a while until they sleep it off?"

"Sure. Todd and one of the other guys can come up," he said. "I'll get them on the road right away."

I was glad they arrived before dawn; I was beginning to worry a little. Todd seemed happy to see me and told me he was getting out of running the hay machine that afternoon. "Good for you," I said, patting him on the shoulder. Gavin and I went to bed shortly afterward and I was glad to lie down. The summer heat was a little wearing, even on a vampire.

It turned out to be a good thing that Todd and the other werewolf (he'd been introduced to me as Dennis) were still there when Phil got up before the others and went out for a while. He came back with two werewolves and six humans and all hell broke loose.

* * *

I KNEW something was wrong even before I woke; the noise was enough to wake the dead (no pun intended), and I had to command my sluggish body to rise, although the sun hadn't completely set that night. Gunshots were erupting from beyond the deck, with answering gunfire from inside the house. There was shouting, growling, howling. I think I was praying again, something I seldom do. Grabbing a bag of blood from the fridge, I was drinking it as quickly as I could but still felt like I was moving in slow motion. I finished my meal the moment the sun slipped below the horizon.

Phil and his army were lined up just off the deck leading to the French doors. The deck itself was built of heavy redwood planking and stood around four feet off the ground. Phil and his allies were ducking below the deck while intermittently firing at Winkler and the others inside the house. With the answering gunfire coming from the house, every window at the back was shattered and the French doors were hanging off their hinges. A bullet thunked into the frame while I watched and a chunk of wood flew off. Phil, for whatever reason, was making a challenge and not in the traditional werewolf fashion. If Winkler could only hang on for a few minutes, help was on the way. I intended to get the head of this snake right off the bat and see if the body fell apart. Turning to mist before I left the guesthouse, I floated out the door, slipping behind Phil and hovering there for a few seconds. He and his buddies were still taking pot shots into the house; I saw bags and containers of extra rounds lying at their feet. No doubt about it, these guys were prepared for a siege. I had no idea what kinds of weapons Winkler had inside the house since guns and ammunition weren't something I went snooping into closets for.

Backing up just a little, I got as low to the ground as I could. None of Phil's bunch were watching behind them, they were watching what was in front of them. It was almost peaceful there, the occasional bullet whizzing overhead notwithstanding, as I made my turn back to corporeality.

Phil's neck was broken when I tossed him aside before turning to the one next in line and smashing his face in with my fist. Now they were aiming guns at me, but just as I'd done with the bunch in Dallas, I snatched their guns away and whacked them in the head with the stock. I was moving too fast for them to get a good shot off and one of them blasted a companion in the face, trying to hit me. They would have done more damage—the werewolf members, anyway—if they'd turned and tried to bite me. Winkler, realizing that something was going on outside, came out with Davis and started helping me. It didn't take long after that. A bullet graze was all I had and I was brushing hair out of my face when Gavin finally made his appearance.

"You get to help clean up," I told him snippily, "since you weren't here for the work." He just raised an eyebrow at me and went to sling Phil over his shoulder.

Todd called Sam's dad, who was there in an hour with a box van. Phil and his bunch were unceremoniously loaded into it and Winkler growled while assailants' pockets were emptied. I got the idea that Phil had recruited from other Packs and Winkler was planning to hand information over to Weldon, who'd deliver the news (along with a reprimand) to waiting Packmasters. "I know somebody who has fishing boats," Sam Sr. informed Winkler, once the bodies were locked inside the van. "We'll weight the bodies and dump them about ten miles out in the gulf." Gavin went with Todd and Sam Sr. to do just that.

"You need a new Second," I told Winkler, who nodded. "Why the hell did he turn on you now?"

"The program," Winkler said. "I know you weren't awake for the argument we had before they all started shooting, but he'd pitched in with somebody who offered him ten million for the program if he'd deliver it and my head on a platter."

"I sort of like your head where it is," I said. "But you know this could happen again."

"I know." Winkler raked fingers through his hair. I think if I closed my eyes, I could see that gesture; it was so much a part of him.

"Well, come on," I took his elbow. "You probably need something to drink and I want to talk to you." This talk needed to be private, just between Winkler and me, so we shut ourselves inside the bedroom that Whitney and Sam used when they came to visit. I laid out what I thought was reality for Winkler. I gave him the best advice I could that night and he said he'd think about it. He thought about it for three days and then called a press conference. He'd gone to Dallas to hold the thing and every major network and most of the minor ones were there. I saw a sea of reporters in front of the Dallas house on television. Gavin and I had stayed behind at the beach house.

"I waited as long as I could to make this announcement," Winkler said. Gavin and I were sitting in the media room inside the beach house, watching the huge flat screen on the wall. It beat our small TV inside the guesthouse all to heck.

"I know you all have been waiting anxiously for me to finish my recognition software, which will assist in the capture of known criminals," Winkler went on. "The preliminary tests were so promising, but I have come to tell you tonight that the project is a complete failure. The software kept developing glitches, which defied me at every turn. So much time and effort has been spent on this project and it breaks my heart to have to abandon it at this juncture, but the sad truth is, it just doesn't work. I know everyone was hopeful that this would help capture some of the world's most notorious criminals, but it just wasn't meant to be. Not for me, anyway. Perhaps someone, somewhere down the road, will be able to develop something that will work. I wish them well." Winkler stepped down from the podium, unwilling to take any questions.

"When is he coming back?" Gavin asked, turning toward me.

"Day after tomorrow," I said. "He told me he wants to take care of some business while he's there. I think it probably has to do with naming his new Second. I hope it's Davis. Glen and Phil were a little too close for my comfort." I picked up the remote and turned the television off. "I think I'll go roof-sit for a while."

Gavin went off to the beach; I saw him after a while, walking southward. He came back about half an hour later, taking an occasional turn around the house. I wondered if Winkler would need as many guards as he now had. I doubted it. More than likely, the human ones would go for sure. I didn't know about the wolves. Winkler's announcement to the world that the software didn't work would more than likely get the enemies off his back, which was the ultimate goal and sole reason he'd done it in the first place. We'd had a talk, he and I, about how much money was enough and if notoriety was worth your life. Winkler had made his decision.

I didn't need to walk the perimeter that night; I could see everything just fine from my rooftop vantage point. The night was quiet and peaceful around me, and the only sounds came from the insects, singing their endless song.

* * *

I'D HAD my shower and my almost pint of blood, brushed my teeth and got dressed in my usual jeans and t-shirt, ready to go to work the following evening when Gavin appeared in my doorway. "What do you need, Gavin?" I asked, tying my athletic shoes.

"Lissa, come here," he said. Puzzled, I looked up at him. I had no idea what he wanted, but went to him anyway. I should have run. I should have leapt out the window, turned to mist or done any other thing to get away from him. But I didn't. I had no way of knowing. I do now.

"Lissa," Gavin's voice had suddenly gone as dark as midnight, "You will do only what I tell you to do from this point forward."

I actually felt the compulsion settle over my brain, taking over my will and leaving Gavin in complete control. I shuddered, my eyes wide. The small part of my mind that could still think was thinking furiously, although I couldn't move a muscle. Gavin hadn't given permission for me to move. Gavin was *vampire*. Who knew how many other compulsions he'd placed on me to forget this or that? I never remembered seeing him eat anything. Or relieve himself, or do any other number of human things. And—the thought hit me and I might have fallen if I'd been able or commanded to by Gavin—Gavin wasn't just any vampire. The Council had found me, long ago. Why had they waited so long to take me? I shuddered again. Was he going to kill me? Right there, while I couldn't move? Winkler would come back and find a pile of ash (or whatever it was that vampires turn into) in the doorway to my bedroom. Would he know it was me? I was sure by that time that Gavin had not only been placing compulsion on me all along, he'd been doing it to Winkler and the others as well.

My skin quivers when I'm frightened, and it was quivering then. I felt it shivering, but perhaps Gavin had no control over that part of me. He left me standing there while he pulled a packed suitcase out of his bedroom and then started throwing clothing into my bag. Was he getting rid of evidence or was I going somewhere else to die? My ribs ached, I was so frightened.

"You may blink," his voice floated down the hall as he walked toward the kitchen, and he was sucking on a unit of blood when he returned. I blinked and tears formed. His voice had changed—the accent was definitely different. How much of a chameleon was he?

Gavin ordered me to pull my own bag and I did so obediently. I had no choice, following along behind him as he carried his own bag toward the road. A car was parked there, waiting for us. Gavin ordered me into the back seat after stowing both our bags in the trunk. He then climbed in on the passenger side.

The driver smelled a bit like Gavin, only with a much lighter spice. Gavin didn't introduce him; I didn't need to know. I was dead and it didn't matter. I did know, now, that the driver had to be vampire. I just hadn't sorted out the complexities of the scent, yet. There wasn't any time to explore that now.

I looked straight ahead; Gavin hadn't told me I could move from my present position. I sat there, my hands in my lap, still shivering and blinking. Gavin never turned his head, never looked back at me and never said anything to his companion while he drove. I saw we were at the airport after a while, where another private jet waited. This one was larger than Winkler's. Two more vampires waited on us when we drove up. Gavin came and ordered me out of the car while one of the others opened the trunk and got our bags out. I wanted someone to explain to me where I was going and what they intended to do with me, but nobody was speaking to me.

"Go up the stairs, turn to the right and wait for me," Gavin commanded. If I'd ever thought myself Winkler's puppet, that was nothing compared to what Gavin was doing to me now. My teeth were chattering by then, my breaths shaky and almost sobs, but I dutifully walked up the steps to the jet, turned to the right and waited. Gavin grabbed my arm and pulled me toward the back of the plane. Two chairs were there, with manacles and heavy chains attached to them. Gavin shoved me into one of those seats and proceeded to wrap the chains across my body, hooking them into clips on the sides before fastening the manacles on my wrists and ankles. Did he think I was going to escape his compulsion? That was ludicrous. I could no more do anything other than what he told me than I could have flown at that moment.

"Do you think that's necessary?" One of the other vampires finally spoke, nodding toward the chains that held me to my seat.

"Are you questioning me?" Gavin snarled.

"No. I'd never dream of questioning an *Assassin*." The vampire backed off but I'd caught the tiniest bit of contempt in his voice. He might not have meant for me to hear what followed that comment, but I did. "The mighty Gavin Montegue, afraid of a tiny female."

Gavin moved the chains aside and sat in the seat opposite me while the others found seats toward the front. There were three vampires, aside from Gavin and me, sitting in the body of the plane with another two up front—a pilot and co-pilot. *Vampires flew planes.* If I hadn't been so frightened, I might have found it slightly humorous.

Gavin could have done any number of things during the flight to keep me from being so frightened, but he did nothing. I sat there with heavy chains crossing over my body, staring straight ahead while the jet took off and flew to some unknown destination.

Dawn was only an hour away when we landed in New York. I only knew that because one of the others mentioned it, but that's all I knew. Gavin unhooked my chains and ordered me to exit the plane. A limousine waited to whisk us to an unspecified location. Someone said *safe house*. I had no idea what that meant. Was this where I was going to die? In a safe house? If so, then they were using a different dictionary than I normally did. But then these were vampires. I wanted to laugh hysterically at that thought. I was vampire, too, but these were so far removed from what I was at that moment it was frightening. It was almost like watching a humanoid race appear from outer space and change everything you ever knew until it was no longer recognizable.

We arrived at a three-story brick building where I was escorted to the basement. Gavin pointed me to a bedroom where there was a bed in the center and a cot over to the side. I was ordered onto the cot and told to sleep. My eyes closed immediately and darkness descended.

* * *

"YES, WE HAVE HER," Gavin was speaking into his cell phone. "We should arrive roughly two hours before dawn." He listened for a few seconds. "I can hold her at the prearranged site, but is there no way to convene the Council sooner?" Another period of listening followed by, "Of course, Honored One. I do understand." Gavin snapped his cell closed and glanced over at the sleeping Lissa. She hadn't wakened; he hadn't told her she could. He sighed.

* * *

"WAKE." That was the first word I heard. I was still alive. Perhaps it might have been a blessing if he'd just killed me while I slept. Easier for both of us. Gavin was an Assassin. I hadn't imagined that from the night before. "Take this," a unit of blood was placed in my hands. "Drink." I drank. I couldn't finish it but he'd told me to drink. I drank it until it was gone and then coughed up half of it. Gavin cursed and ordered me to clean myself up with a towel he brought from the bathroom. He then flung clothes at me and ordered me to change. Had I said mercurial, before? If there was a greater polarity between Dr. Jekyll and Mr. Hyde, I was seeing it now.

"Shit, Gavin, what did you do?" Gavin flung my bloody clothing into a trash compacter while instructing me to walk in front of him. The others looked like they were ready to leave. The one who'd spoken to him the night before was questioning him again. At least somebody wasn't afraid of him all that much. I hoped he lived over it.

"She can't finish an entire unit of blood," Gavin grumbled. "I forgot about that."

"Well, hell, look how tiny she is. What the fuck were you thinking?"

"Will, this is not the time," Gavin growled.

Will had straight, dark brown hair and more than likely was quite attractive, if I'd been in my right mind to notice such things. Not as tall as Gavin, though, or as wide across the shoulders. "Come," we were back to one-word commands. Once again we loaded into the car and drove to the airport. Once again I was chained to my seat, looking straight ahead while we took off and flew for hours.

Somebody said Heathrow when we landed and I knew where we were. London. Where Daryl said the Council was. I was being taken to the Council. It was going to be a public execution. I blinked away tears. I wanted to sob, but Gavin hadn't said I could. How big a criminal, according to vampire law, was I? What had I done? I suppose I might find out when I stood in front of nameless, faceless vampires. Would Gavin kill me while I stood there, helpless and under his compulsion?

"She's crying." Will again.

"Turn the fuck around," Gavin growled. Will turned around. We taxied in, coming to a stop where another car waited for us. The driver brought out silver manacles and Gavin handled them gingerly while he snapped them on my wrists and ankles. Silver didn't burn a vampire's skin. It made me feel weaker, though. Another chapter for the FVM. There wasn't any need for a manual, now. I was on my way to die and would have no use for it.

"That one looks dangerous, eh?" Definitely a British accent.

"She killed twenty werewolves," Gavin snarled.

Was that my crime? Killing twenty werewolves to save the Grand Master? Did the Council have something against him? Did they want the peace to fail as well? Why hadn't they killed me in Texas? At least I would have been somewhere close to home. I was glad Don wasn't alive to worry over me, now. I was far from home, facing death and I had no idea why.

We drove more than an hour, and I was placed in some sort of cell when we stopped. The manacles were left on my wrists and I was locked in a nine-by-nine cube made of concrete, steel and titanium. The cube was furnished with a small bed only, bolted tightly to the floor. I might have liked a bath, but that didn't seem to be an option. Gavin told me I could move freely but couldn't attempt to escape. I huddled on the bed instead, picking at my silver chains. They were alloyed with something else I could tell, perhaps steel or titanium. I found myself wishing more than once that I'd died from the werewolf bites. It would be over now. I'd always been something of a reincarnationist; the Eastern religions had appealed to me more than others traditionally held in the United States. What had I done in a former life to deserve what I was getting now? Somehow, I knew when the sun rose and I slept.

"Come," Gavin was back and holding the door open. He handed a towel to me when I walked through the door and I was instructed to go before him down the long hallway. At the end was a doorway with a shower off to the side. Gavin unlocked my chains and set them on the sink, ordered me to disrobe, turned the water on and instructed me to get inside the tiled cubicle. The water was colder than I liked, but I hadn't been allowed to speak. I couldn't tell him I wanted it warmer. The taps tempted me as I washed under his watchful eye but I hadn't been allowed to touch them. I was paraded naked down the hallway after drying myself at Gavin's command. Clothing had been left inside the room for me while I bathed. I dressed after Gavin told me to do so. He replaced my chains, too, while someone that I couldn't see beyond the cell door handed off a unit of blood.

"Only drink until you're full," Gavin told me this time. I did so, passing back a third of the blood when he held out his hand. How pitiful was I? There hadn't even been a mirror in the bathroom as I combed my hair with a cheap plastic comb. I suppose it was to prevent anyone from making a weapon from it. I couldn't even begin to imagine what kind of weapon I might fashion from a thin excuse for a comb.

Everything Gavin was had been a lie. From his name and accent to those times he'd been almost gentle. Was he only trying to reel me in or placate me, somehow? And I was back to the time frame, as well. Why did he wait? What was the purpose in it? Was he only postponing my capture until I had enough rope to hang myself? Too many questions and no answers. Zero. Nada. Nothing.

Gavin locked me in again and I was back to waiting. He never said when the Council would see me to pass judgment, and I wasn't allowed to speak in order to ask. My prison was underground, so there was no way to get to the sun. Yes, I would have gladly walked into it, if I'd been able. It brought back the memory when he'd instructed me not to mention that again. I had no idea why.

CHAPTER 14

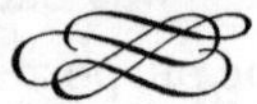

"Grand Master, we have a problem." Winkler was on the phone and he looked like hell. The beach house looked worse. He'd turned to wolf and shredded the place. Even the huge, flat screen television had been tossed through the newly replaced French doors. He'd found the note when he'd returned from Dallas. Gavin had fooled them all. Most vampires could lay an effective compulsion on werewolves, including the Grand Master.

"I have her," the note said. *"She is rogue and will be sentenced by the Council. Under the Peace Agreement, we each punish our own. She is dead to you now."*

Winkler read the note to Weldon and then waited while Weldon expressed his own rage. Winkler berated himself, over and over, for not taking Lissa to Dallas with him. She might still be safe. Might be. At the moment, he had no idea if she lived or not.

"Winkler?" Davis crunched over broken glass as he stepped inside the beach house. Davis was Winkler's second, now. He'd chosen and the Pack had agreed. Glen didn't challenge. Davis saw Winkler was on the phone and didn't disturb.

"There's really nothing we can do," Weldon was back, resignation in his voice. We can't even lodge a protest or Wlodek will feel free to do the same with us in the future."

"This makes me want to tear into the first vampire I see and tempts me to go out and hunt one down." Winkler was back to growling.

"I know. You have to fight that urge. This is bigger than either one of us right now. Winkler, this is an order, leave the vampires alone."

"That fucker placed compulsion, I know he did," Winkler was back to something else he could sink his teeth into.

"And he failed to harm any one of you. His target was Lissa all along. I just can't fathom why the fuck he took so long about it."

"Toying with his kill?" Winkler snarled.

"I've never heard of that before. Of course, that doesn't mean it might not happen."

"What if she's dead?" Winkler was close to howling out his misery.

"Winkler, she most likely is. You have to deal with this. You have to. You've seen wolves go down before. This is no different. A member of your Pack is dead. You must move on."

Winkler sighed morosely at the Grand Master's words and ended the call.

Weldon, however, had just thought of something. He couldn't lodge a protest; Wlodek might retaliate. But there was something else he could do in memory of Lissa. He had no doubt she was dead. Vampires were swift with their justice, as the werewolves were. Opening a drawer in his desk, he pulled out a form edged in gold, with a place at the bottom for his official seal and signature. Weldon began to write.

"Honored One, this came in the mail for you—it's from the Grand Master." Charles handed over the large manila envelope.

Curious, Wlodek held out a hand to accept it. "Any idea what this is?" Wlodek asked.

"None." Charles was just as curious as Wlodek was, perhaps more so. Wlodek opened the metal clasp and pulled the flap back, withdrawing an official-looking document. Setting it on the desk before him, Wlodek began to read.

* * *

I WAS HUDDLED in a corner of my cell when Gavin came for me after nightfall. He almost didn't see me at first; I was cowering behind the bed. I felt small. So very small. Was this part of my punishment? Dragging out my fear until I was immune to it and wishing for death when it finally came? "Lissa!" Gavin's voice was harsh and commanding. I rose unsteadily, my chains clinking a little. I still couldn't speak. I'd been told I could move freely, but permission to speak had not been granted.

"You will once again only do as I tell you," he said and what little free will I'd been granted disappeared. "Come. Walk ahead of me." I came. I walked ahead of him. There was a car waiting for us above ground and I was instructed to sit in the back seat. That was where I sat. Gavin climbed into the passenger seat, only it was where the driver's seat would be at home. I wasn't home or anywhere near home. I wanted to whimper except that I couldn't. Tears fell and I couldn't raise my hands to wipe them away.

The drive took nearly an hour (as close as I could reckon it, given my emotional state of mind). When Gavin opened my door and ordered me out of the car, I found myself in a park-like area with trees dotting the landscape. I had no idea where I was and I wasn't going to find out, in all likelihood. "Sleep," Gavin commanded. I dropped bonelessly to the ground.

* * *

WLODEK TWIRLED a gold pen in his hands as he watched the two captives closely. Edward Desmarais and Sergio Velenci stood at the side of the cave chamber, compulsion keeping them quiet and subdued. Sergio had done the actual turning; that was his crime but at the suggestion and with the complicity of Edward. Despicable, the both of them. Charles was sitting beside Wlodek, busily hooking up the portable power supply to his laptop. Wlodek knew the machine was very efficient but he missed the days of a pen scratching on paper, along with the occasional dip into an inkbottle. He also knew how upset Charles actually was. The younger vampire was tight-lipped and uncommunicative, going about his business and refusing to make eye contact. Charles had been that way ever since Wlodek informed him (barely two hours earlier) that the female would be tried along with the others. Now the entire Council was assembled, waiting patiently for Gavin and the remaining prisoner to arrive.

Gavin carried Lissa as he strode inside the tunnel entrance, finding Stephan and Will guarding it. Will looked Gavin's burden over before turning his head away. It wasn't hard to see what Will thought of the whole thing. Stephan's mouth tightened but he also didn't speak. Russell and Radomir were inside guarding Wlodek, along with any other Enforcers who might be in London at the moment.

The cave where the Council met was a part of the Chislehurst caves, but this particular cave was separate from the portions the public visited, with its own carefully guarded entrance. Most of the caves were man-made; flint and chalk had been mined there in the past. This cave was natural and had stalactites hanging in the back, with the occasional plink of moisture dripping off them. Gavin walked down the long tunnel that led to the cave, carrying the uncon- scious Lissa. No vampire other than Council members, Enforcers, Assassins, and the occasional invited guest was allowed to see the entrance. Prisoners were either blindfolded and led in or carried in unconscious. Lissa was one of the latter.

Wlodek watched as Gavin brought the girl in. She was small. At times, it was difficult to determine from a photograph or an image on television just how large or small someone was. He was only now seeing the reality. Gavin lowered the girl until her feet were nearly touching the floor of the cave. "Wake," he said. The girl woke and shrank back immediately.

* * *

THERE WAS dim lighting inside the cave where I woke. A horseshoe-shaped stone table stood before me, with a group of vampires sitting behind it. The smell almost overwhelmed me at first and my skin automatically began to quiver. I knew that smell; had finally worked it out. The older the vampire, the spicier and more exotic the scent, and here were some very old vampires. The one sitting in the center of the table frowned and I couldn't help it, I shrank back a little. Gavin pushed me forward again, not gently, and then backed away. I still wore my manacles as I stared straight ahead—I hadn't been instructed to do otherwise.

"She is under your compulsion?" The oldest vampire, the one sitting in the center of the stone table, asked. He appeared young, as did all the others in the room. His hair was dark, his eyes almost black and he had old-world, ruggedly handsome features.

"Yes, Honored One." Gavin's voice, from behind me.

"I will place my own so that you may remove yours," he said.

"Of course, Honored One."

"Lissa Beth Workman," the vampire looked me in the eye and if I'd thought Gavin's voice was midnight, this was the blackest of velvet that held steel underneath. "You will do as I say from this point forward," he went on. "When Gavin removes his compulsion, you will be under my control only."

Gavin came around to face me. "You are no longer under my control," he said. Part of the blanket over my brain fell away. The other remained, however. I was still held immobile, unable to do anything unless the old one said.

"You may blink," the old one told me. I blinked.

"First, we will deal with Sergio Velenci and Edward Desmarais," the old one said. "All of you have the records before you, and have taken the opportunity to question these prisoners, prior to this meeting?"

Paper shuffled around the table, but I was staring straight ahead and could only see a bit off to each side with my peripheral vision. It was hard to make out features of the Council members; the dim light came from behind them, casting their faces in shadow. The vampire sitting next to the old one though—he was not old. He had light brown hair, hazel eyes and seemed completely out of place among the others inside the cave. His scent was much lighter than theirs and he was tapping quietly away on a laptop. Vampires had joined the electronic age.

"Are there any questions or comments concerning these two before we pass judgment?" the old one was asking. I couldn't see either of the vampires who'd changed my life forever, sitting in a bar making a wager. They were likely under compulsion as well and had to stand there, staring straight ahead.

"The reason or purpose of the turning?" One voice, male, from the right.

"Shall we ask?" the old one spoke as the younger one tapped away on the computer. "Sergio Velenci," the old one commanded. "Give us the reason you made the turn."

"A wager, Honored One."

That caused a lot of paper shuffling around the table and furious tapping at the computer.

"What was this wager?" the old one asked.

"Edward bet me that the woman would take at least nine days to turn."

"And the amount and type of the wager?"

"One million pounds," Sergio replied. His voice was empty, emotionless.

"So, you made a wager with Edward that the woman would take less than nine days—that was your part in this, other than the turning?"

"Yes, Honored One."

"Very well. Does that satisfy your curiosity, Cecil?"

"Yes, Honored One."

"Any further comments or questions, before sentence is passed?"

"It is in my opinion, although it no longer has bearing on the case, that Edward lost the bet." Another voice—female this time.

There was a snicker or two. "Ilaisaane, while I appreciate the humor, it has no place in these proceedings."

"As you say, Honored One."

"Any further comments or questions before sentence is passed?" Several minutes went by while nobody said anything. "Very well," the old one sighed. "We will pass judgment. In the matter of Sergio Velenci, what say you?"

"Guilty." A voice at the far left.

"Guilty." A voice right next to that one. Calls of *Guilty* continued until eight voices had expressed that opinion.

"I also vote guilty," the old one said. "It is unanimous; let the record reflect the vote." The younger one tapped away. "Russell, move the female over to the side, please."

A vampire to my left (I hadn't been able to see him before) came and took my arm, moving me over to the side. I was now facing the center of the room and could see quite a bit more than I could earlier. I stood there, immobile, blinking like an owl.

"Bring Sergio forward." Another vampire brought Sergio forward. I recognized him, all right—the dark good looks and cruel mouth I'd seen outside my car door in the parking lot of a bar. If I could have moved or spoken, I imagine I would have rushed forward to slap him and curse him while I did it. As it was I watched, frightened out of my wits. I was seeing what would happen to me in only a few moments.

"Gavin, would you like to perform this service?" the old one asked.

"With pleasure," Gavin snarled, pacing forward. I saw something then that I hadn't known was possible. Gavin's eyes went red—as red as blood—and his fangs descended. Then, very lengthy claws formed on his fingers and with one slicing blow, he decapitated Sergio Velenci.

Sergio's head rolled away and his body dropped to the floor. That was when I saw what happens to a vampire when they die. The clothing was intact but the body began to flake away until something like gray ash formed. It was only a matter of minutes until the entire body was completely decomposed, bones and all. Another vampire came forward and lifted the clothing away, carrying it toward the cave entrance. I didn't see what he did with it.

"Now," the old one said. "In the matter of Edward Desmarais, what say you?"

Once more, the vote passed from left to right with every vote guilty. "Very well, the vote is unanimous. Let the record reflect the vote. Bring Edward forward." Edward was brought over and stood amid Sergio's ashes. "Gavin?" Gavin, who hadn't changed his appearance one bit, sliced the head from Edward Desmarais. He, like his partner in crime Sergio, flaked away while I stared in horror. Edward's clothing was removed, just as Sergio's was before. If Gavin thought to frighten me by leaving claws and fangs out, he was doing an excellent job. I was scared witless just by looking at him.

"Now, let us turn to the matter of Lissa Beth Workman. Russell." Not even a gasp or a pause came as two lives were snuffed out. Russell led me back to the center of the room and now I was standing within the ashes of Edward and Sergio. Would Gavin take pleasure in my death as he had the others? I hoped mine would be as swift as he'd made theirs. I wanted to cry again but that would show weakness. I didn't belong there. I belonged in a small town in Oklahoma where I might have mourned my husband in peace, gone back to my job at the courthouse and had lunch with my co-workers now and then. Instead, here I was, in something so far removed from my previous reality I might as well have been on another planet.

"Now," the old one said, "I originally sent Gavin to terminate this one, since she had been turned in complete disregard of protocol, with no legitimate sire or instruction. She managed to offer her services to William Winkler, who hired her as a bodyguard." There were a few indrawn breaths around the room; they all recognized Winkler's name. "As you know, I, as well as many others in this room, was dreading the completion of the software he was creating because it would give any potential enemy the tools to recognize us and hunt us down, should we be exposed. That we could not have. Therefore, I sent Gavin in as a spy of sorts, to wait this thing out and see how it progressed. His job was two-fold—to watch this one," he nodded toward me, "and to report on the software being developed by William Winkler. Gavin has performed admirably in both respects." At that moment, I think I wanted to kill Gavin. He'd sold Winkler and me both down the river.

"However," the old one continued, "things often change, once we become involved in them. Gavin watched while this one learned how to feed herself properly. And then used every bit of talent and logic she had to find William Winkler where he'd been buried in a wheat field. After that, she was sent to protect the Grand Master of the werewolves, Weldon Harper. I wish to hear this story in her own words. Please bear with me before we pass sentence."

"Now," he looked at me, his eyes hard, "you will tell me what transpired when you rescued Weldon Harper from the challenge. You will only speak the truth and you will answer every question asked inside this chamber. Do you understand? Speak now."

I hadn't spoken any words in ten days. My voice was raspy as a result when I began. "I was sent to Grand Forks, North Dakota, to protect the Grand Master while he met with Packmasters from across the United States," I said.

* * *

"So, you had a bad feeling?" one of the Council members asked. I couldn't explain it any better. My skin had been crawling.

"My skin was crawling," I explained. They probably wouldn't accept that any more than the bad feeling, but that's what I had.

"Let us move on," the old one said. "You went after Weldon Harper. Where was he?"

"About five miles away and the wolves were beginning to turn. I hovered over them, waiting for them to run. I intended to follow along from above, to watch over the Grand Master."

"Wait. What did you just say?" a Council member to the left asked.

"I give you permission to turn your head," the old one said. I turned to look at the Council member who'd asked the question. He was a tall black man. "Which part do you want me to repeat?" I asked him.

"You said you hovered, is that the correct term?"

"Yes, sir. I hovered over them. I intended to follow along, overhead." There was rustling now, along with muted conversation.

The old one was now interested. "How were you hovering overhead?"

"I turned to mist before I got to the wolves," I said simply. "It was the easiest way to do it. I can't imagine that I could have just walked into five hundred werewolves, they would probably have torn me apart."

"You turned to mist." The old one was repeating my words.

"Yes, sir."

"Can you turn to mist now? I wish to see this."

Feeling as if I'd made a gaffe of some sort, I concentrated. They could all probably turn to mist in a matter of seconds. For me, it took about four or five minutes, to the best of my calculations. My feet turned first, I could see them disappearing, and then my hands, followed by the rest of my body. I heard Gavin's swift intake of breath behind me and had no idea why. The compulsion held me in place so I couldn't escape or go anywhere. I imagined myself flying free, however. Soaring through the entrance to the cave and far away, where I could spend my last night in freedom before walking into the sun. It might not be as swift as Gavin's decapitation, but at least the choice would be mine.

"Very well, turn back, now," the old one commanded. I turned back, taking another four or five minutes to make the change.

"So." The old one shuffled his papers a little. "Tell us what happened next."

I explained how I'd descended at an angle so I could make the change on the way, landing next to the wolves that attacked Weldon. I went over how I'd thrown him over my shoulder after telling Daryl to wade into the main body of Wolves to protect himself. I then described how I'd taken Weldon up a tree and left him, dropping back down to lead the attackers away from the Grand Master and toward the river.

"I stood in the river and turned to mist again, before going back to the tree. With Weldon over my shoulder, I climbed down and rushed him to his home to get help. Fifteen more werewolves followed us. I fought them off until only six were left and then three Wolves came to assist."

"And this nearly killed you?"

"Yes, sir. I was covered in bites. I almost died. I wish I had died. That would save you the trouble, here and now."

"It might interest you to know what I have here, under my hand," the old one informed me, lifting a paper. "This came from the Grand Master. According to the Peace Agreement, we do not interfere with the punishment of werewolves and they do not interfere with the punishment of vampires. The Grand Master believes you dead already, so he sent this to me. This, in itself, is unprecedented. I will read it to you."

"Be it herewith known among the Werewolf Race now residing upon the Earth, that the following name shall be added to our registers and be forthwith recognized as a member of the Pack from this day forward. And therefore, whether the recipient be living or dead, they will have all honor bestowed upon them, for services rendered to the Werewolf Race."

"Your name, in full, is written here," the old one turned the paper for me to see.

"It is signed by the Grand Master himself, also by his son, Daryl, along with Packmasters Martin Walters and Thomas Williams Jr. As far as I know, no vampire has ever received this honor. What do you make of that?"

CHAPTER 15

"*I* suppose it's good he wrote living or dead on it."

"Yes, I suppose it is," the old one agreed. "Now, Gavin here tells me you were able to contact him through mindspeech. Is this correct?"

"I wasn't sure he heard me," I said.

"Robert, will you come forward?" The old one motioned for a vampire at the back of the room to approach. "Robert can use mindspeech, along with his brother. I would like for you to listen and see if you can hear what he is sending."

A vampire came forward and stood near me. *What is your favorite color?* He sent.

Blue, I sent back to him.

"Honored one, she just answered my question," Robert said.

"Ask her this question," the old one wrote something on a piece of paper with a gold pen and handed it to Robert.

He wants to know what your mother's first name was.

"My mother's first name was Harriett," I said.

"I am convinced," the old one said.

I had no idea why I was jumping through these hoops. They were just going to kill me. Maybe it was the cat, toying with the mouse before they ate it. They'd had Sergio and Edward for a while, it seems, and questioned them. I was the new toy.

"Now," the old one continued, "I would like to hear you ask for your life. Tell me why you deserve to live before we pass sentence."

Frantically searching my mind, I failed to come up with any answer. What did the old one want from me? Did he want me to fall to my knees and beg? My tears hadn't moved Gavin or any of the others. Would they become impatient while I tried to defend myself and my actions? Would it make any difference? Finally, I realized that I had no answer. "I can't," I said, taking a shaky breath. "How can I say I deserve to live, instead of somebody else? Who's to say they're deserving? Maybe deserving over this one, but not that one. Am I a saint? I don't think the Pope has my name on a list. Am I the scum of the earth? That answer is no as well. There's nothing that separates me from most people, except that now I don't get to walk in daylight. I tried that and got burned. I took on a pack of werewolves and almost got bitten to death. I stood in front of a young werewolf and took three bullets in the back because I didn't think he deserved to die. I sent desperate mindspeech to someone I considered a friend because terrorists were about to blast their way through a wall and I was afraid he'd get hit. I misted behind a man who was trying to murder people inside a house and killed him, because the people in the house were the only friends I had. I stand before you now because two morons who belonged to your race decided to have some fun at an old woman's expense on the day her husband died. I have no idea why I deserve to live. Do you?"

The young vampire who'd been tapping at his computer now sat there, his fingers still, his mouth open in surprise. I think I'd just insulted the entire vampire race as a whole.

Russell pulled me toward the tunnel that led into the cave at the old one's command. Russell never said I couldn't move, so I paced around a little inside the tunnel, my chains swaying and clanking while the vampires inside the cave had a confab. They were deciding to kill me. That was the only conclusion I could draw. Gavin? He was probably sharpening his claws.

"Slow down, little Miss," Russell said. He hadn't used compulsion but I figured he was tired of hearing my chains rattling. I backed up to the tunnel wall and leaned against it, brushing yet another stray tear off my face. Russell didn't smell that old; his scent was close to that of the young one sitting next to the oldest one at the table. Both scents were different—I could pick them out of a room full of vampires, now, but their smell had the same quality or weight to it.

Gavin's, on the other hand, was heavier than most inside the chamber. Only the Council members had a more exotic spice to theirs. I suppose they could all do that; tell from the scent the approximate age or who was older than whom. We were far enough into the tunnel, too, that I couldn't hear anything of the discussion. Probably just as well. I'm sure Gavin was laughing over how he'd duped me all that time. If my life hadn't been about to end, I might have considered sending him mindspeech just to tell him how despicable he was. I didn't think I had sufficient vocabulary to curse him or justify the contempt I felt for him.

Robert was the one to come for us. I couldn't tell anything from his eyes; they were hooded and it was dark inside the tunnel, even for a vampire's sight. Robert walked in front of me, Russell behind as we reentered the Council chamber. Gavin now stood slightly to the side so I could take my place amid Sergio and Edward's ashes. I wanted to laugh a bit hysterically over who would come to clean up their (and my) mess afterward.

The old one looked at me for a moment. "Are there any further comments or questions before we pass judgment?" I was back to shivering at his words. There was nothing, now, to prolong my life or delay my execution. "In the matter of Lissa Beth Workman, what say you?"

I had to bite my lower lip to keep it from trembling and I was desperate to keep the tears in my eyes from falling. I wondered how many prisoners, (who still had some of their mental capacity left, anyway) prostrated themselves before the Council at this point and begged for mercy. I decided to go out with as much dignity as I could. I kept telling myself, again and again, that it would be over quickly.

"Guilty," came the first voice. I trembled but stood up straight.

"Not guilty." It was the black Council member. I couldn't send a thank you from where I was headed, but I appreciated his vote all the same.

"Not guilty."

"Not guilty."

"Guilty."

The voices droned on until eight members had called out their votes; four guilty, four not guilty. One of the females had voted for me, one against. It came down to the old one's vote and since he was in charge, I no longer held any hope. Gavin was going to pull out those claws—I had no idea where they'd come from—and just slice my head from my shoulders.

"Well, it is my vote that decides, is it?" The old one's features belied his scent, which was very, very old to me. "For the ones I vote with, I hold my own judgment in this and it is not your votes in this matter which sway me. For the ones I vote against, I instruct you from this point to withhold your opinions on the subject. I do not wish to hear any future discussion or denouncement. Let the records reflect that Wlodek, Head of the Vampire Council, votes not guilty."

The tears fell then. I couldn't hold them back and I was sniffling like a baby. My sobs I was holding back, however. I didn't want anyone to have that vision of me in their minds. "Lissa Beth Workman, there are conditions that come with our granting of your life," Wlodek informed me after giving permission to move my hands and arms. "We must find a surrogate sire for you and I must take time to ponder the matter and make my offers to see if anyone is willing. You must follow his teachings and instructions, once that sire accepts responsibility for you. If you do not, you may well find yourself standing in this very same spot and the vote will not go kindly the next time. Do you understand this?"

"Y-yes," I stuttered a little and nodded. I was still wiping tears away. Vampires must not have any emotions or the impenetrable mask must be part of what they learned early on. None of them had any expression showing.

"I will leave my compulsion in place until your sire is found. I command you now not to attempt to escape and to follow the instructions of all other vampires that I send to you. Is that clear?"

"Yes, sir."

"Very well. Radomir, please take her to the side. She will come home with me until a sire may be found. See to her needs." Wlodek waved a hand imperiously and another vampire, darkly handsome and tall (just like most of the rest of them), pulled me over to the side of the cave. There was still some Council business to tie up and Wlodek was instructing Charles, the younger one typing on the laptop, on what to include in the official record.

Radomir produced a beautiful silk handkerchief from somewhere and handed it to me. I thought it a shame that I was going to wipe my tears with it. They're almost clear but not quite. I suppose you could call them a pale amber color, since they're made from serum, after all. I was going to stain that snowy whiteness. Gavin also moved away from the center of the chamber since his services hadn't been needed. I wondered how disappointed he was over that. He was standing at the back of the cave beside the entrance, almost at attention, staring over the heads of the Council members.

It's strange, the feeling I had after they'd passed sentence. I felt numb. That's the best way I could describe it. Maybe later I'd jump up and down with joy, but it was something else I was going to have to deal with. There had been little joy in my life for a while and I wasn't sure I knew what to do with it. What I can tell you is this—after that night in the Council chamber, I could have picked out any member just by their scent, along with the scents of the Enforcers or whatever they were, standing around the perimeter. That was a strange feeling. Of course, I could do the same thing with any of the werewolves I knew. I'd know Winkler from a quarter of a mile away, if the wind were blowing in the proper direction.

The meeting was over, finally, and members began filing out. The Enforcers split up, escorting Council members out of the cave two or three at a time. Russell and Radomir remained to protect Wlodek and Charles. The other one that remained was Gavin. Wlodek didn't have to say anything; Charles packed up his papers and things in a satchel along with his laptop which he handled with care, and then hefted the satchel over his shoulder. At some unspoken cue, Radomir motioned for me to follow him. Gavin went out first, Wlodek next, and then Charles and Russell. I walked between Russell and Radomir, who came out last of all.

There was a limo waiting for Wlodek, and he was put in the car first. I was led to the other side and seated inside the spacious, black leather interior. Gavin had disappeared already; I didn't see him anywhere. Russell and Radomir rode in the back of the limo facing us and guarding Wlodek, I'm sure. As if he needed guarding from me. At that moment, I felt weak as a kitten, drained completely from my ordeal and still wearing my silver manacles.

"We will remove those when we arrive at the manor," Wlodek said, nodding toward my chains. I wanted to huddle in my corner of the car and hug my arms around myself with my knees drawn up to my chin. That wasn't suitable behavior so I sat there, not saying anything. My hands were clasped in my lap and my eyes were on my athletic shoes, which still showed signs of ash from Sergio and Edward. Charles sat up front with the driver, and except for Wlodek's one sentence directed at me, nobody had spoken a word. I stared as we passed through tall, wrought iron gates before parking on a wide, circular drive somewhere in the English countryside. I would later learn it was in Kent, but I had no way of knowing where I was at that moment. Charles was standing outside the limo, talking on a cell phone when Radomir opened my door to let me out. "Have her clothes sent over," Charles instructed someone before ending the call. The manor we'd parked near was three stories high and quite large. I tried not to gape as I was led up the front steps. The wide front door opened from the inside and the vampire who stood back to allow us entry was nearly seven feet tall with broad features and large hands. He nodded respectfully to Wlodek who walked in first.

"Thank you, Rolfe," Wlodek announced, sweeping inside. At least Wlodek wasn't dressed in a cape and a red bow tie or anything. He had a dark pin-stripe suit on, with a very tasteful tie. The others were dressed similarly, I was only now noticing. I suppose if your life is hanging in the balance, what people are wearing sort of goes right past you.

"Come on," Charles set his satchel inside the door and grabbed my arm, leading me through the entryway and then to the left and down a short hall until we made another left into the kitchen. The only appliance in that kitchen that didn't look more than a hundred years old was the refrigerator (or should I say bank of refrigerators), and freezers. They took up an entire wall, all in stainless steel, and Charles opened one of them to pull out a pint of blood. "You look like you could use this," he said. "Not that you're not pretty or anything," he held up a hand. "It's just that you look worn out. Drink as much as you can, it'll help."

I was a little embarrassed to drink in front of him, but I did eventually bite off the little top and sip until I'd gotten about half of it down.

"We were told you couldn't finish a whole one," Charles took the bag back. "I'll leave this here in case you get peckish again." He then produced a key from a pocket and unlocked my manacles, setting them on the counter nearby. I rubbed my wrists a little.

In case I got peckish? Yes, I knew what the British meant when they said peckish. It meant a little hungry. "Do you mean I can walk through the house? I'm not going to be locked up?" My face must have indicated my shock because Charles came and hugged me, rocking me gently for a moment or two before pulling away a little.

"You just can't try to escape," his eyes peered into mine. "And Wlodek will want to see you, sometime before dawn. He'll tell you that you can't attempt to hurt anyone in this house, but that's standard." He let me go. "I'm sorry, I didn't mean to get so friendly. It's just what I am. They tell me you're from Oklahoma. Do they still have Indians there?" I stared, dumbfounded for a few seconds over Charles' question before I found my voice and my sense—enough to answer him, anyway.

"Of course there are. In this day and age, you can look up just about anything on the internet, including what's going on in Oklahoma. I saw you tapping away on that computer. Don't tell me you haven't done some surfing."

Charles' cell phone rang. He answered and I did my best not to listen in. "Your clothes are here," he said, leading me out of the kitchen. "Actually I do surf, whenever I have time," he said. "That's how I found out about you. Some kid who was buying drugs said he saw his dealer get bitten by a female vampire." Charles sounded a little guilty over that admission.

"Oh lord," I sighed. "First crack out of the bag and I get caught."

Charles grinned suddenly, transforming his face. Honestly, I was glad somebody was able to smile. Those other vampires were just too serious. Rolfe had my suitcase in the entryway when we walked in. "Where can I take this?" I asked, lifting my bag. I really wanted a shower; I just didn't know how to tell Charles that.

"Come with me, I think there's a room on the second floor," Charles said as we walked down the hall until we came to a hidden set of stairs. These were much narrower than the grand staircase that split and went down each side of the huge entryway.

"This set of steps is closer," Charles said as we walked up. We reached the second floor and came out a door at the top of the steps. The hall ran the length of the manor and was wide, with occasional mirrors and tables interspersed down its length. The dark blue carpet underfoot was so soft and deep I sank into it. At that point, I was hoping not to spread Edward and Sergio on Wlodek's rugs. I ventured to say that to Charles and he had to stop, he was laughing so hard. His cell phone rang and I could hear, as plain as day, Wlodek asking Charles what the unholy racket was.

"Lissa's spreading Edward and Sergio on your carpets." Charles was still snickering. Wlodek's communication was cut off and I heard laughter from one floor above us.

"He needed a good laugh," Charles said and led me forward a little farther. "You get this room," he said, opening a door to a suite.

It was period and quite beautiful. The walls were a sky blue with white trim, but the bathroom and closet off to the side were very modern. Walking into the bathroom, I sat down on the tiled edge of the Garden tub and sighed.

"Go ahead and clean up, I'll come back when Wlodek wants you," Charles said, closing the bathroom door behind him.

I didn't take long to shower, although the huge tub looked like a good place to soak. I had no idea how long I'd be staying, so there might not be enough time. Cursing Gavin's packing skills later, I pulled out my blue top and black slacks. They'd been wadded up and tossed inside, along with half my other things. I had to settle for wearing jeans again with the plum top; it wasn't horribly wrinkled. I was hanging up some of my things, hoping the wrinkles would come out of them when Charles knocked. At least this time my hair was braided and looked nice. I'd caught my reflection in the bathroom mirror before I cleaned up and I'd looked like hell.

"Well, this is an improvement," Charles said, looking me over. "Follow me. The boss is waiting." I thought it must be nice to be able to call Wlodek the boss. For me, he'd held my life in his hands. He could have just as easily crushed it out of existence with a flick of his fingers.

"Sit down," Wlodek said as Charles ushered me inside his study. The man had money, that's all there was to it. I wasn't up on antique rugs or desks or furniture, for that matter, but everything in that room had a huge, invisible price tag. There was a wall of bookcases stuffed with books of all kinds and an authentic Monet hanging on the opposite wall. "A gift, from Russell," Wlodek caught me staring at the painting. "It belonged to his sire and when Xavier was killed, Russell gave the painting to me. I'd often admired it in Xavier's study. Russell is using the room for something else, now."

"Do you want me to stay, Honored One?" Charles asked politely. I guess he didn't call him boss to his face.

"You may stay, Charles. I will require your help with the transfers anyway." Charles sat down in the chair next to mine, pulling a pad of paper and a pen out of his suit coat pocket.

"Ms. Workman, your official sire is deceased, now," Wlodek began.

I knew that. I'd seen Gavin off him myself and the image was still burned in my brain. Nodding seemed to be a good idea so I did.

"Sergio's sire is also deceased." Well, I hadn't thought of that possibility before. I nodded again. "Normally, if a vampire is brought up on charges and sentenced to death by the Council, their assets are liquidated and handed over to the Council unless they have legitimate issue."

Oh, lord, legal terms. Sergio didn't have any legitimate children. I wasn't legitimate by any stretch of the imagination. Winkler said that the child had to be registered with the Council. I wasn't registered. I wondered if my surrogate sire would have to do that. "And I'm not legitimate." The words were flat.

"That is no longer specifically true. When the Council decided to spare your life tonight, you gained a bit of legitimacy. Your new sire, whomever that may be, will then petition the Council on your behalf to get you fully registered. Mind you, do not step out of line or that will all be revoked in an instant."

"Yes, sir."

"And since your legitimacy and registration are now only a matter of time, Sergio's assets will pass to you. Your surrogate sire will advise you on its use and in what manner it may be invested."

"Like a trust," I said. Hey, I used to work for a judge.

"Exactly. When your five year period of learning is up, the funds will be yours to control."

"Funds?" I started to shiver.

"You look frightened, Ms. Workman," Wlodek observed. Only because I was. Funds sounded like money. Lots of it. "Charles has pulled up the records on Sergio's holdings." Wlodek held a piece of paper in his hands. "They include a home in Spain, a building in London and cash, investments and other holdings in excess of four hundred million pounds."

My fingers were twisting together in my lap. It was a good thing somebody else was going to be controlling all that for me. I had no idea what to do with it. None at all. I gulped a little. "I hope my sire doesn't mind working with that," I said. "I wouldn't know where to start."

"That is what he will be there for, among a great number of other things." Wlodek almost smiled. "It is refreshing to hear your honesty. Charles will make the transfers when the time comes and I'm sure you will be provided with a monthly stipend of some sort. Also, an official identity will be established for you. The unfortunate part of that is you must leave the name Workman behind. You may keep Lissa if you want; it is a pretty name, but your last name will be tied too easily to your former existence so you must not use it again. Haddon is also no longer an option, since many people might recognize that as well."

"Here." Charles rose and pulled a book off the shelf against the wall.

"Baby names?" I couldn't believe it, Charles was handing me a book of baby names.

"It's a legitimate source," he sniffed, pretending to be wounded. Flipping through the book, I looked at this name or that until I found something. It wasn't even in the female section, either. It was in the males and one of the meanings for the name in the book was *rogue*.

"Huston," I said. "Is that all right?"

"Sounds good," Charles was writing that down. "We can have an ID for you in a couple of days, along with a birth certificate and a passport."

"Holy crap, you guys are good." I slapped a hand across my mouth. That probably wasn't a wise thing to say in front of the boss. Wlodek shuffled things around on his desk for a minute.

"Now," Wlodek said, focusing on me again, "just a few other things. You are not to harm anyone inside this house unless they are threatening me, Charles or Radomir."

"Radomir's a decent person," I said.

"Am I chopped liver?" Charles complained.

"Honey, you're pure caviar," I said. "Not anywhere close to liver. I was just thinking along the line of Enforcers. And Assassins."

"You got all that from such brief exposure?" Charles was staring at me.

"It wasn't hard," I said. "And if anyone's threatening you and it isn't Radomir or the Honored One, here, I'll be happy to slap a knot on their head for you."

"Is that something they say in Oklahoma?" Charles was smiling.

"Yes. And half the judges on the bench pack a gun in the courthouse. Welcome to the Wild West. The only place that might be a little weirder is Texas."

"We're well-versed on Texas," Wlodek observed dryly. He didn't elaborate.

* * *

THE BED WAS WONDERFUL. I made a point to lie down on it before dawn caused me to pass out. The windows had all been blocked inside the bedroom by retractable panels that could be drawn back by pressing a button. The twilight sky was overcast when I woke the following evening; I found the button and checked it out. Wouldn't do to forget to shut those things before dawn since the windows were right in front of the bed. I found that Charles was waiting for me when I went down for my dinner. "Wlodek asked me to take you into London. Your wardrobe is, well, tiny," he said, grinning a lop-sided grin.

"I have some cash," I said. "But it's U.S. Dollars. Is there someplace to exchange it?" My envelope of cash had been inside my suitcase but Gavin left my purse behind. The purse had held my fake ID, the cell that Winkler had given me and the company credit card I'd used. *Gavin.* Just the thought of him made me want to growl and allow my fangs to slip out. I wanted to slap him. Give him a knee in the groin. The sad thing? I'd never be able to get close enough to do that. All he had to do was place compulsion and it would be *sit, stay, blink.* Fuck him. Fuck him and the vampire sire that made him.

"Keep your money for now. Wlodek said to buy what you need and use his card." Charles flashed a card at me. "We can get yours exchanged later."

Charles drove and except for my limo rides, it was the first time I'd really experienced riding in a car in England. I got to sit up front with him, too, and aside from grabbing the *Oh God* handle once in a while when I was convinced he was about to get us killed, it was a fascinating trip.

I'd heard of Harrod's before, but never thought I'd shop there. They have casual designers. International designers. Luxury collections. Designer shoes. I almost hyperventilated. Charles had to fan me to keep me on my feet and he grinned the whole time I was going through the lingerie department. Thank goodness we were vampires; there were so many bags after a while they would have required a pack mule if I'd still been human. Charles was determined to buy everything he thought I might look good in while I was trying to calm him down. "He'll kill us both," I hissed when he slid a designer dress off the rack. It was gorgeous but it cost a thousand pounds.

"I pay all his bills," Charles grinned maliciously. "He told me to get what you need. You might need this."

"Charles, we've known each other for a whole day or so. Put that back." I hung the dress up. "I'll buy it myself if I have to have it." We went to the salon after that, so I could get my hair cut and styled before the store closed.

"That's perfect," Charles admired my hair. He'd gone off to look at a few things for himself while I was getting my haircut.

"How long does it take to grow hair out, anyway?" I asked. He knew I meant it in the Vampiric sense.

"We may grow half an inch of hair in a year. That sort of thing is very slow," he said. "And I've never had to shave since I was turned."

"Well, that's interesting." I hadn't shaved my legs or my pits either, but I wasn't going to discuss that. Charles was all male, too, no doubt about that, even though he did enjoy shopping with me. I don't think Charles gets to go out much with someone who's as young or younger than he is. All the vampires in the house are older.

"Is it impolite to ask who turned you?" I asked when we got back to his car.

"It depends. I don't mind telling you, but you need to get to know anyone else before you ask."

"All right," I nodded.

"Flavio turned me. He was the Council member who was sitting to my left."

I'd seen him, all right. He may have been the most beautiful man I'd ever seen in my life. "He voted not guilty," Charles was smiling.

"I remember," I said. I knew the scents of every one of those Council members, in addition to which ones had voted for and against me.

"I thought he was going to crush the table in his fingers when he saw you cry," Charles said. I wasn't sure what to do with that information, so I kept quiet. Charles likes to talk and he adores information of any kind. He kept up a constant conversation all the way home.

* * *

"CHARLES and I have gone through the records and there isn't another one anywhere," Wlodek looked across his desk at the vampire who sat there. "You need to teach this one carefully, as her abilities might be more than useful. She must be brought to the idea of working for the Council in a gentle manner. The possibilities are almost endless if she does so willingly."

"I hope you do not intend to send her out as a prostitute." The voice was chilling.

"This one would never consent to that," Wlodek said. "And it would be distasteful in the extreme to do that to her. Wait until you see her; she is quite lovely."

"I have no interest in that."

"I know. I hope you do not treat her indifferently, however. She needs someone to genuinely care for her."

"I will do my best. I will certainly not mistreat her."

"Good. Here are the financial holdings," Wlodek handed over a thick folder. "The building in London needs renovation. I don't believe Sergio used it for the past fifty years."

"I'll see to it. Anything else?"

"Let her stay here, tonight. I'll send her over tomorrow."

"All right." The vampire sighed as he rose, nodding to Wlodek on his way out.

* * *

"I HAVE FOUND someone who has agreed to act as your surrogate sire," Wlodek informed me as I sat in the same chair I'd taken two nights before. The information caused me to draw in a shaky breath. "He has several turns to his credit and every one of them has had much success. Unfortunately, he lost two of them, three years ago. I think he still feels the loss so do not vex him overmuch."

"All right." I knew about loss. No way was I going to rip into those wounds if I could help it.

"Charles will drive you over tomorrow. Your new sire's home here in England is about twenty miles away. He owns property in New York and other locations as well. I can only imagine that he might take you traveling with him at times."

I could only nod. My life was about to take another turn and I wasn't sure I was ready for it. "Pack up your things except for what you need tonight and tomorrow. Charles will drive you to your new home as soon as you are ready tomorrow evening." Wlodek turned back to a stack of papers on his desk. I'd been dismissed. I wanted to ask questions. He hadn't given me the vampire's name or any other information about him. This was worse than a blind date. What if he was another version of Gavin? That would be untenable and there wasn't any way I could ask for a different sire if I didn't like this one. My legs were a little unsteady, I think, when I rose from my chair, mumbled my thanks to Wlodek and left his study.

"I think you'll like this," Charles said as he drove me the following evening. I'd dressed in slacks and a new top that was a cranberry color, leaving my hair loose. I didn't know what else to do. I had four suitcases, now; Charles had dug up some expensive stuff from *the basement*. That's what he'd called it. I didn't realize that Wlodek had a basement, but it made sense. Vampires needed those things to survive most of the time.

Charles helped me unload everything on the wide porch of my new home. It was another three-story, I saw, but it looked newer than Wlodek's. A maid answered the door and she was human, I could tell right away by the scent. We carried the bags in and left them in the entry hall. There was a single, wide set of steps leading up to the next floor in this one.

"Hopefully he'll let you have a cell phone," Charles said when it came time to say goodbye. "Here's my number, this'll get you right to me," he handed a slip of paper over. I tucked the number inside the pocket of my slacks. Charles shocked me by giving me a quick hug and a kiss before taking off, and the maid closed the door behind him.

"The master is out at the moment but he'll return after a bit," she said. She was short and perky, probably in her late thirties with light brown hair and blue eyes.

"What's your name?" I asked.

"Lena," she said. "Actually, it's Lenora, but I prefer Lena."

"Then Lena it is," I agreed. She showed me upstairs to a bedroom, and its windows were closed off in a similar fashion to the ones at Wlodek's place. This bedroom was more modern with a nice comforter on the bed, lots of pillows and shams, a sitting area, dressers and an armoire, plus a walk-in closet to die for. The bath was Italian marble in a light sandstone color with a tub and separate shower. Did all vampires have money running out their ears? This place had to cost a fortune. I also found myself wondering as I took two bags up at a time, if Wlodek was going to come over and remove his compulsion after a while or if he intended to leave it in place and my sire (yes, I was having trouble with that word) would place a second one. The brief period that I'd had both Gavin's and Wlodek's compulsion wasn't the most comfortable I'd ever been.

"Come downstairs and meet Franklin," Lena said after I'd dumped my second set of bags in the bedroom.

"All right," I said, following her down the stairs. Franklin was human as well—I could tell that right away. He was cutting up fruit for a fruit salad when I walked in. His thumb was bandaged, and the wound was making it difficult to use a knife. Franklin was tall, with a bit of gray hair running through dark brown. He also had a nice face, although it was lined a bit with age. I estimated him to be in his early sixties.

"Here, let me do that for you," I said, walking over to him and taking the knife. "I'm Lissa," I extended my right hand.

"I know, we're expecting you," he held out his hand and I shook it. He handed the knife over with a smile, so I started slicing up apples, pineapple and peaches. Franklin sat down while I washed the grapes and strawberries and added them to the glass bowl. "Are you ready to eat this now or are you going to serve it later?" I asked. You never add bananas until the last minute; they look terrible after a while.

"Lena and I are about to eat," Franklin grinned.

"All righty, then," I said and cut up the bananas.

Franklin asked me questions while he and Lena ate. He asked me where I was from and then said he'd never been to Oklahoma.

"You know, I get that a lot," I said. "It's just like anywhere else. It has its share of really nice people."

"Do people actually have oil wells in their yards?" That was Lena. "I saw a movie once where these people had an oil well in their yard."

"If you're meaning the pump jacks," I made the rocking motion with my arm and she nodded, "Then yes, I've seen that before. People have gas wells in their yards, too, and on their farms."

"Franklin?" The voice came from down the hall. I had the feeling I was about to meet my surrogate maker. I stood up quickly and straightened my outfit. I'd been sitting on a barstool, leaning my elbows on the granite island and talking comfortably with Franklin and Lena. Now I was shaking.

Maybe he wasn't quite as handsome as Flavio, but he had black hair, piercing blue eyes and I knew right away that he wasn't just vampire. There was a scent about him that had the telltale exotic spice, but there was more than that and it smelled to me like a fresh wind in a spring field. The exotic spice part was old, but the other—I had no idea. This man, whatever he was, had *power*. What had Wlodek done to me? Of course I wasn't about to point any of this out to my new sire, and I had no idea how much trouble I might be in if I tried. I just kept my mouth shut.

"Lissa, this is Merrill," Franklin stood to make introductions. I stared for a few seconds while all those thoughts chased themselves through my head.

"Sorry, didn't mean to stand there like a gaping fool," I said, holding out my hand. Merrill took it, then leaned in and kissed me lightly on the cheek.

"Welcome," he said, smiling.

"Thanks," I said.

CHAPTER 16

*M*errill waited until the following evening to get started and we both sat in his study. It wasn't as elaborate as Wlodek's; there was a computer and a stack of newspapers on his desk.

"You can speak freely around Franklin, he knows everything," Merrill advised me right away. "Lena knows not to disturb us during the day. A light compulsion takes care of that. She thinks you have a skin condition," Merrill smiled. My bedroom came equipped with a small fridge in the bathroom, already stocked with bagged blood. I'd have to find out where the supplies came from. I suppose Merrill would tell me.

"I like Franklin. And Lena," I said.

"Franklin is quite impressed with you. Anyone willing to help in the kitchen is good with him."

"Well, I'll cook for him sometime, then," I said.

"You still cook?" Merrill was surprised.

"Yes. I haven't forgotten how. I cooked for the werewolves. Those guys can eat, let me tell you."

"You're joking?"

"No. Why?"

"Most vampires become ill if they prepare food. They generally don't want to be exposed to any food that isn't blood."

"I never had that problem, I guess."

"Lissa, show me your fangs."

"What?"

"Just do it." He walked over and knelt down beside my chair.

"All right, this isn't awkward or anything," I muttered, feeling embarrassed.

"Please. I don't wish to lay compulsion."

The shakes came. I'd never tried to force my fangs out, before. I'd never even noticed that they'd come out unless I was about to feed, and the one time Tony had kissed me on the beach. "Lissa, show me your fangs." It was an order, wrapped in compulsion. If the house had been hit by lightning, it wouldn't have felt as forceful. My fangs came out and Merrill reached up, lifting my upper lip gently. "All right," he sighed, "you may retract them." Merrill returned to his seat behind the desk.

"No wonder the first man you drank from thought you'd only kissed him," Merrill said. "Your fangs are tiny. Not just thin, but short, too. Amazing."

"What does that mean?" I asked.

"It means that it's a good thing you don't need much blood," he said. "Otherwise you might have a feeding problem."

"Great," I grumbled. "What else is wrong with me?"

"Lissa, I'm going to go ahead and remove Wlodek's compulsion—I told him I would," he said. "And when I place my own, I'll be telling you to forget that I can do that. It's not something that the normal vampire can do."

"But Wlodek knows you can do it?"

"Yes, he does."

"Good enough," I shrugged. Merrill went ahead and did it, right then.

"You are freed from all other compulsions," he said, and just like that, all of it went away. I felt light-headed, it was such a relief. "I'm sorry to place another so quickly, but it must be done," he said. "From this point forward, you will do as I instruct, within reason. You will protect the members of this household and you will not attempt to escape or disobey a direct order from me."

That one slipped over my brain like a light blanket. I nodded. What else could I do except follow his commands?

"What if somebody else tries to place one?" I asked, thinking of Gavin.

"They will not be able to get past mine," Merrill assured me. I wasn't so sure. I knew how heavy handed Gavin's had been. It was almost a physical pain and the humiliation and betrayal that had come with it was still unbearable to me. I'd trusted him. I would never trust like that again.

"Now," Merrill said, "it is time to talk about what you are. And I will be placing further compulsion for you to hide some of these things. Most vampires are not like you, Lissa. You are almost a queen and likely should still be considered one, although you are susceptible to compulsion."

"Someone in a bar called me that one night," I said. "I didn't know at the time that he was vampire and I certainly didn't know what he meant."

"That was a pick-up line," Merrill said. "Many male vampires will use it if they find a female vampire. First off, Lissa, female vampires are rare. Very, very rare. In fact, at this moment there may be less than sixteen in total."

"Are you sure?" I asked. "I saw two in the Council chamber."

"Those two are the two oldest female vampires. Female vampires are extremely difficult to turn, Lissa. Those two fools who turned you were toying with your life when they attempted the turn. I saw the records from the questioning that Wlodek performed. They have done this sort of thing many times, but only with males until you. All the males died quickly afterward, at Edward and Sergio's hands. It was a game to them, Lissa, as vampires can take from three to seventeen days to turn, depending upon their age and physical condition at the time of their turning. You were the one female those two attempted, and they found you in your human shape so pitiful and beneath them that you weren't a sentient being anymore, you were a plaything that they could pick up and discard."

"Too bad they're dead now. I think I might try killing them myself," I muttered angrily.

"As your sire, if they weren't dead already, I'd try killing them," Merrill agreed. He was vampire after all, so he'd heard my quiet muttering. "Now, back to female vampires. It is unfortunate, but any female that is turned has a seventy-five percent chance of walking into the sun or finding some other way of eliminating themselves after sixty years of existence as a vampire. We have been unable to find the root of this problem. I am asking you now to please not consider that."

"So that's what happens," I said, mulling it over for a bit. Then his previous statement hit me. "I'm one of sixteen? How many males are there?"

"A little over two hundred thousand. We had three times that number, fifty years ago."

"What happened?" While two hundred thousand vampires sounds like a lot, if you spread them out across the earth, it's not that many.

"Technology and better weapons happened to accelerate the war between vampires and werewolves. Now do you understand just what it was you did for both races when you preserved the Grand Master's life? He was the first Grand Master willing to make the compromises necessary. His death would have destroyed all of us, I think."

"Were you depressed when you first were turned?" I asked, going off subject for a moment.

"A little. But I was dying in battle, and my sire found me as I was slipping away. I wasn't all that upset, and I have enjoyed my life. Now, Lissa, let's talk about you. And what you can do that is so unique that you are an anomaly—an impossibility, as it were."

"It's not just because I got turned by two morons?"

"Wlodek told me you called them that." Merrill's mouth quirked into half a smile. "He found it humorous, but it is never wise to say something out of turn to the Head of the Council. He has a temper, little one, and you do not wish to see it aimed at you. Every one of those Council members knew how rare you were and still four of them called for your death. To me, that is unacceptable. You are capable of mindspeech, Lissa. At this time, there are only three known male vampires with that talent."

"I met Robert," I said.

"His twin brother, Albert, also has the gift," Merrill informed me. "They are both Enforcers but their gift is short-range only. The other one with the talent is Radomir. He has only experienced it sporadically, however, so it is not labeled as one of his gifts."

"I liked him," I said.

"Radomir is an Enforcer and Wlodek's child. Anything you tell Radomir you tell Wlodek," Merrill said. "The other talent that you have is misting. You are what we call a mister, Lissa. You can turn your body to mist, along with anything you are wearing at the moment. Wlodek was shocked when your chains turned along with everything else. He will be experimenting with his Enforcers to see if they can do the same thing."

"The Enforcers can mist, too?"

"No. Only two now hold that talent. It is as rare as mindspeech and according to the records, never has misting and mindspeech appeared in the same vampire. And most certainly never in a female. You are rare and precious, Lissa. That does not mean that Wlodek will allow you to get away with anything, so do not attempt it. He has warned you that if you appear in front of the Council once more, it most likely will be for the death sentence to be passed."

"Yeah. He said that already." I was twining my fingers together, my eyes on my lap.

"Little one, you did not ask to be placed in this position. You were rogue through no fault of your own, but the laws are in place for a reason. The vampire race is hidden from humans because they fear us and for good reason. We are stronger and we drink from them. The first Vampire Law is *never kill your donor*. I'm sure you've already guessed that one yourself. And with your fangs, it would be difficult for you to kill them with the bite. You could easily kill them in other ways, however, from exerting your strength to placing a compulsion for them to drive off a cliff."

"Geez, that's awful," I said.

"Not every vampire agrees. Some revel in the kill or the struggle and do not place proper compulsion on their donors. We do not have as much difficulty with this now as we once did." Merrill grimaced a little. He leaned back in his chair and steepled his fingers.

"So, some vampires still kill the ones they take from?"

"They are not allowed by law. That does not mean they don't achieve it from time to time. Most vampires feed themselves from the blood banks now. The Council keeps records of those who order blood and those who do not, as well as those who only order sporadically. They also watch to see if humans come up missing regularly where vampires keep residences or even nearby. If suspicions are raised, Enforcers are dispatched to investigate."

"The Council has a tough job."

"Yes. With that power comes a heavy price. You have seen the Council's justice. They do not hesitate and every living vampire knows this."

"So in your opinion, vampires are alive and not the undead? Because I have to tell you, that term has always bothered me. Undead to me means the opposite of dead, which by definition means alive, at least in some way."

"Vampires are alive in their own way," Merrill said. "Their hearts do not beat but they do breathe while awake, which causes some sort of metabolism. It's just that our bodies process things differently. We consume blood and it feeds us. If we did not metabolize it in some way we wouldn't have to consume more every day."

"That makes sense," I agreed.

"Good. Do you have any questions for me tonight? I have business to attend to this evening. We will continue tomorrow night. On Wednesday, I will be away for two days but back on Friday."

"Nothing for tonight. I'll think about it all and if I have questions, I'll let you know."

Merrill smiled at me. "You are something of a miracle, Lissa. I am glad to have this opportunity to teach you."

I left his study and went to Franklin. "Do you think he'll mind if I walk outside?" I asked. I hadn't been able to roof-sit in a while.

"Just don't go far. I'm sure he's already told you not to escape." Franklin smiled at me.

"He did tell me that," I nodded. "I just want to sit on the roof for a while."

"You know, if you were human I would be shouting the house down for Merrill to come and stop you," Franklin's eyes sparkled when he laughed. "But since you are what you are, don't damage the roof tiles."

It was my turn to laugh, then. "I haven't damaged any so far. That I know of, anyway," I said and went to find the door.

Merrill and I talked again Tuesday night and just as he said, he was gone Wednesday and Thursday. Thursday evening after I showered and fed, I went downstairs to see if Franklin needed help in the kitchen or anything else. He and Lena were already eating but he pointed to a small box on the corner of the island that had a note attached.

"That came for you today," Franklin said. I went over to look at it; the note had only my first name written on it. I opened the box first and inside was a beautiful gold bracelet made of links that looked like tiny hibiscus flowers. A small diamond winked at the center of each flower.

"That's really pretty," Lena said, looking over my shoulder. The envelope and note card were a cream color and expensive, I could tell. *Who would be sending me gifts?* I wondered as I opened the note.

"Lissa, I wanted you to have this. I miss you.

Gavin."

"You like this?" I held the bracelet out to Lena. "It's yours." I dropped it into her palm and tore the note into pieces, tossing the paper bits into the wastebasket on my way out of the kitchen. I was fuming when I went to the roof that night and I didn't come down until nearly dawn.

* * *

"SHE GAVE the bracelet to Lena and tore up the note. I rescued the pieces and taped them together so you could take a look," Franklin passed the note over to Merrill.

"Ask Lena to bring the bracelet to me. I'll get her a replacement," Merrill murmured as he read the note. "This is the one who brought her in," Merrill tapped the note with a finger. "I'll do a little research."

Merrill placed the gold bracelet in his desk drawer and gave Lena money to buy something as a replacement. She was happy with the exchange and Merrill placed compulsion for her to forget about the first one.

* * *

"THE SECOND VAMPIRE Rule is *protect the race*. Obviously, it is tied to the first rule. We generally reveal ourselves by drinking from humans and or killing them in the process," Merrill told me Friday night. "If a human sees what we are, a compulsion must be placed so that they forget."

"Has there ever been a human that we couldn't place compulsion on?" I asked.

"Ah, there's the question, right there," Merrill sounded proud of me for some reason. "Do you know what makes a true vampire Queen? She is not susceptible to any vampire's compulsion, even the strongest ones. She can be either a danger or a blessing. A danger if she decides to break the laws and go rogue, because she must be tracked and destroyed. A blessing if she is the one to uphold the laws, since none can make her deviate from them."

"Are there any Queens alive?"

"None. The last one walked into the sun more than four hundred years ago," Merrill said and shook his head sadly. "Her name was Sarita."

"So, do you know when they're human that they'll be a Queen?"

"At times. If we drink from them and the subsequent compulsion has no effect, there are steps we must take. We are forced to take them with us and detain them until the strongest compulsion may be tried. Failing that, there are only two choices left—attempt to turn her or kill her. This must be done in order to protect the race." Merrill was watching me closely.

"Well, that sucks," I said. "I don't suppose you let the woman decide?"

"No, little one. We do not."

"Crap."

"That is why we should not feed from donors unless we are forced to do so."

"That schmuck, Gavin, let me go on out and feed from the population while he more than likely had a fridge full of blood," I flung out a hand in disgust. "It's like he was just waiting for me to do something to hang myself."

"The fact that you existed without your sire's supervision would have been enough to hang you, little Lissa. If other issues hadn't cropped up, you would be very dead right now."

"Yeah, rub that in a little more," I grumbled.

"On a brighter note, I have petitioned the Council to complete your registration. The paperwork has been submitted. I also have," Merrill pulled open a drawer at the side of his desk, "These." He handed a large envelope over to me. Inside were new U.S. and British driver's licenses, a birth certificate and a passport.

"Wow. Charles wasn't kidding," I breathed, examining my new identification.

"He wants you to purchase a cell phone so you can speak to him from time to time. He also asked if he could take you to see a film sometime soon."

"Gee, dad, can I borrow the car?" I grinned and waved my new licenses.

"Only when I am sure you are capable of driving on the proper side of the road."

"Bummer," I said. Merrill smiled.

* * *

"I don't believe she wishes to see you," Merrill leveled his gaze at Gavin. "She attempted to give away the bracelet and ripped up the note. I now have both in my possession."

"Fuck," Gavin paced and cursed a little. He and Merrill were both inside Wlodek's study. Wlodek had arranged the meeting with Lissa's surrogate at Gavin's request. Gavin had no idea the surrogate would be Merrill. Legends surrounded Merrill and his abilities, and none knew his age or the extent of his strength, although many guessed that it might eclipse Wlodek's.

"I believe you may have been too heavy handed with your compulsion," Merrill went on, ignoring Gavin's outburst. "She is new and fragile. More than likely you placed one so heavy it caused physical pain, not to mention the emotional side of it. You betrayed and humiliated her, Assassin. What do you expect?"

"How was I to know she would live over this?" Gavin was still pacing. "I was ordered to eliminate her. And I would have. That does not mean it wouldn't have killed me to do it."

"Ah," Merrill said. "Well. Perhaps someday, you will learn that love means protecting what you love. I am done, here," Merrill nodded to Wlodek and left the study. Wlodek displayed no emotion as he watched him go.

"He didn't say you couldn't keep trying," Wlodek said after Merrill was out of hearing. Gavin stared at the Head of the Vampire Council.

* * *

Anthony Hancock reviewed the results from the first test of the department's new software. The terrorist had been apprehended in Barcelona, just before he'd boarded a plane for Madrid. The software was a work of genius; it not only had feature recognition but mannerisms as well and that was how they'd made the collar—the terrorist had been heavily disguised. Tony wished he could thank Lissa for this as she'd given his card to William Winkler and suggested he offer the program exclusively to the NSA. It had been worth the exorbitant price tag since they were the only buyer. Winkler could have made a hundred times more money selling it on the open market, but he'd had too many attempts on his life. This option had worked out better for both sides. Tony had very fond memories of Lissa and wondered if he'd ever see her again.

* * *

"THE THIRD VAMPIRE Law is this: *A vampire may not contact his former family or friends.*" Merrill toyed with a letter opener at his desk. I wondered if this were boring to him. "Former is the key word, here," Merrill went on. "The vampire race is your new family and friends."

"What about Franklin and Lena?" I asked. I sat on my usual wing-back chair inside Merrill's study. It was my classroom, now.

"Franklin is as much my child as any of my others," Merrill informed me. "He was an orphan, a runaway on the streets of New York when I found him and took him in more than fifty years ago. I taught him to read and sent him to school with the help of a housekeeper."

"He loves you," I said. Merrill had sounded a little defensive there for a moment. I didn't want to upset him.

"I know," Merrill sighed.

"And I know not to drink from him or Lena," I said. "Not that I would, anyway, but because I would never mistreat someone I cared for. And in my book, that constitutes mistreatment."

"Are you sure you're a vampire?" Merrill asked, lifting an eyebrow slightly.

"If I'm not, then I've been drinking blood for nothing and went through that whole *we're going to decide if you live or die* crap for nothing, too. Not to mention nearly frying in the sun. That was almost as bad as the werewolf bites."

"I've never been bitten by a werewolf," Merrill said.

"Lucky you," I told him, my words bitter. "Maybe it wouldn't have been so bad if there weren't so many bites, but I was pretty much covered. Those claws would have come in handy I think, if I'd had them."

"You haven't gotten your claws?" Merrill was up and standing for some reason.

"No. Is that a bad thing?"

"You fought werewolves without claws?"

"Yeah."

"Stand." I stood. "Force out your claws, Lissa." We were doing the compulsion thing again. Somehow, slowly, long claws emerged from my fingers. They were around a foot in length and smaller than Gavin's, but then his hands were huge.

"There we are," Merrill breathed as he came around the desk. Careful not to touch the claws themselves, he lifted one of my hands in his, examining my newly formed talons. "They look almost delicate," he said, turning my hand to look at the underside. Gavin's claws had been nearly black while mine were pale, almost the color of my normal fingernails.

"I need a manicure," I was having trouble talking around my fangs, they'd come out with the claws.

"Retract you claws and fangs, Lissa," Merrill said and they disappeared. "Now, go to mist for me." I went to mist. Merrill timed it. "Four minutes thirty-two seconds," he said. "Now turn back." He timed that, too. "Four minutes forty-six seconds," he said. "Very good. The others take at least five minutes."

"I'm not as big as they are."

"True." Merrill patted my shoulder and went back to his chair.

* * *

"HERE, LET ME MASH THE POTATOES," I told Franklin while he worked on the pot roast for his and Lena's dinner. I made the mashed potatoes, putting in butter and half-and-half like I always did. "I hope you don't have cholesterol problems," I said as I put them in a bowl on the island.

"Isn't that what medication is for?" Franklin laughed.

"Franklin, don't kid about things like that, my husband had heart problems. I let him cheat now and then but all the time is a bad thing."

"I don't cheat often," he was still smiling.

"Where is your husband now?" Lena asked.

"Dead," I said. "I'm a widow."

"Lissa has had a difficult life, although she looks so young," Merrill came into the kitchen. "Lissa, Wlodek wants to see you a little later. Why don't you go change and I'll drive you over."

"Did I do something wrong?" I was suddenly terrified.

"No, sweetheart, you didn't do anything," Merrill had his arms around me quickly. He let me go after only a few seconds and sent me off to my bedroom. I didn't know what to wear at first, but eventually decided on slacks and a V-neck sweater. Even summer in England can be on the cool side and it was raining out that night. I pulled my hair back in a French braid and put low heels on so my pants wouldn't drag the floor.

"That looks nice," Lena complimented me when I returned to the kitchen twenty minutes later.

"Thanks."

"These mashed potatoes are wonderful," Franklin was having more.

"Hey, now," I pointed a finger at him.

"You can't make them again for two months," Franklin grinned. I went to hug him. Merrill came in a few minutes later, car keys in hand. I hadn't even been into the garage yet and there were parts of the house I hadn't explored. I did find the indoor pool and hot tub but I didn't have a swimsuit and there was no way I was going in naked.

Merrill had a Maybach. I couldn't believe it. Well I could, but it was amazing. He also had a Rolls, a Bentley, a Range Rover and a Cadillac. Go figure. No wonder he wouldn't let me drive. I wondered if Charles were going to be there as we climbed into the car. I wouldn't mind saying hello. I really didn't want to date him seriously, but he would be a good friend, I thought. And since there was a dearth of female vampires, what else was I supposed to do?

Rolfe let us in the door of Wlodek's mansion before we had a chance to knock. They were expecting us after all, and any vampire would have heard the Range Rover crunching over the gravel drive. Charles met us in the entryway, giving me a sly wink before he led us up the stairs to Wlodek's office. I almost hissed when we arrived; Gavin was standing beside Wlodek's desk. Merrill noticed my flinch when I saw Gavin.

"Lissa, do not allow him to hold this power over you," he said quietly, so I slowly straightened up and went to sit in one of Wlodek's chairs. I was shivering again, I couldn't help it. Merrill took the other chair. "You wished to see us?" Merrill raised an eyebrow at Wlodek.

"Yes. We are in need of Lissa's talents, Gavin and I," he said. "And this was my idea, no one else's," he held up a hand.

I wanted to tell him that I wasn't about to cooperate with Gavin, but Wlodek had me over a barrel and he knew it. One step out of line and Gavin's claws wouldn't be held back from my neck a second time.

"Why do you need her?" Merrill asked, voicing my own question.

"We require a mister and the others are engaged elsewhere," Wlodek replied. "We have a confirmed rogue killing tourists in Florida. A mister would be a tremendous help." They were going to make me go. They were going to make me go with *Gavin*.

"Lissa, please do not make me place compulsion to stop this fretting, I don't like doing it," Merrill told me on the drive home. I drew in a shaky breath.

"I'll be fine," I whispered. "I just have to deal with this." Gavin and I were scheduled to leave the following evening. The private jet would be flying us to Tampa where a safe house was available for us to use. Wlodek said that Charles had already arranged to have blood delivered and stocked in the fridge for us. The weather would be much warmer in Florida, too—it was July and I was thankful for the shopping trip with Charles. I'd gotten quite a few sleeveless and short-sleeved things, all of which would be useful for a trip to the eastern edge of the Gulf Coast.

I used up some of my fretting energy to pack two bags, using the expensive ones that Charles had given me. "Do you need anything from the city?" Franklin knocked on my door and walked inside when I answered and invited him in.

"Franklin, you don't have to run after me," I told him.

"I have to go anyway," he shrugged.

"I need shampoo," I sighed, grateful I didn't have to worry about it. There were a couple of other things—my favorite soap and toothpaste —so Franklin wrote it down and told me he'd have it for me when I woke the next evening.

"Don't let that one upset you," Franklin said before leaving my bedroom. "Gavin was treating you as a criminal before because that's how Wlodek and the Council saw you. He was just doing his job. I don't know how he thought you were going to turn on a dime, though, and let all that go." Franklin shook his head in confusion over the whole thing.

"He didn't have to be such an asshole about it either," I said, tossing shoes into one of the bags. "I couldn't even blink without his permission after he laid compulsion, and he chained me up anyway inside the jet. I wasn't able to look out the window or anything." I think I was close to tears.

"Lissa, vampires are a different breed. Some of them are as cold as the Arctic while others can be as warm as a summer day. They're like people, only they tend to go to the farthest of extremes. I know your turning wasn't supposed to be and that is a sad thing. But if they hadn't done it, here I would be, never having tasted the best mashed potatoes I've ever eaten." Franklin smiled.

"I told the Grand Master of the werewolves that he had to tell his grandchildren that he was rescued from a tree by a cookie baking vampire," I gave a shaky smile in return.

"And what did he say?"

"He said he would."

Franklin had placed my shampoo and other items in a plastic bag and set them outside my bedroom door when I got up the following evening, so I packed those things last, zipping up my cases. I had to force myself not to get the shivers again. Putting Gavin out of my mind forcefully worked temporarily, Merrill helped get my bags into the trunk of the Cadillac and we drove to the airport where the Council's private jet waited. This rogue wouldn't be coming back with us; Gavin intended to kill him but I was going along to help track him if I could. The rogue would be able to scent Gavin, but when I was mist, I didn't have a scent. I have no idea at all how that works, but it's true for all misters.

"If you need me, use this," Merrill placed a new cell phone box in my hand. "It's already charged up and programmed with my numbers plus Franklin's if it's an emergency and you can't reach me. He can get to Wlodek if he has to. And here's this," he handed a credit card to me that had my new name on it. I gulped.

"It's a freaking black American Express," I whispered, staring at my surrogate sire.

"Yes it is. Use it."

I'd put my envelope of cash in one of my bags. I still had more than forty thousand, mostly in large bills. I hadn't spent the reward money Winkler had given me and precious little of my paychecks. I stuffed the credit card into the small purse I carried and Merrill hugged me. "Be safe," he told me as I went toward the plane.

Gavin was already there, buckled into his seat. I didn't say anything to him and barely spared a glance in his direction. He'd taken a seat near the middle of the plane and since I had no desire to sit anywhere near him, I sat down and strapped myself in two rows in front of his. Maybe he would have preferred that I sit next to him, but he wasn't getting that. Nope. Not from me.

There was a car waiting at the airport when we arrived in Tampa —one of the local vampires had gotten it for us. Gavin barely thanked the local before getting in on the driver's side of the black Lincoln Town Car. I thought about getting in the back but didn't want to fight with Gavin over it, so I climbed in on the passenger side instead. I remembered when he'd first started working for Winkler and I'd thought he was a normal person that smelled really, really wonderful. Those were the good old days, all right.

"How are your lessons?" he asked as he drove. The GPS in the car was telling us where to turn as Gavin navigated through Tampa.

"Fine," I said, refusing to look at him.

"Is Merrill a good instructor?"

"Merrill is very good. I couldn't ask for better." I considered the conversations I'd had with Tony and how much fun those had been. Now Gavin was speaking to me and all I could do was shiver.

"What have you covered so far?"

"Rules one through three and a few other things. He tells me my fangs are so small that if I didn't drink so little blood I might have a feeding problem. And he had to force my claws to come out since they'd never done that before."

"You didn't know you had claws?"

"Not until I saw yours," I said sullenly.

"Christ," he muttered. "How did you kill those werewolves?"

"By breaking their necks or throwing them so far they broke most of the bones in their body and couldn't move or kicking their heads in or whatever else I could do. I wasn't thinking about it at the time, there wasn't any opportunity to analyze my fighting methods." I pulled my knees up so my feet rested on the edge of the seat and wrapped my arms around myself.

"I know why you do that. You're uncomfortable," he said, glancing my way briefly. I didn't answer.

The safe house was nice. It was a block east of the beach and about five miles south of Tampa, with a basement beneath the house. Yeah, it was unusual for a home to have a basement in Florida, but vampires have their own rules. We went through a heavy door in the floor of the master bedroom closet and found two bedrooms and a tiny kitchen below. Gavin punched in a code on a hidden keypad to get us into the basement in the beginning, closing off the door afterward and locking us inside. That wasn't frightening or anything. I was locked inside a basement with Gavin. He checked the fridge first thing, checking our blood supply. There was only one bathroom in the small space so we'd have to share. Also not comfortable. Gavin flipped on the television and found a local station that did re-runs of the evening news. I stood and watched as journalists were reporting the disappearance of yet another tourist.

The man had gone nightclubbing and never returned to his hotel room.

"Fuck," I mumbled.

"This is the fifth one," Gavin said, hitting the mute button.

"What is he doing with them—their bodies?" I asked.

"He could be doing anything with them," Gavin said. "Tossing them in the ocean, dismembering them and feeding them to alligators, burying them somewhere, it doesn't matter."

"I might be able to find the bodies if I could smell clothing that they wore or something," I said.

"Lissa, I know you have a good nose—better than mine and perhaps better than most other vampires. But we need to concentrate on getting this thing out of the way. Those bodies could have bite marks and that would be disastrous if they're found."

"I was just thinking that the body might have the vampire's scent all over it and make it easier for me to find him in the first place," I grumbled.

"If problems arise, that might be an option. Let's try to get this done quickly."

"All right." I'd borrowed books from Merrill's library; he had all sorts of things. Franklin read too and kept his books on Merrill's shelves. I'd found a couple of mysteries to bring with me, so I left Gavin in the tiny living area and went into my bedroom to read. As usual, Gavin had gotten the bedroom nearest the exit. I didn't even care how big it was.

CHAPTER 17

Gavin was already dressed and ready to go when I slipped into the shower. Knowing he was likely fretting and pacing while waiting on me to get ready, I hurried as fast as I could. I shouldn't have to feel that way. Shouldn't. But I still had daymares about the compulsion he'd forced on me and the absolute power he'd had as a result. I'd been more comfortable fighting werewolves. At least I'd had some control over my life, then.

"I'm ready." I slung my excuse for a purse over a shoulder. My new credit card, my cell phone and a little cash had gone into it, along with my New York driver's license. I didn't know why they'd picked New York as the state for my U.S. residence, but I did remember that Wlodek had said Merrill owned property there. I wore a sundress with a halter-top to go out sleuthing with Gavin. Charles had loved it the moment he'd seen it, although I didn't think I'd ever have an opportunity to wear the thing. It was a compromise. It only cost three hundred pounds as opposed to the thousand-pound price tag attached to the other dress.

Gavin didn't say anything, raking my body quickly with deep brown eyes before leading me up the stairs to the ground floor of the house. If I'd had time, I wouldn't have minded sitting in the media room and either reading or watching television. We were three blocks away from the gulf and didn't have an ocean view but I could smell the water the minute we walked outside.

"It smells salty and fishy," I said as we climbed into the rental.

"The car?"

"No." I wanted to call him doofus but that would be inviting trouble. I didn't know what he'd been thinking, sending the note and bracelet. How could he even think we'd have a relationship? Relationships allowed teasing. Invited closeness. Formed a bond of trust. There couldn't be any of those things between us.

"Where are we going?" I asked after a while. He hadn't bothered to give me much information. Not that I was surprised or anything.

"The last known places where the humans were seen before disappearing," he said. "Bars and nightclubs."

"Are any of them the same?"

"No."

"He's moving around, then. He might not go back to any of them."

"I know that, Lissa," Gavin heaved a patient sigh. "I want to question the staff. See if they know anything or are hiding something." Gavin did this sort of thing all the time. I was the newbie, so anything I said would likely irritate Gavin. I wondered, for perhaps the hundredth time, why Wlodek had seen fit to send me out like this. At least Gavin hadn't told me to shut up. Not yet, anyway.

"Compulsion." I couldn't help saying it.

"Yes."

That had come to mean something worse to me than any curse word ever could. Curse words for me were a way of letting off steam. I'd known people where I worked, though, who would cringe at a carelessly dropped *damn*. I'd tried not to curse around those people. Not just because it offended most of them, it was a pain to them too. And I didn't like to cause pain—not back then. I drew my knees up to my chin in the car seat and didn't ask any more questions.

The bartender in the first bar had long blond hair that hung halfway down his back and it was tied at the nape of his neck with a leather thong. Gavin had only placed a slight compulsion since the bartender seemed more than willing to answer questions. It was a Monday night, too, so the crowd was light.

"The police asked me already," the bartender answered one of Gavin's questions.

"That isn't what I asked you," Gavin said, strengthening the compulsion. "You will answer all my questions in detail, no matter how many times you've answered them already."

The bartender's eyes went blank for a second and he nodded. "The guy was sitting down there," the bartender pointed to the other end of the bar. We were currently standing at the opposite end, just to the left of the door. "He ordered martinis. Six of them. He talked to several people including three women, but he didn't get very far with them. They decided he was too drunk and took off with somebody else."

"You didn't see him leave with anyone, male or female?" Gavin asked.

"No. One minute he was there, the next he was gone. There was a hundred on the bar when I got back."

"What did you do with the money?" I asked. Gavin turned to me and frowned.

"The cops asked that, too," the bartender replied. "We deposited it the next day. The guy wasn't reported missing until the day after that. Too late to do anything about it."

"So you put the money in the till and then take tips out later?" I asked.

The bartender looked like he was sweating, suddenly. He hadn't been honest with me, but then Gavin hadn't commanded him to answer *my* questions truthfully.

"What did you do with the hundred?" Gavin was now getting forceful.

"I slipped it in my pocket," the bartender whined.

"And then what did you do with it?" I asked.

"Bambalacha."

"Great," I mumbled. No luck getting the vampire's scent that way.

"What?" Gavin didn't know what he'd said.

"He bought marijuana with it," I said.

"How do you know this?" Gavin pointed a deep frown in my direction.

"I used to work for a judge, doofus."

"You will forget you saw either of us," Gavin gave the command to the bartender before gripping my upper arm and ushering me out the door.

"Go ahead, tell me not to call you doofus again," I muttered petulantly as he shoved me into the passenger seat and shut the door.

Gavin didn't say a word; he just slid in on the driver's side, started the car up and drove to the next bar. We met with pretty much the same results at all five bars that night. No, the other bartenders didn't take the cash and run, or buy marijuana (Not that came up in conversation, anyway). Three employees did remember the victims clearly, (two males and three females were missing) and they said that all but one left cash on the bar—mostly hundred dollar bills—to cover the drinks plus a hefty tip. All the cash had gone to the bank or otherwise gotten lost in the shuffle afterward.

"I'm sure the police have already checked with the area banks to see if anybody has done currency exchanges in large amounts," I said as we were driving through Tampa. Gavin looked at me sharply.

"He could be local but I'm thinking not," I said. I wasn't sure how to explain why I felt that way, I just did.

"You think he traveled here just to do this and then planned to go home?" Gavin asked, intrigued.

"Well, yeah."

"Fascinating."

With no idea whether Gavin thought I was an idiot or not, I turned my head and watched the city of Tampa off to the east as we drove across the Sunshine Skyway Bridge. Neither Gavin nor I would ever see that bridge in the sunshine it was named after. Not in person, anyway.

"Here," Gavin thumped a Tampa area Yellow Pages down in front of me after we made it back to our basement. I was sitting at the tiny kitchen table, my purse flopped onto the surface at my elbow.

Looking up at his unreadable expression for a moment, I sighed and opened the book to look for bars. There were a lot of them. I was looking through the many listings when an idea hit me.

"Gavin, do we have any paper and a pencil?"

Gavin was watching news re-runs, checking for further disappearances. Without a word, he stood and went into his bedroom, coming back with a legal pad and a very nice pen. "Now," I said, "I know what bars we went to, but what order were they visited? What's the order of disappearances and the corresponding names of the bars?"

Gavin looked like he wanted to growl at me but went back again and brought out a thick file folder, setting it down next to me. The first page inside the folder had four names of victims listed, along with the name of the bar where they'd last been seen. The information had been printed before the fifth victim disappeared. Adding his name to the list, I wrote the information down on my legal pad in two columns, one for the person, the other for the bar in question. Three out of four fit my theory. It was the third one that didn't.

"The Bearded Manatee, that's where the waitress said she saw the girl but the girl paid with a credit card, right?" I looked over at Gavin, who'd gone back to watching the news.

"Yes." He didn't even turn in my direction when he answered.

"She wasn't abducted from that bar," I said. That got his attention. He was staring at me now.

"And just how do you know this?" A deep frown was aimed in my direction.

"It's likely the police haven't missed this either," I said. "The fifth guy disappeared from Eddie's Bar," I said. "Look at this." I took my list over to Gavin and showed him my columns. "First one disappeared from Antonio's. Second from the Beachcomber. The third one—that bar is listed as the Bearded Manatee, but I don't think that's the one the girl was grabbed from. That bar started with a C."

Gavin grabbed the legal pad away from me. The fourth bar had been Dio's Bar and Grille. "He's going through the phone book, Gavin," I said. "He's making this a

game, just like those two idiots who turned me."

Gavin stood faster than I could see him stand and had his cell phone in his hand in almost as much time. He hit a number on speed dial and I heard it ringing. Wlodek's voice came through, loud and clear.

"Honored One, do we know the whereabouts of Nyles Abernathy, Edward Desmarais' sire?" Gavin asked, ignoring the greeting.

"Charles!" Wlodek's shout for his assistant could have been heard by a human, I think, and Gavin was holding the phone away from his ear and grimacing in pain.

We both listened while Wlodek instructed Charles to get Nyles on the phone. We waited. Nyles had an assistant too, because Wlodek came back to us in a few minutes with the information that *Master Abernathy was traveling.*

"He's striking back at us for us killing Edward, isn't he?" Wlodek said after passing off the information.

"It looks that way," Gavin replied.

"Do you want Radomir to come?"

"Go ahead and send him but I'm still going to try and take Abernathy down in the meantime," Gavin raked fingers through his hair.

"He probably knows we know, now," I said quietly. "I'm sure his assistant was instructed to let him know if we tried to contact him."

"Did you hear that, Honored One?"

"Yes."

"Fuck," Gavin said.

"Heard that too," Wlodek observed dryly. "We have no record of his asking to use a safe house, so he could be almost anywhere," Wlodek went on. Gavin and I had heard Charles say the same thing, off in the distance.

"Dawn is nearly here, Gavin," Wlodek gave him the reminder.

"Thank you for the information, Honored One," Gavin said, ending the call.

"He's been killing with two or three nights in between," I said, but realized that Gavin already knew that. He didn't reprimand me. "I'll go read, now," I said quietly and went to my bedroom, closing the door behind me. Not being able to help myself, I stuck my head out again after a couple of minutes. "Since he knows now, he may step up his attacks." I shut the door a second time and went to find my book.

The page from the phone book containing names of bars beginning with the letter F was in my hand as Gavin drove through Tampa the following evening. I suppose the good thing about hunting a vampire is that he couldn't move in daylight, just as Gavin and I couldn't. He'd be asleep someplace while the sun was in the sky. We were headed toward Farscape, a nightclub near Tarpon Springs. I didn't think Nyles would pick the first name out of the book but Gavin wasn't satisfied with not checking all of them. I smelled plenty of perfume, aftershave, suntan oil and perspiration when we got there, but no vampire. We left.

The next name on the list was Felicity's, inside a hotel. Gavin set the GPS and started driving again. It was humorous to me that vampires were so gadget oriented; Gavin had a nice MacBook Pro. Honestly, I would have taken him for a PC guy. The hotel bar was nice. In Farscape, my feet had stuck to the floor a little. No vampire at the hotel bar either, Gavin knew it as soon as I did. We left. There were only two F bars left—The Fisherman's Bend and Foxy's. The Fisherman's Bend was south of Sun City and not all that big, either. I would have called it a hole-in-the-wall but Gavin had a set look on his face so I didn't disturb him. He was in Assassin mode, I figured, and I sure didn't want to mess with *that*.

The scent was nearly overpowering when we walked inside the bar and it scared me. There were only two vampires that I knew of that were older than that scent and they were Wlodek and Merrill. If this was Nyles, he was older than Gavin. Not fully sure whether Gavin would get anything from me or not, I sent him mindspeech anyway. *Gavin, he's older than you*, I sent. Gavin never moved a muscle to let me know he'd heard.

Instead, Gavin leaned down and brushed his lips against my neck, making me shiver. "Go to the restroom and mist," he murmured against my skin. I headed toward the ladies' room to do just that. There was only one stall and I had to wait precious minutes for it.

Hoping all hell wouldn't break loose while I waited, I tapped my foot until the girl finally came out.

"Leave the bar now," I hissed, placing compulsion. She nodded and hit the door at a trot. I locked myself inside the stall and concentrated on turning to mist. Merrill had timed me at a bit over four minutes and thirty seconds. I had to calm myself down to turn as fast as I could. I was almost changed completely when I heard the screams outside the restroom, along with the sounds of crashing furniture and running feet.

Misting under the door to get back to the bar, I found total chaos inside the place. The humans were shouting and screaming, all of them trying to get out the door at once. What drew my attention was Gavin. He stood off in a corner, glaring at something that wasn't that far away from me. Initially, it had been blocked by fleeing bar patrons. Now I could see it clearly and if my blood hadn't been cold already, it would have become so. He wasn't tall, perhaps five-nine or so, with thick blond hair and a stocky body. If he'd had black frame glasses and a pocket protector, he might have looked like any geek from Silicon Valley. He was dressed in an expensive suit instead, didn't need glasses and was pointing a flamethrower at Gavin.

Anybody holding a flamethrower would be somebody to get the hell away from, but a vampire holding a flamethrower? That had to be a hundred times worse. A man ran in front of the vampire and he fired a jet of flame, setting the poor soul on fire. Instead of dropping to the floor and trying to beat out the flames by rolling, the man ran through the door, his body blazing. His fiery exit caused even more havoc; I heard screams from the crowd outside and I didn't know if there was any saving him after that. All the patrons were now outside the bar. Only Gavin, Nyles Abernathy and I remained inside.

Nyles casually set a wooden table on fire that had been knocked over between him and Gavin. Gavin wouldn't have any way of knowing I was behind Nyles and in my present state that did me no good at all. All Nyles had to do was shoot the flamethrower at Gavin and he would be burned to a crisp. I didn't think vampires and fire mixed all that well.

Wlodek said that he was sending Radomir. I had no idea when Radomir was coming, where he was at the moment or how far I could send mindspeech. I sent it out anyway, because the way things were going, Gavin and I might not make it out of this alive. *Radomir, we're at The Fisherman's Bend Bar in Tampa. Nyles has a flamethrower.* That was the best I could do before I concentrated on turning back to myself behind Nyles as he faced off with Gavin.

Nyles was laughing and shouting at Gavin as I turned, and for fun shot the flamethrower toward Gavin's left to keep him from inching toward the door. I also heard sirens in the distance and knew we didn't have much time. I concentrated harder while Nyles aimed another blast at Gavin. Gavin moved at the last millisecond, barely avoiding being fried. The table continued to burn, along with the wall to Gavin's left. The whole building was going to go up quickly once those flames found their way to the ceiling.

"You should have held your child in check," Gavin said, ducking another shot of flame.

"You think so? Who do you think taught him to play?" Nyles sounded crazed and I figured a crazed vampire couldn't be a good thing. I also didn't think Nyles planned on coming out of this alive. He intended to take Gavin down with him when he went, too. "I wondered how many people would die before you figured out my simple puzzle," Nyles laughed. I was nearly solid again. Only a few more seconds. Those seconds were too long.

"Stand still while I kill you," Nyles' compulsion rang out like a bell and Gavin went completely still. Nyles was firing his flamethrower directly at Gavin when I got back to normal and I didn't even have to force my claws out this time, I was so furious. I slashed out at Nyles' neck, causing him to shoot the flamethrower upward and catching the ceiling on fire.

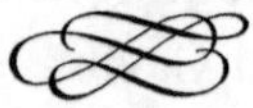

yles stood there, shooting fire into the ceiling for seconds and the entire bar was in flames before he began to flake away. His head never dropped from his body, though, until his knees buckled and he fell to the floor. The flamethrower stopped then but it was already too late; fire was roaring through the building.

Gavin's flesh was still burning when I threw myself on top of him, barely managing to suffocate the flames before the building began to cave in. Water was pouring in, too—the firefighters had arrived. I have no idea what those people thought when I kicked right through the wall of the building, hauling Gavin along with me. The scent of burning was in my nostrils and I couldn't smell anything other than that. Someone came forward to help me and I was trying to fend him off, knowing if Gavin were taken to a hospital somewhere, it would be disastrous.

"Lissa! Lissa, it's me!" Radomir was trying to get through to me somehow, but it took precious time to do it. When I realized who it was and allowed him take Gavin, Radomir rushed us through the gathered crowd who parted to let us pass. Gavin was laid in the back seat of a rented SUV, Radomir tossed me into the passenger seat and in a blink, we were on our way out of there. I started crying. Gavin was dead and everything was awful.

"There's blood in the cooler in the back," Radomir said, doing his best to drive through the city as quickly as possible. "See if you can get him to swallow any." I was sniffling as I climbed through the speeding SUV, carefully wriggling over the back seat so I wouldn't injure Gavin's blackened flesh. Tossing six bags of blood into the floor in front of the back seat, I climbed back over and ripped the top off one of the bags. Gavin couldn't even moan as I did my best to pour blood down his throat. Most of it was coming right back out again, even as I was praying that some of it would make its way inside.

"Come on, Gavin," I wept. "Drink this or I swear I'll never speak to you again." The second bag was now in my hand and I was trying desperately to get it down Gavin's throat. His throat convulsed and he swallowed. And then swallowed again. I almost sobbed and poured the rest of that bag into him before tossing the empty aside and reaching for the third. I had the better part of five bags into Gavin when Radomir drove in the garage at the safe house. He carried Gavin inside and down the steps to the basement.

We convinced Gavin to drink another two bags of blood and Radomir was beginning to look hopeful. Gavin was lying on the sofa in the tiny living room while I was picking charred clothing away from his flesh. "We'll put him in a tub of water shortly before dawn," Radomir told me. "I think we've gotten enough blood down him now."

Radomir handed a unit of blood to me later while I sat at the kitchen table, staring morosely at Gavin's body lying on the sofa just feet away. "Drink some, it'll help," Radomir urged gently. "If you hadn't sent mindspeech, I would never have known where you were," he added. "And it came in, clear as a bell. The plane had just landed at the airport and I was loading my bags into the SUV."

"Thank you for being there." I still felt like crying as I sipped my blood. "I was terrified somebody would try to take him to a hospital and that would have been a calamity."

"Yes, it would have been that for certain," Radomir sighed. He pulled out his cell phone and dialed a number. I heard Wlodek's voice when he answered.

"Child," Wlodek said, "what has happened?" Radomir truly was Wlodek's son, by blood. Not his biological father, but by blood, anyway. I realized I could connect the two by scent.

"Nyles had a flamethrower and burned down a bar along with injuring Gavin. We do not know if he will survive the rejuvenating sleep," Radomir explained.

"Is Nyles still running loose, then?" Wlodek sounded upset.

"No, father. Lissa killed him."

"Put Lissa on the phone." It was an order. Radomir handed the phone to me.

"Honored One?" I was tired and it came through in my voice.

"Lissa, tell me exactly what happened." I told him. About turning to mist and Nyles playing with all of us, terrifying the bar crowd and sending them rushing through the door. About his placing a compulsion on Gavin so he'd stand still to be burned. And then about my turning back to myself behind Nyles to decapitate him.

"Do you think Gavin will live?" he asked.

"I hope so," I sighed. "We got as much blood as we could into him. I guess we have to wait now. His skin is black and just flakes off if we touch him."

"I made the right decision, sending you," Wlodek said.

"Yes, I suppose you did," I agreed. "I just wish it had turned out better."

"I will get some of the local vampires to do damage control," he told me. "There are quite a few in the area. Let me speak to Radomir again."

I handed the phone back to Radomir and went to kneel beside Gavin. Even his hair had been burned. I remembered Charles telling me it would only grow about half an inch a year. If Gavin lived, he'd have short hair for a while. "Gavin," I said softly, "I don't know you well enough to say what you need to hear to make you want to live. I have no idea what that might be. But I can't help thinking that you wouldn't want to leave this way. You strike me as the guy who'd want to decide for himself how that happened, instead of allowing some crazed idiot with a flamethrower to make that decision for you. Radomir says we'll put you in a tub of water after a while, so I'm going to go clean the bathtub a little. I don't want you getting soap scum on your tooshie when we put you in." I touched his forehead lightly and my fingers were blackened with ash when I pulled them away.

The bathtub was as clean as I could make it when we put him in later. "I made the water slightly warm, I hope it's the right temperature," I told Gavin as Radomir lowered him into the tub. The water was black in seconds as the top layer of his skin floated away. We replaced the water three times and it was still draining out gray when we pulled Gavin out. I'd laid towels across his bed as Radomir carried Gavin inside the bedroom and laid him down on top of them.

"Honey, I don't know if you can stand this or not, but I'm taking a chance anyway," I said and covered Gavin lightly with a sheet.

"I'll sleep in here, over in the floor," I told Radomir. "You can take my bed." Radomir didn't argue when I went to the other side of the floor and sat down. I keeled right over the minute dawn came.

* * *

THE MOAN WOKE me when night fell, making me jerk upright. I'd been in a curled up position, having fallen over in the floor the minute the sun had come up, almost. Scuffling over to the bed on my knees, I peeked over the edge to see what was happening. Gavin was moving just a little. His skin looked bright pink, as skin sometimes does after a scab drops off. "I'll get some blood for you," I told him and rushed off to the kitchen.

Having no idea how much he might need or be able to drink, I grabbed three bags and ran back to the bedroom. Gavin was moving around, trying to sit up. "Here," I said, pulling him up as best I could while trying not to hurt him. He was naked, didn't seem to care and nearly bald on top of that—there were still a few small patches of hair on the back of his head. His dark eyes examined me briefly before tearing into the first bag of blood and drinking it quickly. I had the top off the second one and passed that to him so he could start on it. He got halfway into the third one before he sat back, closed his eyes and sighed.

"Did you get the asshole?" he asked.

"Yes. Asshole gone now. Gone, gone."

"Why are you talking like that?" he demanded, opening his eyes and frowning at me.

"Ooh. Tarzan thump mighty chest," I said. His mouth quirked into a smile.

I cleaned the bathtub out again before any of us took a shower. We left the keys to our rental car under the mat; the local vamps were going to return it for us. Radomir and I loaded everything into Radomir's rented SUV. Radomir told Gavin to rest while he and I did all the work. That didn't sit well with him and he grumbled, but did as he was told anyway. He kept his eyes closed most of the flight back, and I think he slept off and on. Will and Russell met us at the airport and helped with the bags. Radomir bundled Gavin into the Limo Russell brought and we all drove to Wlodek's manor. I suppose we were debriefed, whatever the hell that means. We just talked about what happened, Gavin and I, while Charles typed it all into his computer for the records. Gavin was exhausted but wasn't willing to let Wlodek know it, suffering in silence mostly, his face an expressionless mask. He only spoke when Wlodek asked a question.

"Nyles' assets will be liquidated and handed over to the Council," Wlodek said after we finished talking. Merrill came in a little later to pick me up. Franklin was with him and they both hugged me. I was really glad to see both of them to be honest, and when we got home it *felt* like home. Franklin went off to bed when we got back but I asked Merrill if I could talk to him for a few minutes.

"Of course," he smiled, leading me toward his study.

"Merrill," I said, "I think there's something you should know. At first I thought all vampires could do this but now I'm not so sure."

"What is it, child?" He was sitting behind his desk while he watched me, his fingers steepled under his chin.

"Well," I began, "when I finally learned that Gavin's scent was the scent of a vampire, I was able to compare that to the scents of other vampires I met afterward. Will's isn't as heavy and exotic as Gavin's. Russell's is a bit spicier than Will's. When they took me into the Council chamber that night, I knew immediately, just from the scent, that Wlodek was the oldest vampire, there. Then the rest of the Council came, according to age, that is, except for Charles, of course, his was light. After the Council, Gavin's came next. I don't know exactly how old any of them truly are but I could line them up in descending order, according to their ages." I looked at Merrill, whose face was now unreadable.

"You can tell this? This is extraordinary," he dropped his hands and lifted his letter opener.

"Yes. I hope this doesn't result in my death," I said. "I know that you would be right behind Wlodek in the age thing. When Gavin and I walked into the bar two nights ago, I could smell Nyles and knew he was older than Gavin. That meant he might be able to place compulsion on Gavin. I tried to send mindspeech to Gavin to tell him, but I don't think he heard me."

One of Merrill's eyebrows was now quirked up as high as it would go. "Lissa, that talent might come in handy quite often," he said, smiling a little. "Vampires don't generally like telling their age and it's rude to ask. However, since you don't know the actual number, we'll leave it at that for now, shall we? I will have to inform Wlodek of this, but if he does as I think he'll do, he'll keep this to himself and only ask you to employ it when necessary. The fewer that know about this the better." I nodded in total agreement with that assessment.

"Now," Merrill said, "dawn will arrive soon. Go to bed, little Lissa and take tomorrow off. Read, watch television or do whatever you want."

"Can I borrow a computer? I want to order a swimsuit online. I don't have one and I'd like to sit in the hot tub or go swimming."

"You're welcome to go in nude," he said. "Although I think you might be too modest to do that. Feel free to use this computer anytime," he tapped the one on his desk. "I'll get an e-mail account set up for you if you want and you can exchange e-mails with Charles if you like." I left Merrill's study after that, heading off to my bedroom.

I had another bag waiting outside my door when I rose the following evening. Two swimsuits were inside—a one-piece and a bikini, both in the right size. There was a note inside from Merrill, saying he'd asked Lena to purchase something for me. That was really nice of him and Lena had done a good job. I borrowed Merrill's computer anyway, sent an e-mail to Charles and passed along a thank you note to Radomir through him. It was the right thing to do.

* * *

"Rad, she sent you a thank you note," Charles was turning his laptop around so Radomir could read the message from Lissa. Radomir sat down in front of Charles' desk to read.

"Radomir, I cannot tell you how much I appreciate what you did for Gavin and me," it read. *"If you hadn't been there, I don't know what we would have done. Had I known something you might like, I would have sent it to show my gratitude. In the meantime, you'll have to settle for my thanks.*

Lissa."

"I don't believe I have ever received a thank you note before," Radomir smiled. "Can we forward this to father?"

"Sure." Charles flipped the laptop around and did just that.

* * *

"She is sitting on the roof," Merrill said, five days later.

"She likes to do that," Gavin agreed.

"Can you get yourself up or do you need help?" Merrill asked, almost smiling.

"I can get myself up. The only thing not fully recovered is my hair."

"I can tell," Merrill wanted to snicker but didn't.

"I had to get my scalp shaved so it will grow out evenly," Gavin huffed.

"Of course," Merrill nodded agreeably.

* * *

I WAS SITTING on Merrill's roof, staring out over the English countryside of Kent, which is quite beautiful, actually. I'd only seen pictures of what it looked like in the daytime, though. What surprised me was when Gavin floated up and landed on the roof. I had no idea he could do that. I almost slid off the roof, I was so surprised.

"What the hell was that? You can just float around?" I asked, dusting off the back of my jeans and climbing up again to sit down in my usual place.

"Some of the older ones can," he replied, sitting down next to me.

"Well, that explains how you got up and down those other times without making any noise," I grumbled.

"Yes. That explains it."

We sat there in silence for quite a while. Finally, he spoke again. "Lissa, I heard you."

"Gavin, you hear me all the time, whether you want to or not," I huffed.

"No, when you mindspoke me. I was so shocked I couldn't even think what to say and I really don't know how that happened."

"And yet you stood there like a dummy and let Nyles place compulsion," I said. "Doofus."

"Lissa, I got a little taste of my own medicine that night," Gavin told me. "I know now what it's like to stand there, facing your own death when you can't move a muscle."

"Welcome to the club," I grumbled. "At least yours lasted only a few seconds. Mine lasted days. You scared me, Gavin. You still scare me. When we're together, I keep reminding myself that you could place compulsion any time and I'd be forced to do whatever you said. Do you know how humiliating it is to have to wait for permission to blink? And you're never running a shower for me again, you jerk. That water was cold."

"I know I frightened you." He reached over and placed his fingers on the nape of my neck, massaging it a little. I drew my knees up to my chest.

"Don't, Lissa," he said, pulling me against him. "I know it's too much to ask for you to trust me. You may never trust me again and I can't say that I blame you. I should have asked Wlodek to send someone else to replace me, but I couldn't do it. I was torn between wanting to be with you as much as I could and jealousy if someone else came to replace me. And I wouldn't have been able to live with myself if someone else took your life and they were cruel about it. I wanted your death to be as swift and painless as I could make it, *ma petite ange,* if it came to that."

"Am I supposed to thank you for that?" I asked incredulously.

Gavin pulled me into his lap. "No, angel. Not at all. All I want, if you are willing, is for you to give me a chance. Let me court you as you should be courted. Without interference. Without the rogue status and the Council and the blackmail hanging over your head. That is what I ask. And no, I will not be placing compulsion to make the decision come out in my favor. Rule four, Lissa, is *never use compulsion for unethical reasons.* Vampires used to take—not just blood, but sex and money and anything else they wanted—by compulsion. That is wrong. You were rogue and that rule is lifted when we go after criminals. Your decisions will be your own from this point forward where I am concerned. Tell me you will consider this." He kissed the top of my head.

I sat there for a few minutes, Gavin's arms wound tightly around me upon the very peak of Merrill's roof. The stars were out and they twinkled brightly over our heads. "I'll think about it," I said.

* * *

WINKLER WAS CHECKING his e-mail and yawning before going to bed. Davis was working out well as his Second and Glen had slipped into the background a little. He and Phil had been friends for a very long time, but even Glen hadn't known anything about Phil's betrayal. Lissa's cell phone and the credit card he'd given her still rested on a corner of Winkler's desk; he couldn't bring himself to get rid of them. They were the only things he had left of her. Lissa's fake ID was missing and he could only imagine that Gavin had taken it with him. Winkler got down to his last e-mail message of the evening. It was from an unknown source. He was just about to hit delete without reading it when he changed his mind and opened it up. He stared at the three words for a very long time.

"*She lives.*

-Gavin"

The End